"Can you make it inside?"

Carrie asked. "Or should I get help?"

Felipe tried to straighten up. "I can make it," he said. He forced a smile. "Thanks for not running away."

"Yeah, well, I should have," she said. "I'm leaving as soon as I get you inside."

"No, you're not. I can't let you."

"Watch it," she said sharply, "or I'll drop you right here and run."

"If you do," he said, "somehow, some way, I will find the strength to follow you."

She turned to look up into his eyes, and he knew that she believed him. She might not have believed his story about his brother, she might not have believed that he was a cop investigating Lawrence Richter, but she *did* believe that he would follow her.

It was a start.

Dear Reader,

Merry Christmas! I hope you'll like Intimate Moments' gift to you: six wonderful books, perfect for reading by the lights of the Christmas tree. First up is our Heartbreakers title. Welcome veteran romance writer Sara Orwig to the line with *Hide in Plain Sight*. Hero Jake Delancy is tough—but the power of single mom Rebecca Bolen's love is even stronger!

Terese Ramin is back with *Five Kids, One Christmas*, a book that will put you right in the holiday mood. Then try Suzanne Brockmann's *A Man To Die For*, a suspenseful reply to the question "What would you do for love?" Next up is *Together Again*, the latest in Laura Parker's Rogues' Gallery miniseries. *The Mom Who Came To Stay* brings Nancy Morse back to the line after a too-long absence. This book's title says it all. Finally, welcome Becky Barker to the line as she tells the story of *The Last Real Cowboy*.

Six books, six tales of love to make your holidays bright. Enjoy!

Leslie Wainger
Senior Editor and Editorial Coordinator

Please address questions and book requests to:
Silhouette Reader Service
U.S.: 3010 Walden Ave., P.O. Box 1325, Buffalo, NY 14269
Canadian: P.O. Box 609, Fort Erie, Ont. L2A 5X3

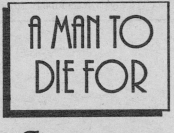

A MAN TO DIE FOR

SUZANNE BROCKMANN

Published by Silhouette Books

America's Publisher of Contemporary Romance

SILHOUETTE BOOKS

ISBN 0-373-07681-9

A MAN TO DIE FOR

Copyright © 1995 by Suzanne Brockmann

All rights reserved. Except for use in any review, the reproduction
or utilization of this work in whole or in part in any form by any
electronic, mechanical or other means, now known or hereafter
invented, including xerography, photocopying and recording, or in
any information storage or retrieval system, is forbidden without
the written permission of the editorial office, Silhouette Books,
300 East 42nd Street, New York, NY 10017 U.S.A.

All characters in this book have no existence outside the imagination of
the author and have no relation whatsoever to anyone bearing the same
name or names. They are not even distantly inspired by any individual
known or unknown to the author, and all incidents are pure invention.

This edition published by arrangement with Harlequin Books S.A.

® and TM are trademarks of Harlequin Books S.A., used under
license. Trademarks indicated with ® are registered in the United States
Patent and Trademark Office, the Canadian Trade Marks Office and in
other countries.

Printed in U.S.A.

Books by Suzanne Brockmann

Silhouette Intimate Moments

Hero Under Cover #575
Not Without Risk #647
A Man To Die For #681

SUZANNE BROCKMANN

wanted to be a cowboy, an astronaut, a spelunker and a rock-and-roll singer when she grew up. Allergic to horses, too nearsighted for NASA and slightly claustrophobic, she took up writing instead and has successfully gone with her characters on trail rides, into outer space and deep beneath the earth. She actually was a rock singer, forming and fronting an original band while attending college in Boston. Suzanne still lives in the Boston area, surrounded by the best family and the coolest group of friends in the world.

Chapter 1

July

It was quarter past midnight before Carrie Brooks turned
off the computer in the Sea Circus office, twenty past before she turned off the lights.

With the laser printout of her environmental coastal report safely tucked in her backpack, Carrie stopped only to
pick up the tranquilizer rifle she was borrowing for tomorrow's expedition to the edge of the Everglades. She was
leading one of her well-known wildlife preserve tours for a
group of college professors from Ohio. The rifle wasn't really necessary. She wasn't planning on using it, but it made
for good show, and it *would* be pleasant to have on hand
should any of the 'gators get nasty, or should one of the
professors get careless.

One of the rifle's double barrels was loaded, she realized
as she locked the office door behind her and headed down
the rickety wooden steps into the hot, humid summer night.
That wastecase, Simon, had no doubt left the gun loaded,
and returned it to the Sea Circus office without even putting the safety on. Didn't he realize it was a weapon? Just

because it shot tranquilizer darts meant for sharks or 'gators didn't mean it couldn't hurt or even kill a human.

Carrie put the safety on, locking it into place as she started across the Sea Circus grounds.

She had to be up and alert and at the marina by six in the morning. By the time she got to her car, drove to the gate, punched in her security code, opened the gate, drove her car out, closed the car, restarted the alarm system and drove all the way home to her little apartment on the other side of town, she'd stand a chance at getting four solid hours of sleep.

Four wasn't too bad, she thought as she cut across the lawn next to the main aquarium tank. She'd be able to nap tomorrow afternoon, maybe take the boat back out and just let it drift. She'd close her eyes in the soft sunshine and work on her tan....

Carrie froze. Was that the sound of laughter that had floated across the sandy grounds, or had it been some lonely seabird, or the sound of the surf?

Listening hard, Carrie heard it again. Laughter. Laughter, followed by a stream of rapid-fire Spanish, then a plaintive voice, complaining clearly in English, "Yo, man, talk American, wouldja?"

Teenagers on the beach, she decided. No one could have gotten onto the Sea Circus grounds without triggering the alarm system. And even if they had somehow managed to get in without setting off all the bells and whistles and bright flashing lights, the fail-safe silent alarm would ring down at police headquarters, and a patrol car would be out in a matter of minutes.

Carrie rounded the corner of the main aquarium tank, heading to her parked car.

And came face-to-face with a group of men.

Good Lord! How the hell had they gotten in?

The scientist that she was, quickly assessed the facts.

There were four of them—that she could see anyway—and they were *not* teenagers. They were grown men in their mid-twenties. Several of them may have been even older.

The take-no-bull Montana rancher's daughter that she'd been for the first eighteen years of her life planted her feet firmly on the ground and cradled the rifle in her arms, making sure they could see it clearly.

"I believe you gentlemen are trespassing," she said coolly. "I suggest you allow me to escort you off Sea Circus property before the police arrive."

One of the men wore a red bandanna tied around his head. On closer examination, he looked to be in his late thirties, with deep-set eyes and gaunt, hollow cheekbones. He merely smiled at her words.

"But we're not ready to leave," he said with a thick Cuban accent.

Another of the men had a nose ring the size of a quarter. He was tall, taller than the rest of them by a good six inches, and he towered over Carrie. He had greasy blond hair pulled back into a messy ponytail at his nape. He kept his eyes carefully hidden behind a pair of mirrored sunglasses despite the fact that it was the middle of the night.

A third man was standing slightly to the left of Bandanna. He had short red hair in a crew cut and a face that still bore the scars of teenage acne. He was wearing a faded Nirvana T-shirt and a pair of cutoff jeans that revealed a pair of skinny legs. "Yeah, baby," he said, leering at her. "Iceman wants to look at the fishies."

"Then he should come back tomorrow," Carrie said tartly, "when Sea Circus is open to the general public."

"We ain't the general public," Nose Ring sneered.

The men seemed undaunted by the rifle she was holding. They moved slowly, spreading out around her, and Carrie realized in another few seconds she'd be completely surrounded. She slipped the safety off the rifle and took several steps backward until her shoulder blades hit the rough concrete of the main aquarium building. Better to have a wall behind her than God-knows-who and his even uglier brother.

In one quick movement, she hoisted the solid barrel of the rifle to her shoulder and cocked the trigger, closing one eye and squinting to aim directly at Bandanna—the man who was clearly the leader. At this proximity, shooting the tranquilizer dart at his head would probably kill him. The dart would shatter the bones in his skull, then penetrate his brain. He'd be tranquilized—permanently.

Bandanna seemed to realize this, too, and he gave a brief command in Spanish.

"Back off," another man translated, a man who had been standing slightly out of Carrie's sight, in the shadows behind Bandanna.

Carrie glanced in his direction.

He was the only one of the four who looked as if he might actually be nice to stand downwind of. He was more than average height—which meant that he stood a good nine inches taller than Carrie—and his clothes were pure American Urban. Despite the heat, he was wearing a black leather biker's jacket over a white T-shirt, and a pair of faded blue jeans that fitted him like a second skin. Snakeskin cowboy boots with pointy toes and silver-chained boot bracelets added the final touch.

His hair was long and thick, curling down around and past his shoulders. He had wide, angular cheekbones that spoke as clearly of his Latin heritage as did his gentle Hispanic accent.

He was a handsome man. No, forget handsome. He wasn't handsome. He was drop-dead gorgeous, Carrie realized as he stepped out into the light—but not because of his cheekbones or his shiny hair or his trim, muscular body.

It was his eyes.

Soft and black, his eyes were incredible—the color of the midnight sky—surrounded by a fringe of thick, dark, almost femininely long lashes. They held a gentle serenity, a quiet confidence, like that of a priest or a minister, that contradicted his macho leather-and-chains getup. But then that look shifted, and there was something else in his eyes, too—a glint of excitement, a flare of fire and power, a sense of very real danger. Part priest maybe, but also part devil.

This was not a man to mess with.

Holding Carrie's gaze, he stepped in front of Bandanna, shielding the older man from her rifle. But he didn't stop there. He kept going, slowly moving closer and closer to her.

"We were only cutting through. We *will* leave, but first you must give me the gun," he said. He smiled at her, showing a set of white, perfect teeth, and added, "Please?"

"Pwetty pwease?" Crew-cut said, then laughed loudly. "Yo, Carlos, man, you forgot to say 'Mother, may I.'"

Carlos. The man with the midnight eyes was named Carlos.

"Freeze, Carlos," Carrie ordered him, training the gun on the center of his forehead.

But he just kept coming. "Give me the gun, miss," he said again, "so that no one gets hurt."

"You don't want anyone to get hurt?" she asked, her anger making her sound breathless and afraid. "Then turn around right now and leave."

Bandanna spoke again in Spanish.

"Iceman says we will," Carlos said, translating. "But only when we are ready." Was that genuine remorse that flashed in his eyes? Or was it amusement?

He was almost within an arm's reach of her rifle. Carrie moved the barrel down slightly, so it was aimed steadily at his stomach. He smiled, and she knew *he* knew she didn't have the nerve to kill him. But if he came any closer, she *would* pull the trigger. And God only knows how the human body would react to the fast-acting tranquilizer intended for a four-hundred-pound marine mammal.

"Take another step and I'll shoot," she warned him.

He stopped. And laughed. "You would, too, wouldn't you?"

"Damn straight," she said grimly.

"And then what?" Carlos asked his eyes glittering, reflecting the dim glow of the floodlights that lit the park grounds. "I fall." He shrugged. "But there are three others. And I doubt that my friends will wait patiently while you reload your gun. No, if you shoot me, you will be in serious trouble. I cannot recommend it."

"Let's skip the trouble, shall we?" Carrie said. "Now, you boys just hop back over that fence and clear on out of here, and we'll call it a night."

"You sound like one of them thar Western movies," Crew-cut said, mimicking and exaggerating Carrie's drawl.

"Like a cute little cowgirl." He smiled, revealing a variety of cracked and broken teeth. "Come on, baby, why don't you show us your spurs and whips?"

Carrie glanced at Crew-cut for only a fraction of a second, but that was all it took to give Carlos an edge.

He moved, faster than she thought it was possible for a man of his size to move, quickly closing the gap between his hands and her gun.

She squeezed the trigger, but it was too late. He knocked the barrel of the gun up, and the dart shot harmlessly into the night sky.

The recoil caught her off-balance, and Carrie went down, hard, into the sandy dirt. She scrambled quickly to her feet, straining her ears for the sound of police sirens. But there was only silence.

Bandanna, Crew-cut and Nose Ring stood in a semicircle around her, just watching. Carlos was looking at her gun, releasing the spent cartridge and making sure there wasn't another round in the second barrel.

"She was gonna shoot ya, man," Crew-cut said to Carlos.

Carlos just smiled serenely.

Now what? Carrie was still breathing hard, trying to control the crazy hammering of her heart. The situation wasn't looking very good. She was unarmed, in a deserted spot, in the middle of the night, with four scary-looking men. Could things get much worse?

Bandanna said something to Carlos in Spanish.

Carlos answered evenly.

Bandanna spoke again, gesturing toward Carrie.

Carlos smiled at Bandanna, smiled at Carrie and nodded his head. *"Sí,"* he said. *That* she understood. *"Sí"* meant yes. But yes *what?*

A police siren wailed faintly in the distance, and Carrie held her breath. But it was moving away from her, getting softer and softer until she couldn't hear it anymore. Dammit, where *were* those police?

And still the conversation in Spanish went on.

Crew-cut finally exploded, voicing all of Carrie's frustration, letting out a stream of foul language. "I'm feeling left out here," he added. "If you guys aren't discussing the balmy weather, then translate, for chrissake."

"Iceman said he wants to see the dolphins now," Carlos said, clearly tongue in cheek.

Nose Ring scowled. "Cut the crap, Carlos."

"Time to go," Carlos said evenly.

"What about her?" Crew-cut asked, pointing to Carrie with his chin. "We can't just leave her here."

"Sure you can," Carrie lied. "You clear out of here, I'll forget I ever saw you. No harm done, right?"

Carlos laughed, humor lighting his face.

"What?" Carrie said defensively. But she could tell from his eyes that he knew if they simply left her here, she'd run up to the office and call the police faster than they could sneeze.

"I'll take care of her," he said to Crew-cut. "You go with Iceman. I'll catch up."

Bandanna and Nose Ring were already walking away, heading for the other side of the park.

"No way, man," Crew-cut said, his voice cracking. "Why do I want to go on ahead when *you're* having all the fun?"

Carlos shrugged. "Suit yourself." He turned to Carrie. "Do you have a car?" he asked.

Her blood felt icy cold despite the evening's heat. Take care of her? How was Carlos going to "take care of" her? Still, she stuck out her chin. "Maybe."

"Please give me the car keys."

"I don't have 'em," she lied.

He leaned the rifle against the side of the aquarium and stepped toward her. "Give me the keys, please," he said, "or I'll have to take them from you."

"And I'll help," Crew-cut said with an ugly smile.

Carrie crossed her arms. "You boys planning to steal my car now, too? Aren't breaking-and-entering charges good enough for the lot of you?"

One arm. That's all it took for Carlos to hold her while he quickly searched her pockets for her car keys. Both her arms were pinned and her face was pressed against the sweet-smelling leather of his jacket. If he hadn't been wearing that jacket, she would've bitten him, but she didn't even try, since all she would've gotten was a mouthful of cowhide. She pulled back her leg to kick him, but he found the keys in the front pocket of her shorts and let her go before her boot connected with his shin.

Carrie was gasping indignantly, but Carlos was unruffled.

"Thank you," he said politely, as if she'd handed him the keys. He slipped them into his own pocket.

A strand of her long blond hair had come free from her ponytail, and she pushed it back off her face, looping it behind her ear. "I have three more payments on that car," she said hotly. "If you think I'm just going to let you steal it—"

"No one's going to steal your car," Carlos told her.

"Wait a minute, man." Crew-cut looked at Carrie. "What kind is it?"

Even Carlos looked exasperated. "Get lost, man," he said to Crew-cut. "You're cramping my style, you know?"

But Crew-cut didn't budge. "If *you* get to have fun," he said with a petulant set to his square jaw, "*I* get to watch."

Watch? Watch what? The fear was back, fear for her personal safety, fear for her very life. But the fear brought a new wave of anger—anger that her father and brothers were going to be proven right. She *couldn't* take care of herself. She had had no right to leave the safety of their isolated Montana ranch and move to a crime-riddled Florida city. Dammit, she could just imagine them saying "We told her so," as they morosely gathered around to identify her body at the St. Simone morgue.

Carlos took her gently by the arm, but she pulled free, glaring at him.

"Where are you taking me?" she asked.

He countered with a question. "Where's your car parked?"

She didn't answer, so he answered for her.

"Not in the parking lot outside the gate," he said, "or I would have seen it there. It's probably somewhere inside the fence, no?"

She stared at him silently. If he so much as touched her, she'd throw up on him. That's what she'd always been told to do in the event of a sexual assault, right? It sure wouldn't take much effort on her part. She was already feeling queasy.

"Are you going to walk?" Carlos said patiently, "or perhaps I should carry you?"

"Yo, Carlos, *I'll* carry her," Crew-cut volunteered.

"I'll walk," Carrie said quickly.

"Oh, man," Crew-cut said, exaggerating his whine. "I don't think she likes me." He pretended to pout. "But, baby, you know, I like *you....*"

He reached out to touch her, and Carrie jerked back out of his grasp. "Don't you come near me," she said sharply, including Carlos in her glare.

What were her options here? She could stand passively by and wait to see what they were going to do with her. Or she could run. She could dart away into the shadows and hide. She could slip into the seal tank and swim to the covered hutch that could only be accessed underwater.

She glanced toward the seal tank. It was more than a hundred yards away. If she was smart, she'd run in the other direction first, lose these jerks in the shadows underneath the main aquarium bleachers, and then head back to the seal tank. Once she was under the water, they'd never find her. Not in a million years.

"Don't even think about it," Carlos murmured, as if he could read her mind.

"Think about what?" she asked innocently. And bolted toward the bleachers.

Seven steps. That's all it took before Carlos tackled her, pulling her down onto the hard sand with him. He pinned her to the ground, her hands above her head, the full weight of his body pressing against her.

Carrie struggled to get away, struggled to bring her knee up to kick him, but she couldn't move. Her heart was pounding and she was nearly blind with panic.

"Madre de Dios," Carlos said. "You are a handful and a half, aren't you?" He brought his mouth closer to her ear, lowering his voice. "Look, I'm not going to hurt you. I'm a—"

Carrie bit him between his shoulder and his neck, right through the white cotton of his T-shirt collar.

He swore sharply, and pulled away from her. She scrambled into a sitting position and tried to back away, but he grabbed her ankle with one hand. With the other he rubbed his neck.

"A biter, huh?" Crew-cut said, crouching down next to them. "Oh, baby, you can bite *me* anytime."

Carrie was shaking uncontrollably, and she couldn't stop the tears that had flooded her eyes. One spilled down her cheek and she wiped it fiercely away. She'd be damned if she was going to let these bastards see her cry.

Carlos muttered something in Spanish, pushing his hair out of his face. One dark, curly lock caught on his eyelashes, but he didn't seem to notice. The priest look was back in his eyes, making his entire face seem warm and compassionate and full of remorse. Would he look at her that way after the devil took over again, after he'd forced himself on her?

Carrie spit at him, and he closed his eyes as the spittle hit him full in the face.

"Oh, gross," Crew-cut exclaimed. "Slap her, man. Don't let the bitch get away with that. Hell, I'll slap her for you."

"No, thank you."

"Aw, come on—"

"I said, *no.*" Carlos kept his eyes closed until he'd wiped his face clean with his hand. When he opened his eyes again, Carrie could see no anger there—only patience. He smiled apologetically at Carrie. "I'm sorry," he said. "I didn't mean to frighten you."

"You're telling her you're *sorry?*" Crew-cut said. "*She's* the one who should be apologizing."

Carlos exchanged his hold on Carrie's leg for a steady grip on her arm and got to his feet, pulling her up with him.

She tried to pull free, but he wouldn't let go. "If I let you go, you'll just run again," he said, "so I'm not going to do it."

"You're hurting me," Carrie said.

"Don't pull, and I won't have to hold you so tightly," Carlos said.

He led her around the corner of the main aquarium, and there was her little sports car, bright red and very shiny, even in the dimly powered floodlights.

Crew-cut gave a low whistle. "Nice wheels."

The trunk was open, the way she'd left it when she'd come to the office that evening. She'd been airing out the fishy smell that seemed to follow her around.

"I guess I didn't need those keys after all," Carlos said, pulling her around to the back of the car. He was still holding her arm with his right hand, so he gestured grandly toward the trunk with his left. "Get in."

Carrie stared at him, not understanding. What did he want her to do?

"That's it?" Crew-cut sputtered, disappointed. "You're just going to lock her in the trunk? Man, if it was me, I'd've taken her right here, in the front seat of her car."

Carlos was going to lock her in the trunk of her car. He wasn't going to force himself on her; he was just going to make sure she couldn't call the police. He *wasn't* going to hurt her; she was going to be all right. Except, Lord, that trunk was awfully tiny, and with the hood down, it would be incredibly dark and hot and . . .

Crew-cut reached out and ran one grubby finger down the side of Carrie's face. She pulled away, slapping at his hand, disgusted by his touch. On further thought, maybe being locked in the trunk wasn't such a bad idea.

Crew-cut drew back his hand to slap her, but Carlos caught his wrist.

"Rumor has it," he said dryly, "that sex is more pleasurable when the woman is willing."

"Yeah, well, this would be better than nothing," Crew-cut said with a shrug, jerking his hand free.

"No," Carlos said firmly. "In a case like this, *nothing* is best."

"Aw, come on, man," Crew-cut said. "I think she's kind of cute, so little and pretty. Look at all this blond hair."

Her hair had come free from its ponytail, and it hung around her face in a smooth blond sheet. Crew-cut ran his fingers through it, and Carrie yanked her head back, nearly toppling over. Carlos steadied her, and she realized she was grateful for his presence, grateful for the warmth of his body behind her. Crew-cut was the one she was afraid of. Carlos didn't want to hurt her. At least she *hoped* he didn't.

"Come on," Crew-cut said again. "Take me five minutes, ten minutes tops. I bet she's a real screamer." He leered at Carrie. "I bet you'd like to sink those sharp little teeth in me, huh, baby?"

"If you so much as touch me," Carrie snapped, "I'll kick your family jewels through the roof of your mouth."

"And that's after *I* get finished kicking your family jewels through the roof of your mouth," Carlos said mildly. "Back off, T.J."

"Why? You don't want her—"

"I didn't say that," Carlos corrected him. "On the contrary. You're right. She *is* very pretty. And I like her spirit. Very much so. No, I didn't say I didn't want her."

Carrie's eyes flew to Carlos's face. Her heart was pounding so loudly she could barely hear. She searched his eyes, looking to see if he was serious, or if he was joking—or if he'd been joking all along and he really meant to force himself on her, and then let his horrible friend take a turn.

"Shh," he said softly, as if he could see the sudden flare of panic in her eyes. "No one's going to hurt you."

His eyes were unreadable, an odd mix of heat, excitement and...*kindness?* Carrie was confused, and terribly frightened again. If this was some kind of head game Carlos was playing with her, he was winning, hands down.

"Just do her, man," Crew-cut urged. "You know you want to."

"But the real question is, does *she* want to?"

"Try it, and I'll kill you," Carrie whispered.

"Unlike you," Carlos said to Crew-cut, "I am quick to recognize a no when I hear one, and that sounded like a very definite no to me." He turned to Carrie. "Get in the trunk, please."

But Carrie couldn't do it. She couldn't move. As much as she wanted to be away from Crew-cut and Carlos, she couldn't bring herself to climb into that tiny, dark, airless trunk. Never mind her childhood claustrophobic fears of being locked in a closet or trapped in her parents' camper's tiny bathroom. Lord, in a few hours, the hot Florida sun would rise, and that trunk would turn into an oven. She'd bake. She'd dehydrate. Her body temperature would soar, and she'd be dead in a matter of hours.

Carlos scooped her up, holding her, one arm behind her shoulders, the other supporting her knees, and lifted her easily into the trunk.

"No!" She clung to his neck, afraid to let go, afraid that his would be the last face she'd ever see, afraid of the hood closing down on her, trapping her, entombing her.

"You'll be safest here, *cara,*" Carlos murmured, prying her fingers loose. "Trust me," Carlos said to Carrie, his dark brown eyes so gentle, so kind. "You have to trust me."

The hood of the trunk closed with a frightening finality. She was alone, alone in the dark.

"C'mon, man, we're going to be late," T.J. said, running his hand anxiously across his crew cut as he looked across the dark marine park. "Iceman's gonna start the meeting without us."

"I'm not ready to go," the man known as Carlos said calmly, stopping at a row of pay phones near the closed and shuttered concession stand.

"This ain't the time to call your girlfriend," T.J. said, watching him dial. "911? What the hell . . . ?"

"Someone's got to get the girl out of the trunk before the sun comes up," Carlos said in his gentle Hispanic accent.

"Yo, we can let her out on the way back." T.J. smiled. "*I'll* come back this way and—"

"Yeah," Carlos said into the phone. "I'd like to report a woman locked in the trunk of a red Miata inside the grounds of Sea Circus. Yeah, that's Sea Circus—down on Ocean and Florida Streets? The car's *inside* the park, not out in the lot."

T.J. shook his head. "You're a stupid sonuva—"

"No, I wish to remain anonymous," Carlos said.

"We gotta go," T.J. growled.

Carlos put his finger in his ear, blocking the sound of T.J.'s voice. "How do I know there's a woman in the trunk of a red Miata?" He laughed. "Because I put her there. Just send a patrol car down to let her out, okay?'' There was a pause. ''Good,'' he said.

He hung up the phone and smiled at T.J. ''Now I'm ready to go.''

Chapter 2

January—six months later

Felipe Salazar adjusted his bow tie in the mirror of his furnished suite at the ritzy Harbor's Gate Apartments, then wiped imaginary dust from the shoulder of his tuxedo.

It was a very nice tuxedo, carefully tailored so that his shoulder holster and gun didn't disrupt the lines of his jacket.

This penthouse suite was very nice, too. It was four times bigger than his tiny one-bedroom apartment on the other side of town. Of course, the monthly rent was much higher than four times that of his little, airless apartment. But luckily for him, he wasn't paying it.

In fact, he wasn't paying for anything these days. The hotel, his expensive clothes, his meals, the two thousand dollars in spending money he carried around in fifties and one hundreds were all courtesy of the St. Simone Police Department.

It was one of the perks of working a round-the-clock dangerous job. In fact, it was the only perk most people would understand. Very few people would call the danger, the risk, the *thrill* of being an undercover police detective a perk.

But Felipe Salazar wasn't most people.

And tonight, he wasn't even Felipe Salazar.

Tonight, as he'd been for the past five months, he was Raoul Tomás Garcia Vasquez. Raoul Tomás Garcia Vasquez had quite good taste in clothes. He wore expensive suits and Italian shoes and underwear that cost more than a police detective's daily salary.

Felipe looked at himself again in the mirror. Yes, the tux fitted him very nicely. It was a far cry from the leather jacket and worn-out blue jeans he'd worn on his last assignment. He'd been called Carlos for that one, and he'd infiltrated an uneasy alliance of street-gang leaders out to make a fortune in the world of illegal drugs. As Carlos, he'd come face-to-face with Caroline Brooks, that intriguing blonde at Sea Circus and . . .

He shook his head. This was no time to think about blondes, particularly about *this* blonde. Unfortunately, there was never any time. He'd gone straight from being Carlos to being Raoul Vasquez. He couldn't remember the last time someone had actually called him Felipe. But such was the nature of his job. Felipe glanced into the mirror again, and Raoul Vasquez looked back at him.

Raoul was fresh out of prison, and ready to start over. He'd come to St. Simone—or so his story went—after cashing in some favors, some *big* favors. His old boss, Joseph Halstad, the head of a minor crime syndicate in Washington, D.C., had offered him his old job back, but Raoul wanted a fresh start, someplace new, someplace where the police didn't recognize his face.

So Halstad had phoned Lawrence Richter, the man who ran Western Florida's organized-crime outfit, and called in a few favors of his own.

Of course, Richter didn't know that Halstad had made that phone call as part of a deal struck with the Washington D.A. over certain racketeering charges.

And Richter *wouldn't* know—at least not until Felipe had gathered all the proof he needed to cement this case shut and send Richter and all the men and women in his syndicate to jail for a long, long time.

After five months, Felipe was immersed in Richter's organization deeply enough to put Richter and many of his underlings away. Strangely enough, even with all the drug and weapons sales, the prostitution, gambling and racketeering that went on, it was the importation of illegal aliens that was going to bring Richter down.

On the surface, it seemed innocent enough, benevolent even. Lawrence Richter, humanitarian, was helping the poor and impoverished into America. He was helping them get a start, helping them find that American Dream.

Felipe knew all about the American Dream. His own parents had made the move from Puerto Rico to Miami, searching for a better life for themselves and their five children. But Miami had been hot and angry, and they'd moved on, across to the west coast of Florida, to the city of St. Simone.

Some American Dream.

Felipe's father had worked himself into an early grave, trying to keep his floundering auto shop afloat. Raphael, Felipe's older brother, had run with the wrong crowd, nearly overdosed on drugs and ended up doing time in a state maximum security prison. His oldest sister, Catalina, had married a man who'd been killed in a car accident by a drunk driver, leaving her alone to raise their two small children. His other sister, Marisela, had given up her own dream of going to college and had taken over their father's garage with the help of Roberto, their youngest brother, who was still in high school.

And Felipe? Felipe had become a cop.

He smiled wryly at himself in the mirror. His father, the dreamer, had been disappointed in Felipe's choice of profession. Yet it was Felipe who was most like the old man. Out of all his brothers and sisters, it was Felipe who was the idealist. It was Felipe who still believed in good versus evil, in right over wrong. It was Felipe who still believed in the criminal justice system and the rule of law. It was Felipe who was keeping alive the American Dream.

And that meant putting away Lawrence Richter, who was bringing entire families of illegal immigrants into the country and turning them into little more than slaves. In exchange for safe passage into America, the land of opportunity, Richter would squeeze years of indentured servitude from these people. He'd contract them out to work in factories and sweatshops at much lower than the legal minimum wage. Then he'd keep most of their paycheck, giving them only barely enough to get by. If they complained, they'd get delivered into the hands of the immigration department, speaking hardly any English and knowing only the assumed names of the men who had brought them into the country.

Felipe had seen many of these people, trapped into working sixty-hour weeks for money that they would never see, money that would line Lawrence Richter's pockets. Felipe had looked into their eyes and seen the despair and desperation—and utter hopelessness.

For them, the American Dream had become a nightmare.

Shutting Richter's operation down would mean deportation for many of them. But some would slip through the cracks, free at last to pursue that elusive American Dream.

Still, as close as Felipe was to nailing Richter, he had to wait. Because last week, something he'd suspected for quite some time had become more than a mere suspicion.

Richter had a partner.

And Richter's partner was someone relatively high up in St. Simone's government. He was someone with power, someone with clout, someone who, it seemed, could make the entire police force turn their heads and look the other way if need be.

And before he took Richter down, Felipe Salazar, faithful believer in right over wrong and staunch defender of his father's American Dream, was going to make sure that this other man, this man Richter had nicknamed "Captain Rat," whoever he was, fell, too.

Bobby Penfield III was *the* most boring man Carrie Brooks had ever met in her twenty-five years of life.

Yet she sat across from him at their table in Schroedinger's, St. Simone's most elegant restaurant, located on the ground floor of the glamorous Reef Hotel, and tried to smile. *This* was why she didn't go out on dates, she reminded herself sternly. The next time some relatively nice-looking man that she didn't know asked her to dinner, she would definitely find some excuse to stay home.

Sure, some women might have found Bobby Penfield III and his endless stories about the ad agency wars exciting. But frankly, Carrie couldn't see how choosing a man over a woman to plug some paper towel on TV could really make that much difference in the future sales of those paper towels. And it certainly didn't warrant nearly an hour of dinner conversation. Besides, as an avid environmentalist, she'd prefer it if the entire world stopped using paper and turned to reusable cloth towels instead.

Carrie wished that he'd change the subject. She wished that he'd talk about *any*thing else. Hell, she'd rather discuss last week's sensational mob-related killings—the "Sandlot Murders," the press had so cleverly dubbed them. Everyone across the state was talking about it. It had even made the national news. Two mobsters, Tony Mareidas and Steve Dupree, had been executed in a vacant lot downtown—a vacant lot that happened to be next to an elementary school. Children had discovered the bodies, and the city was in an uproar, searching for the man or men responsible for the bloody crime.

But Bobby Penfield III rambled on about his paper products, and Carrie was forced to smile cheerfully back at him. She was here because Bobby's ad agency was going to produce a series of commercials and print ads about Sea Circus, at quite a discount off their regular rates. Or so Hal Tompkins, the aquarium's business manager had told her. And when Hal had brought Bobby over to see the dolphins run through their afternoon training session with Carrie, and when Bobby had asked Carrie to dinner and Hal had widened his eyes at Carrie in a silent plea to be nice to Bobby, Carrie had stupidly accepted the date.

So here she was in her own personal level of hell, in a much too posh restaurant, underdressed in the fanciest dress she owned—a simple blue-flowered sleeveless dress with a short, swingy skirt—sitting across the table from a man she had nothing, absolutely *nothing* in common with. Except maybe for the fact that they both liked the new two-piece bathing suit Carrie had been wearing during that afternoon's dolphin training session.

Across the restaurant, a long banquet table caught Carrie's eye. It was filled with men in tuxedos and their beautiful wives. Or dates. Dates, Carrie decided cynically. Their wives were probably all home with the children.

A silver-haired man sat at one end of the table, smiling benevolently at his guests. Yes, this was his party, Carrie decided. Silver-hair was definitely the man who'd be picking up tonight's check.

Bobby Penfield droned on about marketing disposable diapers, unaware that Carrie's attention had long since wandered. As she watched, across the room, Silver-hair stood up and made a toast. Another man, a man who had his back to her, stood also and bowed graciously to polite applause.

Carrie leaned forward, trying to get a closer look. Something about this man, something about the set of his shoulders—or maybe the way his tuxedo fit those broad shoulders—was oddly familiar. She studied the back of his head, silently willing him to turn around.

But he didn't. He sat back down without giving her a chance to see his face. Whoever he was, he wore his long, dark hair pulled tightly into a ponytail at his nape.

Carrie knew plenty of men with long, dark hair that they wore in a ponytail. But none of the men *she* knew had ever worn a tuxedo—let alone a tuxedo that had so obviously been altered to give its wearer such an incredibly precise fit.

Carrie looked up, startled, suddenly aware that Bobby had stopped talking. He was looking at her as if he was waiting for her to answer a question.

She did the only thing she could. She smiled at him. And asked him where he went to college.

Bobby was only too happy to keep talking about himself. He didn't even notice she'd never answered his question.

Carrie wasn't sure he'd heard a single thing she'd said all
night—except the questions she'd asked about him.

Lord, somewhere, someplace in the world, there had to
exist a man who actually listened to the words another person spoke. But whoever he was, he sure as all hell wasn't
named Bobby Penfield III.

Of course, she wasn't exactly listening to *him*, either. She
sighed. She'd known from the moment she'd gotten into his
car that this entire evening was going to be a disaster. She'd
picked up on their incompatibility that early and wished
now that she'd had the nerve to bow out gracefully.

Except Bobby still seemed to harbor hopes that Carrie
would go home with him after dinner. She could see it in his
eyes, in the way his gaze lingered on her breasts and on her
mouth.

Carrie sighed again. This was truly the pits.

But it sure wasn't as bad as being trapped in the trunk of
her car for two endless, nightmarish hours, the way she'd
been back in July.

It still haunted her, even after all these months.

Those two hours had seemed more like two years.

Carrie had gone ballistic at first, flashing temporarily
back to the time she was locked in the tiny bathroom of her
parents' camper when she was nine years old. Just as she'd
done when she was nine, she'd cried as if the world were
coming to an end. She'd cried, and kept crying, until she'd
groped around and found the old flashlight she kept in the
trunk of her car for emergencies. The main bulb was out,
but it was one of those big box flashlights with a bullet-
shaped red light attached to the handle, and *that* light was
working.

The trunk had been absurdly tiny and terrifyingly confining in the red glow from the flashlight. But at least the
darkness hadn't pressed in on her anymore, suffocating her.
And there had been fresh air—or at least there had been after she'd pulled the foam sealing strip from between the
trunk hood and the frame. Her trunk would probably never
be watertight again, but fresh air had been her immediate
concern.

Then, lying on her back with her legs scrunched up and her face only a few inches from the inside of the hood, Carrie sang. She sang to keep herself from losing her mind. She sang every song she'd ever learned, and some she hadn't. She sang all of the top forty hits from the year she'd entered eighth grade. She sang all of those annoying Broadway musical show tunes that her mother had loved so much. She sang every song from Patty Loveless's two most recent compact discs. She sang until her throat was raw.

It truly had been hell, lying there, sweating, trying to keep the panic from engulfing her, feeling the walls closing in even tighter....

Carlos.

Her thoughts continued to return to him every now and then, even after all this time. In the first few weeks after he'd locked her in the trunk, she'd thought about him often.

Oddly enough, he still sometimes showed up in her dreams, too. Even odder, those dreams were steamy and erotic, filled with entangled legs, and cool, smooth, muscular skin, and long, dark hair hanging down around her face as he slowly bent to kiss her, as he sensuously, languorously, exquisitely moved inside of her—

She'd wake up with a start, surprised and sometimes a little disappointed to find that she'd only been dreaming.

Six months ago, she'd gone to the police station and sworn out a complaint, but the man named Carlos and his three friends still hadn't been caught.

Lucky for them, she told herself fiercely. If she so much as set eyes on any of those sons of bitches again...

Across the room, Silver-hair's guests stood up, stretching their legs. The women moved off, almost in one body, toward the ladies' room. The men shook hands and—

No.

It couldn't be.

Could it?

Carrie had gotten only the briefest glimpse of the man's face, but those exotic cheekbones were unmistakable.

She wouldn't be absolutely positive until she saw his eyes, but either she was going crazy or the man with the long dark ponytail, the man in the well-tailored tuxedo, was *Carlos*.

Of course, it was entirely possible that she *was* going crazy.

It had been six months, and Carrie *still* thought she spotted Carlos everywhere—in the mall, in the grocery store, at the movies, and even in the crowd at Sea Circus. She'd see a tall man with long, dark hair and she'd stare and take a closer look. But then the man would turn his head and she'd realize it wasn't Carlos after all. It was just someone who looked a little bit like him.

But *this* man didn't turn around and give her a second chance to see his face. He stared toward the lobby door with his back to her.

"Excuse me," Carrie said to Bobby Penfield as he paused to take a much-needed breath. She folded her napkin and set it down next to her salad plate. "Excuse me for just one minute. I'll be right back."

She pushed back her chair and hurried toward the lobby after the tuxedo-clad men.

Schroedinger's lobby was splendorous, with lots of plants and high ceilings and chandeliers and big wall mirrors that seemed to make the room twice the size it really was. The man who might be Carlos was standing near the checkroom, talking to Silver-hair. Several of the other men stood nearby.

Carrie stopped short at the sight of the long-haired man's face in one of the mirrors.

It *was* Carlos. Lord in heaven, it really was him.

He was smiling, with that gentle, priestly smile, at something Silver-hair had said to him. Silver-hair said something else, and the smile exploded into a devilish laugh, complete with a full view of perfect white teeth.

Despite all her dreams and various pseudo-Carlos sightings, Carrie had forgotten exactly how handsome this man was.

At that exact instant, his gaze flickered in her direction, then landed squarely on her face. For the briefest second, Carlos froze, recognition darkening his eyes as he looked at Carrie.

She'd known him six months ago for all of half an hour, but during that time, even when she aimed her rifle directly at his head, she'd not seen anything besides confidence and calm control in his eyes. But now, suddenly, she could see panic. Sheer, total panic. It flared for an instant, and then it was gone, and his face and eyes were oddly expressionless.

He was afraid of something. Afraid of *her*, probably.

Damn straight he had a reason to be. He'd locked her in the trunk of her car, for Pete's sake. All she had to do was point her finger and scream loud enough, and the entire St. Simone police force would be down upon his head.

Slowly, deliberately, Carrie started toward him.

Chapter 3

He was looking at the cause of his death.

Felipe Salazar was standing in the lobby of Schroedinger's, and looking directly at the cause of his certain death.

It was the dolphin-riding cowgirl from Sea Circus, and she was heading toward him, a small, tight smile on her perfect lips, and the fires of hell gleaming in her pretty blue-green eyes.

She'd traded her clunky boots for a pair of brown leather sandals, and her grungy shorts and T-shirt for a sleeveless, short, blue-flowered dress that would have sent his heart into his throat—if it hadn't already been there for an entirely different reason.

Her blond hair was longer than it had been six months ago, and she wore it down around her shoulders, parted on the side, a straight sheet of gold that shimmered in the light from the chandeliers.

She wasn't wearing much makeup, just a hint of eye shadow and lipstick, maybe a touch of rouge. She hadn't tried to hide the charming splash of freckles that dotted her delicate nose and softly rounded cheekbones.

Madre de Dios, but she was even lovelier than he remembered. And dear God, he'd spent an awful lot of time remembering, those first few weeks after the showdown with Iceman and the rest of his gang. Felipe had even gone back to Sea Circus, just to see for himself that the girl was really all right.

Her name was Caroline Brooks, nickname Carrie.

He'd caught most of her dolphin show, and seeing her dive into the huge tank with the enormous sea creatures, seeing her actually ride on their backs, seeing the gentle way she treated them, seeing her smile and laugh without that tinge of panic on her pretty face, and yes, seeing her in that amazing red, form-fitting Speedo bathing suit, he'd almost approached her. He'd almost gone up to her and finished that sentence he'd started, that sentence she'd interrupted with a bite from her sharp teeth.

I'm a cop.

So why hadn't he told her?

Because he liked her way, *way* too much. Because in his heart, he knew that even if he were able to seduce her, one or two nights simply wouldn't be enough. Because he knew in a matter of days, he'd be gone, deep under cover, infiltrating Lawrence Richter's crime syndicate as Raoul Tomás Garcia Vasquez. And, most of all, because he knew that any romantic involvement with him would place her in potential danger.

So he'd made himself forget about her.

Or at least he'd tried.

At the very least, he'd stayed far, far away from Sea Circus and pretty Caroline Brooks.

How very ironic to realize now that *not* approaching her, *not* telling her he was a cop, *not* revealing his true identity to her, was going to result in his own death. And, dear God, probably her death, too.

Because, coming over here the way she was, with that bright light of justice and retribution in her eyes, Felipe had no doubt that she was going to blow his cover to kingdom come.

And if Lawrence Richter had the slightest reason to believe that Felipe was a cop, then Felipe was soon going to be a very dead cop. There was no way—not knowing what Felipe knew—that Richter would let him live.

Felipe hadn't spoken to his best friend, Jim Keegan, in more than four weeks. That thought flashed crazily into his head and he wondered briefly how Jim—or Diego, the Spanish version of James, as Felipe was fond of calling him—would take the news of his friend's death.

The best defense is a strong offense. That's what Jim always used to say back when they were partners on the vice squad, before Jim took a coveted spot on the force as a homicide detective. *There's always a way out. You've just got to find it,* and *Keegan's Rule Number One: Nothing is impossible.*

If there was a way out of this mess, it would involve somehow keeping Caroline's smart mouth tightly shut.

And that wasn't going to be easy.

"Excuse me, please," Felipe murmured to Lawrence Richter. "I have to head off an...old girlfriend."

If the older man saw the bead of sweat drip down the side of Felipe's face, he didn't mention it. He merely looked from Felipe to Caroline and back, and smiled.

"Of course," Richter said.

Felipe moved quickly then, intercepting Caroline Brooks a good ten feet away from Richter. Maybe, just maybe, they were far enough away to keep him from overhearing their conversation....

"Well, what do you know?" the tiny blond woman said, gazing coolly up at Felipe as if she were the one who was almost ten inches taller. "We meet again, C—"

Carlos. She was going to call him Carlos, in a voice loud enough to carry around the entire lobby. But he wasn't Carlos now. He was supposed to be Raoul Vasquez.

Felipe shut her up the only way he could.

He covered her mouth with his and kissed her.

She tasted like the house salad dressing, fresh and spicy and delicious. She drew her breath in sharply, pulling back to look him in the eye, and Felipe knew in that one fraction of a second he hadn't imagined the electricity that had sparked between them that night at Sea Circus. It was still there, still fierce and hot. And he also knew without the slightest doubt that if he'd gone to her the way he'd longed to, if he'd told her the truth, told her he was a cop and apologized for treating her so roughly, he would've been able to seduce her. Or, *Madre de Dios,* maybe she would've seduced him.

Regret coursed through him, regret that he'd missed his chance, regret that he'd probably never have another opportunity to kiss Caroline Brooks, let alone make love to her. Because unless Felipe took her arm and dragged her away from Lawrence Richter and his right-hand triggerman, Tommy Walsh, his life was about to end.

"Darling," he said smoothly, while she was temporarily silenced, "how nice to see you again. Come, let's step outside where we can talk privately."

He took her by the arm and drew her toward the main entrance.

But she wasn't having any of it. She pulled her arm free and laughed. "You're crazier than I thought if you think I'd go *any*where with you," she said coldly in her Western twang.

Felipe could feel Richter's eyes on him, watching. Richter was always watching, always aware of every little thing that went on around him. It was one of the reasons he was so successful, and one of the reasons he'd never been apprehended.

"I know you've missed me," Felipe said, loudly enough for Richter to overhear. "And I'm sorry I haven't called you, but I've been busy. Please don't be angry—"

"*Missed* you?" She laughed in disbelief. "You locked me in the tr—"

Near desperation, Felipe kissed her again. Anything, *any*thing, to make her stop talking. He kissed her harder this time, drawing her body completely against his and holding her tightly in his arms.

Again she was temporarily silenced, and he took advantage of those few precious seconds.

"Please," he said, again loudly enough for Richter to hear. "I know you'll find this difficult to believe, but I've stayed away because I care for you so very much and—"

She hit him. She pulled her right arm free and hauled off and punched him, hard, in the stomach. Felipe saw it coming and tightened his stomach muscles. She probably hurt her fist more than she hurt him. But it was enough to catch the attention of the restaurant staff.

"Mister, you are *so* full of crap," Carrie said, her coolness gone. She was livid with anger.

"Is there a problem here?" the maître d' said, smoothly sidling up.

"No, no," Felipe said almost desperately. "Everything is fine—"

"Yes, there most certainly *is* a problem," Carrie said. "This . . . this . . . *con* man is trying to make it seem as if he and I have known each other for longer than the thirty minutes we spent together over at—"

"Caroline," he said quickly, interrupting her. Con man. Better than cop, but not by much. One glance at Richter told Felipe that the older man was still watching him. Watching and listening. "I think the gentleman would like us to continue this discussion outside and—"

Carrie's eyes narrowed. "How do you know my name?"

"She gets like this sometimes," Felipe said in a low voice to the maître d'. "Too much to drink. Will you help me take her outside?"

"Touch me again and I swear I'll scream," Carrie warned him, glaring at both men.

The maître d' backed off, eager to keep the young woman from having a fit in the lobby of his four-star restaurant.

Richter nodded once and Tommy Walsh stepped forward, his pale blue eyes bored and flat. "Raoul," he said in his thick Brooklyn accent, "you need some kind of help here?"

Carrie turned her wide blue-green gaze back on Felipe. *"Raoul?"* she said in disbelief. She turned indignantly to Tommy. "Funny, six months ago I knew him as Carlos."

Six months ago, Raoul Vasquez was supposedly in prison.

"Oh, really?" Tommy said to Carrie. "Is that right?"

"It was August," Felipe said, talking fast and low. "I was just out on parole. It had been eighteen months, man. I didn't want to get married. I just wanted a little relief, you know? I told her my name was Carlos and—"

"It was *not* August. It was July," Carrie said sharply. "And you didn't touch me. You locked me in the trunk of my car, remember?"

She sounded loco. The way she said it, it sounded as if Felipe—or Raoul or Carlos or whoever he was—had turned down an opportunity to spend the night with her. And standing there in that enticingly simple blue-flowered dress that accented her near-perfect figure, with her slender, tanned arms and shapely legs, her shining golden hair, her eyes the color of the ocean and her sweetly pretty face, it didn't seem possible that any man in his right mind would have turned her down.

So Felipe laughed, praying hard that Tommy would get the joke.

He did. Tommy's beefy boxer's face crinkled slightly in a tight smile that didn't reach his eyes. But then again, Felipe had never seen Tommy truly smile.

"She's crazy, man," he said to Tommy, grateful at least for that half smile. He turned back to Carrie. "Sweetheart, I know you must've been upset when I was gone in the morning but—"

Carrie crossed her arms and turned her imperious gaze on the maître d'. "Call the police. I want this man arrested."

"You must be confusing me with someone else," Felipe said, in a last-ditch effort to keep her from revealing his true identity. But he knew it was too late. Yes, Tommy was smiling, but he was smiling as if the joke was on Felipe.

"Oh, no," Carrie said with certainty. "You're Carlos, all right. And it wasn't August. It was July. July 22. You were with that son of a bitch you called T.J. And that other guy you called Iceman and—"

Carrie kept talking, but Felipe didn't hear her. He didn't hear her because she'd just told Richter clear as day that he was a cop.

Iceman. Her mention of Iceman had given him away.

Iceman had been one of St. Simone's hardest-working drug pushers.

And Iceman had owed Richter a cool quarter million at the time of his death. The money had been borrowed in order to make an investment in what was quite possibly the biggest small-time drug shipment to hit the west coast of Florida. The money had been borrowed and never paid back, because when Iceman and T. J. Cerrone and big, nose-ring-bedecked Randall Page, a.k.a. Mule, went to pick up the shipment of cocaine, the police went, too.

Although surrounded and clearly outgunned, Iceman had pulled his weapon and started a gun battle that had injured four police officers and left himself and his two business associates dead.

It had happened last summer, on the night of July 22, to be precise. And if Felipe had been with Iceman on July 22 before his death, it could only mean one thing.

Richter was a smart man. Tommy Walsh, despite the fact that he looked like an aging boxer, was a smart man, too. They could add one plus one, and in this case, one plus one equaled cop.

Richter looked at Tommy and Tommy looked at Richter, and Felipe knew that they'd come to the obvious conclusion.

"You were good," Tommy said quietly to Felipe, speaking to him in the past tense as if he were already dead. "You just weren't lucky enough."

Tommy's pale blue eyes flickered once toward Caroline, and Felipe knew with dreadful certainty that Richter's right-hand man was going to use the petite blonde to make sure Felipe cooperated. Tommy was going to threaten to blow Caroline's brains across Schroedinger's lobby if Felipe didn't go quietly with him out to the parking lot and Richter's waiting limo.

But if Felipe went along for the ride, it would be his last ride. He had no doubts that Tommy would take him into the Everglades and kill him. And then he'd kill Caroline, too, because by then, *she'd* have seen and heard too much. Dear God, she'd probably already witnessed enough to warrant her death in Tommy's mind.

From the corner of his eye, Felipe could see the big glass doors that led out of the restaurant. Outside, a valet pulled an expensive-looking car under the brightly lit awning.

As if in slow motion, Tommy reached under his jacket for his gun.

The valet got out of the car, leaving the door open. He crossed to the other side and opened the front passenger door as the owners of the car, a middle-aged couple, started out into the Florida night.

It was now or never.

Felipe turned, scooped Caroline into his arms and ran for the door.

She screamed in outrage, just as he knew she would. He prayed that drawing attention to themselves this way would keep Tommy from pulling out his gun right there in the lobby and shooting Felipe in the back.

Felipe heard the muffled thud of a gunshot, then a bullet whizzed by his left ear, and he knew with a sinking heart that Tommy wanted him dead badly enough to risk going to prison himself. He shielded Caroline Brooks with his body and moved even faster, hoping desperately that Tommy would miss again. But Tommy didn't often miss, and Felipe knew without a doubt that the gunman's next shot was going to hit him.

The car's owner was still holding the glass door open for his wife, and Felipe knocked them both aside, praying they wouldn't get caught in the cross fire.

Tommy was using some kind of silencing device—most of the people around them were unaware of the gun, unaware of the danger.

"Get down," Felipe shouted, shifting Caroline easily into one arm, drawing and brandishing his own gun. "Everyone down!"

The valets scattered.

As Felipe threw Caroline into the front seat of the waiting car, slamming the door behind her, he felt a slap hit the back of his leg. He scrambled up and over the hood of the car and into the driver's seat. The keys were in the ignition and the motor was idling, and he threw it into gear.

The tires squealed on the pavement as the powerful engine responded. Felipe knew he'd been shot. He knew his leg was bleeding, but the pain hadn't registered yet. It was masked by the adrenaline surging through his veins. Besides, a bullet in the leg was nothing compared to what might have been.

He was alive. He was still alive.

Tommy's aim was usually unerringly accurate, and Felipe knew that it had only been good fortune that had kept the bullets from slamming first into the back of his head, and then into the small of his back. Or maybe somebody was listening to his prayers.

But that somebody wasn't listening to all of them.

In the rearview mirror, Felipe could see Richter's limousine leave the parking lot, bouncing as it took the slope of the driveway too quickly. Tommy was following them. This wasn't over yet.

Next to him in the car, Caroline Brooks had stopped screaming. One glance in her direction told Felipe that she was watching him. Her face was pale and her eyes were big. That and her rapid breathing revealed the fear she was trying so hard to hide.

"Fasten your seat belt," he told her curtly over the roar of the engine.

"Just let me out of the car," she said, talking low and fast, working hard to keep fear from raising the pitch of her voice. "I don't know what your game is, mister, but you don't need me to play it."

"I don't need you," Felipe agreed, taking a hard right turn that took an inch of rubber off the tires. Caroline lost her balance and was thrown across the seat nearly onto his lap. "But you need me."

"Like hell I do." She scrambled back, away from him, and quickly fastened her seat belt.

Sixty miles an hour. He was going sixty miles an hour on shadowy back streets. His mind was going even faster.

Tommy was right behind them. It would take quick thinking and a great deal of luck to lose him—Tommy Walsh was one of the best when it came to pursuit. And even if Felipe *did* lose him, he couldn't be sure he'd actually succeeded. He couldn't be certain that Tommy hadn't simply faded into the background, unseen but ready to blow Felipe away the moment he stepped out of the car.

Even if Felipe drove directly to police headquarters, Tommy would gun him and Caroline down in the parking lot.

There wasn't too much Felipe could do short of driving this expensive car up the front steps and through the double doors of the St. Simone Police Department's Fourth Precinct.

No. He had only one option here. And that was to lead Tommy to a place where Felipe would at least have a fighting chance at defending himself.

Felipe went through a red light, swerving to avoid hitting a pickup truck, and Caroline yelped in fear.

"Look," she said sharply. "Just pull over and let me out."

"I can't do that," Felipe said.

"Whatever you're wanted for," Caroline said sharply, "kidnapping me will only make it worse."

Felipe took a sharp left at Ocean Street, leaving more of the car's tires behind on the street. There was heavier traffic in this part of town, and he kept his eyes on the road, praying that no cars would pull out in front of him.

"I'm not wanted for anything," he told her matter-of-factly. "I'm a cop."

Carrie stared at the man sitting so calmly next to her.

He was a cop?

He'd stolen a car and kidnapped her and now was driving like a lunatic, violating every traffic law in the book. And she was supposed to believe that he was a cop?

She laughed, but it had nothing to do with humor. "Try another one, Carlos. Or Raoul—or whoever you are."

"Felipe," he said in his gentle Hispanic accent, raising his voice only very slightly to be heard over the sound of the racing engine. "Salazar. I'm an undercover detective with the Fourth Precinct. You blew my cover back there, Miss Brooks. Those men I was with, they're very dangerous. We're lucky we're still alive."

Carrie stared at him as she braced herself against the dashboard. "Just pull over to the side and let me out," she said tightly. "And then you can get back to whatever little fantasy you've got going here, okay?"

He glanced at her with those deep chocolate brown eyes, those dark, penetrating eyes she'd seen so many times in her dreams, then looked back at the road ahead of them. His face was glazed with perspiration, and his hair curled damply around his face where it had come free from his ponytail. A bead of sweat traveled down past his ear and plopped onto the lapel of his tuxedo jacket.

"I'm sorry," he said apologetically. His eyes flickered up to the rearview mirror. "I can't do that. I can't stop. There's a man—Tommy Walsh—chasing us. He's not a very nice man. He wants me dead, and I think he's going to try to kill you, too."

Carrie loosened her hold on the dashboard and turned around. She looked over the back of the plush leather seat, through the rear window.

There *was* a car following behind them. It, too, was driving at breakneck speed. Tommy Walsh. He must be the balding man with pale eyes and a boxer's scarred face and muscular build who had approached them in the lobby.

"Well, I think *he's* the cop and *you're* the bad guy," she said. "That's usually how these chases work, isn't it?"

"Not this time," Felipe told her. "I've been under cover for five months and I've witnessed some things that would put Walsh—and his boss—into prison for years. They aren't going to let me get away without a fight."

Carrie looked at the car that was following them, at Mr. Muscles, and then at Felipe. How could she possibly believe *any*thing this man told her?

"All right," she said abruptly. "Show me your ID. If you're a cop, prove it."

But he shook his head, still watching the road. "Do you know what it means to be deep under cover?"

They were rapidly approaching a red light. Carrie could see the traffic crossing the intersection in front of them, but Felipe didn't hit the brakes.

"Lord in heaven," she gasped. "Slow down!"

"Hold on," Felipe said, and gunned the car even faster.

They were going to die. Forget about Mr. Muscles in the car behind them. Forget Mr. Muscles, who Carlos—or Felipe or whoever he was—said wanted to kill them. They were going to die all by themselves, without anyone's help.

Carrie shrieked and held on as they roared through the red light, but her voice was drowned out by the sound of squealing tires and blaring horns as first one, then another and another car swerved. Then one vehicle went into a skid and slid sideways into them. Metal scraped against metal, creating a chilling, awful, screeching sound.

And then it was over. They were through the intersection, once more going sixty down Ocean Street.

Carrie glanced back through the rear window. Unbelievably, the big, dark limousine was still behind them.

"When a detective goes deep under cover," the dark-eyed man said calmly, as if nothing were wrong, as if they hadn't just nearly been killed in a car accident, as if he hadn't just removed all the paint from one side of this expensive car— this *stolen* car, "when he intends to infiltrate an organized-crime outfit, he does not bring any police identification with him. Hold on again, please."

Felipe yanked the steering wheel hard to the left, cutting across the oncoming traffic to pull into a narrow side street. The car skidded on loose gravel and dirt, hitting a metal garbage can with a bang and a crunch. The windshield was instantly covered with a layer of rotten vegetables.

"Oh, Lord," Carrie breathed, and for the first time since she'd seen the panic in Felipe's eyes at the restaurant, the man seemed unsettled.

He muttered in Spanish, alternately searching the dashboard for the controls to the windshield wipers and peering at the narrow road through a tiny hole in the muck.

Carrie saw it first. Loosening her grip on the dashboard, she reached over next to the steering wheel and switched on the wipers.

"*Gracias,*" Felipe said. "Thanks."

"Don't bother," Carrie said tersely. "It was pure self-preservation."

"I'm sorry you had to become involved in this," Felipe said, glancing at her, then back in the rearview mirror at the car still following them. "It was an unfortunate coincidence that we were both at that same restaurant."

The neighborhood they were roaring through was run-down and unkempt, with crumbling stuccoed apartment buildings, their wooden porches sagging and rotten. The road, too, had seen far better days. Carrie's teeth rattled as they hit another pothole.

"I *had to* become involved?" Carrie said skeptically. "You really expect me to believe that Mr. Muscles would *kill* me simply for talking to you at Schroedinger's?"

"You were a witness," Felipe said.

"A witness to *what?* A conversation?"

"When I turn up dead or missing," Felipe said, taking another sharp right turn, "there'll be a great deal of publicity. You're the only one who can place me in that restaurant lobby with Tommy Walsh—Mr. Muscles, if you will— and Lawrence Richter. It's not enough to base a murder case on, but Walsh is known for his caution."

Carrie glared at him. "There were twenty other people in that lobby," she said. "Is Muscles going to kill them, too? That is, assuming he really does want to murder you."

"Hold on," Felipe said.

"Lord, I hate when you say that," Carrie muttered, bracing herself by bending her knees and putting her feet up against the dashboard.

They were coming to the end of the side street. Felipe could turn either left or right onto Clark Road. For once, the light was green.

Felipe took a left, and then an immediate right, going the wrong way down a one-way street.

Carrie bit back a shout. There was no need to point out his mistake. Because it was no mistake. He knew exactly what he was doing.

"With the exception of the maître d'," Felipe said calmly as if their conversation hadn't been interrupted, "who's probably on Richter's payroll, you were the only one in that lobby who knew me well enough to make a positive ID."

"Know you?" Carrie said. "I don't know you at all. And there's no reason for anyone to think that I do."

"But you're wrong," he said.

He glanced at her again, and in a flash, Carrie remembered those kisses. He had kissed her—twice—there in Schroedinger's lobby, and she knew just from looking at him, that he was remembering it, too. His gaze dropped to her legs, to where her ungainly position had caused her skirt to fall away from the tops of her thighs.

They were barreling, sixty miles an hour, the wrong way down a one-way street, and he was sneaking looks at her legs?

No, not sneaking. He wasn't sneaking anything. There was nothing even remotely clandestine about the way he looked at her legs. His gaze was almost leisurely, appreciative and very, *very* male. And he glanced up and met her eyes afterward, as if he wanted to make sure she knew that he'd been looking at her legs.

That's when she saw it. The car phone. It was in a special case between their seats. Carrie pointed at it. "If you're a cop," she said, "why don't you call for backup?"

"Because I don't have the telephone's access code," Felipe said. "I've already checked. It's got a valet lock. You know, so the parking-lot attendant doesn't make a hundred dollars' worth of long-distance phone calls while the owner's having dinner?"

"You have an answer for everything, don't you?" Carrie observed tartly.

"Unfortunately, no," Felipe said. "I haven't figured out a way to get rid of Tommy Walsh without putting you in real danger."

Real danger? *Real* danger? Their current situation wasn't *really* dangerous? If this wasn't real danger, then what was?

The rear window shattered with a crash.

"Get down!" Felipe shouted, grabbing Carrie and pushing her onto the seat.

The right passenger mirror was blown completely off the car door.

He was shooting at them.

Mr. Muscles, the guy in the car behind them—Tommy Walsh or whoever he was—was *shooting* at them.

With a gun.

With bullets.

Real bullets.

The kind that could kill you.

"Hold on!" Felipe shouted again, and for the first time, Carrie was glad to hear him say those words. For the first time, she actually *wanted* him to drive even faster.

But the way she was down on the seat, there was no place to hold on to, nowhere to get a good grip.

The tires squealed as Felipe turned another corner and Carrie started to slide.

Felipe reached out with one hand and held her tightly, pulling her against him, anchoring her in place.

"He must've stopped and picked up a shooter," he said. "I saw him slow down, but I didn't see him stop."

Another bullet made a hole in the windshield and Felipe ducked.

And then the car phone rang.

Chapter 4

Caroline Brooks turned to look up at Felipe from her rather indelicate position, sprawled out on the seat across his legs, her head down. Normally, the sight of long, fine hair like spun gold fanned out across his lap would trigger rather powerful sexual fantasies. But at the moment, Felipe could allow himself only the very briefest possible flash of pleasure. And even if he had allowed himself to dwell on the possibilities, the fear and alarm in Caroline's blue-green eyes would have quickly brought him back to the task at hand.

Somewhere underneath beautiful Caroline Brooks, the car phone was ringing and Felipe knew exactly who was on the other end.

Caroline scrambled off him, her head carefully kept down behind the protective barrier of the seat back. Gunning the car to over seventy, Felipe picked up the phone.

"*Hola,* Tomás," he said.

There was a brief moment of silence. Then Tommy Walsh spoke.

"Give it up, Vasquez," he said. "Or should I call you *Detective Salazar?*"

Felipe's hand tightened on the phone. He wanted desperately to swear. He wanted to let loose a long stream of the blackest curses, but instead he kept his mouth tightly shut. By knowing his real identity, Tommy Walsh was already one giant step ahead of him. If Felipe vented his frustration by swearing, that would only reveal to Walsh just how badly he was rattled.

Before the silence stretched on too much longer, Felipe made himself laugh.

"Very good, Tomás," he said, taking the entrance ramp to the interstate and pushing the car even faster. Seventy-five. Eighty. "Please extend my admiration to Mr. Richter. His efficiency is—as usual—quite remarkable. Of course, it helps to have an inside man in the police force, does it not?"

It was Tommy Walsh's turn to let the silence turn stale.

"Here's how it's gonna work," Walsh finally said. "You give up and pull over, and I'll make it quick and painless. One bullet in the back of the girl's head, nice and neat."

Felipe glanced at Carrie. She was watching him, her eyes wide in the light from the dashboard, listening only to his side of the conversation.

"I recommend you stop and pick up a dictionary, Tomás," Felipe told Walsh, "and look up the definitions for both 'nice' and 'neat.' A bullet in the head is neither. It's ugly, in fact."

"No," Tommy Walsh said. "Ugly is what happens when I have to chase you all over kingdom come. Ugly is when I make you spend the last few hours of your life listening to your little girlfriend scream."

Eighty-five. Felipe shot past a row of semis that were themselves going well above the sixty-five miles-per-hour speed limit.

"So that's it," he said. "Option A or option B?"

"That's what it boils down to," Walsh replied.

Ninety.

"You know, man, there's always option C," Felipe said. "You give yourself up to me and plea bargain for your freedom in return for testifying against Richter—"

"Three more miles," Walsh interrupted him. "You pass the next exit, and we do it the ugly way."

The phone line was cut as Walsh hung up.

Carrie was still watching him. Felipe smiled ruefully. "I don't think he liked option C," he said, reaching over to put down the telephone.

"I want to get out," she said. "Just pull over and let me out. I'd rather take my chances with him." She gestured with her head back toward the car that was still following them.

One hundred. How much faster could this car go? Or a better question—how much faster could the limo Walsh was in go?

"I'd reconsider," Felipe said. "He just offered to put a bullet into your brain."

"That's what *you* say," Carrie said. "And we both know I have absolutely no reason to trust *you*."

Felipe nodded. "That's right," he said. "You don't. But if I were you, I'd test this situation with something smaller and less important than my life."

One hundred and five. One hundred and ten.

The exit was approaching, the green sign reflecting their headlights in the darkness. It was the point of no return. *Madre de Dios,* don't let him regret this. The thought of having to watch and listen as Walsh tortured Caroline Brooks was excruciating. But to simply pull over and quit... No. If they were going to die, they'd die fighting.

They shot past the exit, and sure enough, the shooter in the limo opened fire, trying for one of their tires.

At nearly one hundred and twenty, if they lost a tire, they'd be smeared across the road. But at nearly one hundred and twenty, the limo was hard-pressed to keep up. If only this car could go a little faster, they'd lose Walsh. Unfortunately, Felipe, too, had maxed out, with the gas pedal to the floor. Now all he could do was pray.

Pray, and turn off the headlights and rear running lights. Why give them a lighted target?

They were barreling into the darkness, with only the lights from the other cars and trucks to guide them.

But then, suddenly, the shooting stopped.

Felipe glanced into what was left of his rearview mirror.

He could see inside the limousine. The interior lights were on and Tommy Walsh was on the phone again. Walsh hung up and the limo began to slow.

As Felipe watched, Walsh moved into the right lane. As he raced up to the crest of a hill, he looked back and saw the limo's headlights turn away as the car exited the highway.

What the hell . . . ? Was Tommy Walsh giving up? Man, what just happened here?

Felipe had a sudden bad feeling in the pit of his stomach as he lifted his foot from the accelerator and the car began to slow. Something was wrong. Something was *seriously* wrong. The only time he'd ever seen Walsh back away was when his prey was dead. The implication was that in Walsh's eyes, Felipe and Caroline were already dead.

Still, Felipe hit the brakes and turned his lights back on. He could feel Caroline's eyes on his face as he searched the rearview mirror, watching for some sign of a trap. But there was nothing. There was no sign of the limousine, no sign they were being followed by anyone else.

He exited at a rest stop, pulling onto the ramp at the last instant, keeping his signal light off.

Caroline peeked over the back of the seat. "Did we lose them?"

"No," Felipe said tersely. "They lost us. Something's wrong."

"Something's *wrong?*" she echoed. "They're not shooting at us anymore. I'd consider that to be something *right.*"

"Tommy Walsh shouldn't have given up so easily," Felipe said, glancing at her. He had to make a phone call, find out what the hell was going on.

He saw a row of pay and credit-card telephones that could be accessed without leaving the car. That was good, because now that the immediate danger had passed, Felipe's leg was starting to hurt like hell. He parked next to one of the phones, leaving the car engine idling.

But even before the car had stopped moving, Carrie was out the door like a shot.

Felipe swore. He'd pulled up to these phones because he hadn't wanted to get out of the car. His pants were wet with blood and his leg was throbbing with an unholy pain. Despite the agony, he slid across the bench seat, leaving a smear of blood on the fancy leather upholstery. Carrie hadn't closed the door, and as he left the car after her, he hit the pavement running. *Man!* His leg hurt like a *bitch,* but he ran after her anyway. If he didn't catch her, she was as good as dead. Worse, he thought, remembering Walsh's threats.

The parking lot was mostly empty. There were a few cars but no people around. She headed toward a brightly lit fast-food restaurant.

"Caroline, wait!" Felipe called, but she only ran faster, harder.

She was fast, but she was small, and her stride was only three-quarters the size of his, even with a bullet in his leg.

He caught her before she reached the wheelchair ramp up to the front door of the restaurant, and pulled her down with him onto the soft grass that lined the sidewalk.

"No!" she cried. "Let me *go!*"

She took in a deep breath to scream and he covered her mouth with his hand, trying desperately to ignore the fire of pain shooting up and down his thigh.

"Stop it!" he hissed into her ear. "I'm not going to hurt you, but Tommy Walsh will. By now, he and Richter know who you are and where you live. You go home, you're *dead.*"

There was fear in her eyes as she looked up at him. But was it his words, or was it he, himself, that frightened her?

He realized with a sudden stab of awareness that he was on top of her, covering her with the full weight of his body. Mother of God, she was so very female, so very soft, and he was crushing her.

Keeping a tight hold on her arm, he rolled off her.

"I'm sorry," he said. "I didn't mean to..."

But now she was looking at him with new horror in her eyes. "Are you bleeding?" she breathed. "My Lord, you *are.*"

Her dress and part of her leg were streaked bright red with his blood.

Still holding her with one hand, Felipe pulled himself to his feet before helping her up. "I need to make a phone call,'' he said, ''and then we need to get out of here. We're not out of danger yet, Caroline.''

He winced as he put his weight on his wounded leg. But he tried not to limp as he led her back across the parking lot toward the car. On the off chance someone was watching, he didn't want them to know he was injured.

''Lord above,'' Carrie said, ''you were *shot*.''

He glanced at her. The expression in her eyes begged him to tell her otherwise, but Felipe nodded his head. ''Yes,'' he said. He had her full attention, and he pressed his advantage. ''This is not a game we're playing here. The bullets are very real, and Tommy Walsh is saving one or two of them especially for you, do you understand?''

He watched her steadily, seeing the doubt and mistrust on her face. What he would have given simply for her to trust him. But she didn't believe him. She didn't buy into what he was telling her. Even so, behind all that mistrust, he could see her concern.

In her mind, he was the enemy, yet she was concerned for his health. Felipe found himself smiling as he gazed at her. Despite her tough-guy exterior, she was softhearted. She was as sweet as she looked. Dear heaven, even with her dress rumpled and stained, and her hair windblown and messy, she still managed to look incredibly sweet.

''You better do something to stop the bleeding,'' she said, glancing up at him. She quickly looked away, but not before Felipe caught the answering heat of attraction in her eyes. Maybe sweet wasn't quite the right word....

''You know,'' he said softly, ''instinctively, you want to trust me, Caroline. Instinctively, there is this powerful attraction between us—''

Carrie laughed. ''I'd be willing to bet that instinctively, there's a powerful attraction between you and every woman on earth,'' she said, carefully not meeting his eyes.

He smiled again. ''Not like this,'' he said. ''Never like this.'' He closed the car door and led her around to the other side. He opened that door and, still holding her wrist, shrugged out of his tuxedo jacket. He handed it to Carrie. ''Use this to wipe off the seat, please, and then get in.''

To his surprise, she took it and tore it cleanly down the middle. She handed him back one of the halves. "Use this to tie around your leg to try to stop the bleeding," she said. "It *is* your leg that's hurt, isn't it?"

Felipe nodded, once again touched by her concern. Still, she wouldn't meet his eyes. "Yes," he said. "Thanks."

But he wouldn't let go of her wrist to tie the jacket around his leg.

"I won't run away," Carrie said.

Felipe just laughed.

In frustration, she took the torn fabric from him and tied it herself, folding a piece of the sleeve against the gash on his upper thigh, forming a bandage that applied pressure to the wound. Damn, it hurt. He had to grit his teeth to keep from crying out. He must have made some sort of sound, though, because she glanced up at him.

"Sorry," she whispered.

And she was. She was tending to him with as much compassion as she'd give a wounded manatee—or shark. Yes, Felipe could imagine her coming to the aid of an injured shark and disregarding its sharp, deadly teeth in the name of compassion.

Her hands were unquestionably gentle, but there was a hole in his leg where the bullet had entered. A hole, with a bullet still inside, that hurt like *hell*.

If she noticed the new layer of sweat that was glazing his face, she didn't mention it. "I've never been shot," she said, tying the bandage into place, "but my brother has—in a hunting accident. It was barely a scratch, but my other brothers had to carry him down from the mountains on a stretcher."

Brothers. Felipe realized in a flash just where they could go to hide. To his brother's. Of course. He'd cut himself off so thoroughly from Raphael, no one in the police force, including Jim Keegan, knew he had an older brother. Not even Richter would be able to track him there.

The pain had subsided to a dull, throbbing ache. Felipe forced his face to relax, then even managed to smile at Caroline. "Well, my brothers are not here right now," he said, "so I'll have to carry myself."

"You should go to the hospital," she said. "I didn't get a really good look at your leg in this light. I can't tell if the bullet's still in there. If it is, you're risking serious infection. If it's not, you still need stitches."

"The hospital can't treat a bullet wound without reporting it to the police," Felipe said. "I can't go in yet. Not until I know that it's safe for both of us."

"Please," she said, still looking up at him. "Just turn yourself in. You're clearly a man of integrity—"

"I'm so glad you've recognized that," Felipe said with a wry laugh.

"I'll go with you," she said. "I'll make sure no one hurts you. I'll help you get an attorney—"

"Caroline, I'm a cop," he said. "I don't need a lawyer."

"If you let me go right now," Carrie said as if she hadn't heard him, "I'll ask them to dismiss any kidnapping charges."

"I'm cop, a police detective," Felipe said again, looking down at her. "There will be no kidnapping charges. I wish you would believe me."

She still gazed up at him. "If you're a police detective, then let's go to the police station," she said beseechingly. "Right now. Let's just get in the car and drive over—"

"I can't."

She stood up. "Because you're not a cop."

Felipe shook his head. "No, because we're dealing with organized crime," he explained, "and they've bought someone in the department. Neither of us would last a day in local protective custody. Richter would be tipped off as to our every move, and he'd bring in a hit man to finish the job. And God knows how many good men and women would die trying to protect us."

Caroline didn't buy it—he could tell from the set of her mouth. "That's a convenient excuse," she said.

They were standing so close, she was forced to tilt her head to look up at him.

"I'm telling you the truth," he said.

She only laughed. "Are you sure you even remember the truth?" she asked. "Or maybe you simply change it with your name, Carlos. Or should I call you Raoul? No, wait, it's Felipe, isn't it? Yeah, Felipe Salazar, undercover cop."

"If you would get in the car, please, and sit down," Felipe said, feeling his patience start to slip, "then I could sit down, too. And I really, *really* would like to sit down."

She climbed into the car, and still holding tightly to her wrist, he followed her, closing the door behind him.

It was cool inside. With the engine running, the air conditioner kept the temperature down to a comfortable level. Caroline was silent as Felipe pushed the button that lowered the window, then reached outside the car for the telephone. He dialed Jim's direct number, glancing over at her.

It was so easy to imagine this woman sitting next to him in his own subcompact car, smiling instead of looking at him with this mixed expression of wariness and mistrust. He could imagine the sound of her laughter; he could picture amusement dancing in her beautiful eyes. And he could imagine bending to kiss her smiling mouth, her face upturned in anticipation of his lips.

"Jim Keegan, Homicide," said a familiar, husky voice on the other end of the line.

Felipe pulled his gaze away from Caroline's face. "Diego, it's me."

"Phil! Jesus! Thank God you're alive."

"Look, man, I need—"

"I'm sure you realize that this line's tapped," Jim said, cutting Felipe off and talking fast, "and that I've got to try to keep you on as long as possible so we can track you."

"Of course," Felipe said. My God, he'd had no idea. His heart sank. Obviously, Jim wasn't in any position to help him.

"An APB came in just a few minutes ago," Jim said. "All available men are looking for you and a stolen car, New York plate HTD-761."

In other words, ditch the car.

Jim Keegan was one of the few people who knew that Felipe had been trying to infiltrate Richter's organization. Why would he make hints for Felipe to stay away, to keep running, to stay hidden?

"You're wanted for the Sandlot Murders, pal," Jim said. "It's not my case, but the word is we've got evidence that ties you to the crime scene."

The Sandlot Murders? They'd happened less than a week ago. Two men with mob connections had been killed in a vigilante-style execution after they'd been released from prosecution on a technicality. Word on the street was that they'd been prepared to deal with the D.A. Now they were D.O.A. and a very obvious warning to the other underlings who worked for the crime bosses.

The media had sunk their teeth into the case because the murders were committed in a vacant lot next to an inner-city elementary school. The children were traumatized, the parents were in an uproar and the newspapers and TV stations were searching for someone to blame.

The triggerman could've been any one of a number of hired assassins. It was a high-profile case with virtually no chance of being solved.

It was the perfect case to use to create a frame.

It was so obvious. Richter's man in the police department, this partner of his, this "Captain Rat," had worked hard and fast to set Felipe up. It was such an obvious frame, it was almost laughable.

Almost.

But maybe, if he could stay alive long enough, the last laugh could be Felipe's. He may not know exactly who Captain Rat was, but he *did* know that there was a planned meeting between this man and Richter in less than three days, at three-thirty in the afternoon. But he couldn't tell Jim about it—not with the line being tapped and God only knows who listening in.

"I'm supposed to try to talk you into turning yourself in," Keegan said. "Just stay where you are, stay on the line and we'll come to you, you hear me?"

In other words, get out of there fast.

"I hear you, man," Felipe said. "Loud and clear." He hung up the phone.

Caroline Brooks watched him in silence.

"Diego can't help us," he told her, even though she had no idea who Diego was.

Diego couldn't help him, but maybe Raphael could.

It was time for a Salazar family reunion.

Chapter 5

Carrie heard the sirens in the distance at the same time Felipe did.

But instead of starting the car the way she expected, he opened the door.

"You're wearing sandals, not heels, am I right?" he asked, looking down the length of her legs to her feet. "Good," he added, not even waiting for her to answer. "Come on."

He was still holding on to her wrist, and he tugged her gently out of the car.

"Where are we going?" she asked.

"The police are looking for this car," he answered, leading her across the parking lot toward a grove of trees, beyond which shone the lights of a suburban street. "We're better off on foot."

"The police," she said. "I thought you *were* the police."

"I am," he said.

"Then how come they're looking for this car?" she asked. "And you, too, I assume?"

"Because they don't know that I'm one of the good guys, and that one of the bad guys is in the department," Felipe said.

His hair had come free from his ponytail, and it curled around the shoulders of his snowy white tuxedo shirt. He'd untied his bow tie and unbuttoned the top few buttons of the shirt, its perfection now marred by darkening stains of blood. He was still shockingly handsome, despite the lines of pain Carrie could see on his face.

His eyes were as soft and as dark as the night sky above her, and equally mysterious. If she could suspend all disbelief, it would be easy to see him as one of the good guys. In a more perfect world, no criminal could possibly have eyes so kind, so warm. If she looked at him for too long, she felt as if she were being pulled into some kind of vortex—spinning, imprisoning, consuming.

She looked away, and from the corner of her eye, she saw him smile at her confusion.

"You really don't want to like anything about me, do you?" he asked as he led her into the cover of the trees. "Careful where you step," he added.

"Let me go," Carrie countered, "and I'll be your best friend."

It was dark in among the trees, away from the lights of the parking lot. The ground was spongy and wet. Mud squished up over the soles of Carrie's sandals and between her toes.

He'd slid his hand down so that he was no longer holding her wrist. Instead, he was holding her hand, their fingers interlocked as if they were lovers rather than captor and hostage.

She could no longer see his face in the darkness, but she could hear his ragged breathing. His leg must hurt him. He stumbled slightly, and his grip on her hand tightened and she heard his quick inhale. He was clearly in serious pain.

But when he spoke, his voice was even. "I can't let you go, Caroline. I'm sorry."

"Then I can't be your best friend," she said.

"That's too bad," he murmured.

Yes, oddly enough, it was.

The sirens were louder now, and despite his injury, Felipe picked up the pace. Together they half ran, half skidded down an embankment to the street below.

One dim street lamp illuminated a row of shabby houses, blue television light flickering from most of the windows. In one of them the volume was up too high. Canned laughter echoed among the cars parked along the side of the road. Farther down the street, a dog barked, but other than that, nothing moved.

Here in the darkness, Felipe didn't try to hide his limp. Still, he moved quickly along the line of cars.

"What are you looking for?" Carrie asked.

He turned toward her, putting one finger to his lips. "Shh." Bringing his mouth up close to her ear, he said very softly, "We need transportation. I'm afraid I'm not up to walking back to St. Simone."

She pulled back to stare at him. "You're going to *steal* a car...?"

"Shh," he said again. "Not steal. Borrow."

Carrie nodded. "Right. Tell that to the guy who owns the car."

Felipe ran his hand across his face. "If there was another way, I wouldn't do this," he said. "But I believe a life— *your* life—is worth more than a 1979 Subaru, don't you?"

He tugged at her arm, and she knelt next to him as he opened the driver's-side door and quickly turned off the interior light. He pulled her in front of him, pinning her between the car and his body so he could use both of his hands.

"I'm worth a vintage Ford Mustang convertible," Carrie said. "Preferably from 1966 and cherry red."

He glanced at her and smiled, his teeth a flash of white in the darkness.

"I'm glad your sense of humor is back," he said, disconnecting a panel from the steering column.

"It's hard for me to keep my sense of humor when I'm being held hostage," Carrie said.

It was also hard to keep her sense of humor with his body pressed against hers the way it was. As he worked to hotwire the car, his arms were on either side of her, his weight against her. Carrie tried to shift away, but only succeeded in wedging herself more firmly against him.

He pulled back slightly to look down at her. "You're not a hostage," he said.

"Are you sure?"

He didn't hesitate. "Yes. You're in protective custody."

"Assuming you are who you say you are, Carlos-Raoul-Felipe," she said.

Felipe shifted his position, then winced as his weight came down more fully on his injured leg. He wiped the sweat from his upper lip. "I'm tempted to take you to my apartment in St. Simone, just to show you my police identification," he said.

"But no doubt you've got some dramatic excuse to keep us from going there, too," Carrie said, trying to ignore the fact that his face was mere inches from her own. If he leaned forward another four inches, he'd be kissing her.

"They're looking for me. My apartment is one of the first places they'll stake out," he said. "It's no dramatic excuse. It's a fact."

"They who?" Carrie asked. "The police?"

"The police and Richter's men," Felipe said. "They'll both send someone around to watch my apartment, assuming I'd be stupid enough to show up there." The car started with a roar. "Quick, get in."

Carrie scrambled across the stick shift and into the passenger seat. She reached for the opposite door and was about to throw it open, when Felipe firmly put his hand on her left knee.

"Give me a break," he said.

"Let me go," she countered.

"Haven't you been listening to *any*thing I've told you?" Felipe said. "Put the car in first gear, please."

With her left hand, Carrie pushed the stick shift up into first position.

With a jerk, Felipe pulled away from the curb.

"If I let you go," he said, trying hard to be patient, "you're dead. Second, please."

Carrie shifted into second gear as Felipe rounded a corner onto a secondary road heading south toward St. Simone.

"I do not want you to be dead," Felipe said, "therefore, I will not let you go. As long as you're with me, I'll keep you safe. Third gear, please."

Carrie snorted, shifting gears. "Oh, you've kept me really safe so far."

Felipe turned to look at her. His eyes were dead serious. "A lot of it's been luck, and circumstance," he said, "but yes, so far, I have."

His hand was still resting on her knee. She looked down at it pointedly. "You can have your hand back," she said. "I'm not going to jump out of a car going forty."

He glanced at her and grinned. "Thirty-five, you'd try it, but not forty, huh?" He squeezed her knee slightly, then put his hand on the stick, shifting into fourth gear. "Short of driving to the precinct or going to my apartment to get my ID, what can I do to make you believe me, Caroline?"

Nothing. Carrie shook her head. "If Silver-hair—this Richter guy—if he's such a threat, how come I haven't heard about him before?"

"He's very low-key," Felipe said. "Some mob bosses, they get off on people knowing who they are and how powerful they are, you know? But not Lawrence Richter. Instead of taking a seat on the city finance committee, or some position where the media would check into his background, Richter joined the public library's volunteer board of directors. The papers and TV reporters don't pay him any mind—he's not paid after all—and, through the contacts he's made, he has the ears of some of St. Simone's most powerful politicians."

"Lawrence Richter," Carrie mused. "Doesn't exactly sound like he's Old-World Mafia."

"The Mafia controls only a portion of organized crime," Felipe said. "These days, organized crime is an equal-opportunity employer."

He used the back of his arm to wipe the sweat from his face. This car's air conditioner wasn't anything to write home about. He glanced at her and tried to smile, but she could tell it was getting harder for him to hide his pain. His face was pale—it looked almost gray in the headlights from the oncoming traffic. She wondered how much blood he'd lost.

"Do you want me to drive?" she asked.

He looked at her in surprise. "No," he said. "I'm okay. Thanks."

She studied his face in the dim light from the dashboard. With his exotic cheekbones and liquid brown eyes, with his elegantly shaped mouth and sensuous lips, with that trim, athletic body, he could have made a fortune modeling for perfume ads or loose-fitting-jeans ads or, hell, even underwear ads. Maybe especially for underwear ads. Or, if he could dance even just a little bit, he could surely have made a bundle every night over at the Chippendale's club at the corner of Gulf and Garden Streets. But he didn't even seem aware of his striking looks—well, except for the fact that somewhere down the line, he'd learned that women responded to his smile. Or maybe that wasn't learned. Maybe it was instinctive.

He could have slid along in life, getting by with that smile and those warm, expressive eyes. Instead—so he claimed—he'd chosen to become a cop.

"What made you decide to join the police force?" Carrie asked.

He glanced at her again. "Is this a test?" he asked. "If I don't have an answer ready, that proves that I'm lying?"

"You're stalling," she returned. "Do you need more time to make up your story?"

"I became a cop," Felipe said without further hesitation, "because of my brother, Rafe. Raphael. He was a robber. I figured someone had to go in the other direction and balance the family out."

"That's it?" Carrie asked. "You just woke up one morning and decided that you had to be Wyatt Earp because your brother was Jesse James?"

He looked over at her. "You really want to hear the whole story?"

She pushed her hair back behind her ear. "Yeah," she said. Oddly enough, she did. "Is Rafe older or younger?"

"Older, by about five years," Felipe said. "He first started using when he was fourteen—I was nine."

"Using?"

"Drugs."

He stared at the road. Carrie could see the sudden tension in his jaw.

"We shared a bedroom," Felipe continued, "and he used to come in wasted and tell me not to tell our parents. He was my hero—how could I tell? Besides, it was a laugh at first. He was funny when he drank or when he got stoned. But then it stopped being funny when he started using the hard stuff.

"It happened real fast—he was an addict at fifteen. By the time I realized what was happening, I couldn't stop him. I don't know how many times I tried to talk sense into him, but you can't reason with an addict.

"I could only pick him up off the street when he was too high to walk, and carry him home. I could only hide his stash from my father. I could only give him the money from my paper route when he was broke and hurting and needing drugs to ease his pain. And I could keep my mouth shut when he started stealing."

Felipe glanced at Carrie, but she didn't speak. She simply waited for him to continue.

"Rafe didn't know it," he said, "but I gave back most of the stuff he stole. He thought he was getting ripped off by some of the other guys in the 'hood, but it was just me, covering his ass." He laughed, but the sound was devoid of humor. "Man, I was the perfect little enabler but I didn't even know the definition of the word. I was Rafe's worst enemy, second only to himself." He turned to glance at her again. "You sure you want to hear more?"

Carrie nodded. His words rang with a certain bitter truth. She actually wanted to believe him.

"Rafe and I did the addict-enabler dance for eight years," Felipe said, his gentle accent like music accompanying the soft hiss of the car's tires against the road. "Then, the summer I turned seventeen, one of the detectives in the local precinct started an outreach program designed to help kids like me—and indirectly, help kids like Rafe.

"By that time, Rafe had a few priors, nothing too big, and no punishment bigger than a reprimand. Still, this detective, Jorge Gamos, added up Rafe's record with what he saw going on in the neighborhood. Gamos actually came out on the street and hung with the kids. He got to know us. He saw that Rafe had a habit, and he also saw my stress levels, which were pretty high by that time. I was seventeen—going on forty-five. I hadn't been a kid since Rafe lit his first crack pipe. Anyway, Jorge Gamos saw what was going on, and he figured out—correctly—that my brother couldn't have lasted so long on the street if it hadn't been for me.

"It took Gamos nearly a year, but he finally talked me into going to a meeting that he helped run—a counseling session for kids who'd lost a brother or sister to drugs. It was…eye-opening, particularly when he told me that I was going to end up right there, with those kids, talking about my brother Rafe. My *dead* brother Rafe."

Carrie wanted to believe him, but his story was probably fictional. Still, it was one hell of a good tale. "Did Rafe die?" Carrie found herself asking, as if Rafe were a real person, as if Felipe really had been a kid who'd lost his childhood to drugs.

He glanced at her, a fleeting smile touching his lips. "Not yet," he said. "I virtually turned him in. He came to me for an alibi, but I wouldn't lie anymore. He was convicted and served an eight month sentence. During that time, he detoxed. When I went to see him in the jail, he thanked me for helping him, and he swore he'd never touch crack again. He was clean and he was going to stay clean. I was attending the police academy by that time. I was going to be a cop. With Jorge Gamos's help, I got Rafe an early release."

Felipe shook his head. "Raphael hit the streets and in a matter of weeks, he was using again. It nearly broke my heart. He'd conned me into getting him out of prison. His apology, everything he'd told me had been nothing but crap. None of it had been sincere. *None* of it." He laughed bitterly. "He ended up back in prison, but after he scammed me, I washed my hands of him. I haven't seen him in years. Apparently, Rafe's been out of jail for a while now. Jorge tells me he's really clean these days, that he runs a halfway house and works as a counselor for addicts and ex-cons. I've heard that counselors who've been addicts and ex-cons themselves are the most compassionate. Man, I guess he's got that covered because he's been there and back.'' He leaned over and tried to turn the air conditioner's fan higher. "That's where we're heading, by the way.''

Carrie blinked. "You mean . . . right now?''

"Yes. To Raphael's halfway house.'' Felipe glanced at her, his dark eyes even more mysterious. "It's time for my brother to pay some old debts.''

By the time Felipe pulled up in front of the A Street Halfway House, his left leg was on fire. He should have ripped off a car with an automatic transmission. Borrowed, he corrected himself. The car was only borrowed. And he'd memorized the plates so that when this was over, he could track down the owner and give him or her money for the mileage, gas and inconvenience.

If he was still alive when this was over. . . .

He looked over at Caroline Brooks who sat quietly in the passenger seat, gazing back at him, unmindful of the fact that they were parked in the most run-down, dangerous part of the city.

"Are you all right?'' she asked quietly.

Her blue eyes were colorless in the shadowy darkness. Her hair looked silvery, reflecting what little light there was. He could smell her perfume—no, that wasn't perfume. It was sun block that he smelled. Carrie wasn't the type to wear perfume. The fresh tang of the lotion suited her better than any flowery fragrance could have. She smelled like blue skies and white sand and warm gulf water. She smelled like paradise.

He'd had a bigger whiff when he'd kissed her back at the restaurant. He thought back to the way her lithe body had fitted against his. . . . Paradise indeed. Oh, what he would give to kiss her again.

"I must be all right,'' he said, finally answering her question. "The thoughts I am thinking are those of a healthy man.''

She turned away. It was too dark for him to see the blush tingeing her cheeks, but he knew it was there.

She was such a contradiction, this Caroline Brooks. Part of her was a tough-talking, rifle-wielding, no-nonsense fighter. But another part of her blushed at his sweet talk.

Felipe reached over and took her hand, and she nearly jumped out of her seat.

"I know it's an inconvenience to hop over the stick shift," he said, "but I need you to come out of the car this way. I can't risk your running again."

Still holding tightly to her hand, he opened the car door and stiffly pulled himself to his feet. Pain hit him in one solid wave and that, with his light-headedness, nearly made him black out. But Caroline was right behind him, and she held him up, looping his arm around her neck and supporting most of his body weight.

"Can you make it inside?" she asked, "or should I get help?"

Felipe tried to straighten up. "No way in *hell* am I going to face my brother on anything but my own two feet," he declared, then realized he had spoken in Spanish. God, he was losing it fast. The concern in Caroline's eyes was growing. "I can make it," he said, this time in English. He forced a smile. "Thanks for not running away."

Regret passed briefly across her eyes. "Yeah, well, I should have," she said, helping him around the car and onto the cracked sidewalk. "I'm leaving as soon as I get you inside."

"No, you're not," he countered. "I can't let you."

"Watch it," she said sharply, "or I'll drop you right here and run."

"If you do," he said, "somehow, someway, I will find the strength to follow you."

She turned to look up into his eyes, and he knew that she believed him. She may not have believed his story about his brother, she may not have believed that he was a cop investigating Lawrence Richter, she may not have believed that Tommy Walsh would kill her as easily as blinking, but she *did* believe that he would follow her.

It was a start.

Chapter 6

Raphael Salazar was bigger than his brother. He was older, harder, leaner to the point of being wiry, and several inches taller. His hair wasn't quite as long, though he, too, wore it pulled severely back from his face in a ponytail at his nape. But the biggest difference was in his eyes. Unlike Felipe's, Rafe's eyes were flat, cold and expressionless.

He didn't bother to greet his brother but simply came into the linoleum-tiled waiting room. Two other men, the two who had answered the door, stood slightly behind him. One was almost as broad as he was tall, his Bugs Bunny T-shirt stretched tight across his belly; the other was just a kid, looking barely even eighteen years old.

Rafe didn't move, didn't even blink. He just stared at Felipe, who was sitting on a hard bench against the far wall, Carrie at his side.

"Yes," Felipe said. "That's right, man. It's me."

Rafe took in the bloodstains and the makeshift bandage on Felipe's leg. Then his cold eyes flickered toward Carrie. He spoke softly, but in rapid-fire Spanish.

"In English, please," Felipe said. "Or she won't understand."

"Figures you'd get a gringa girlfriend," Rafe said. His voice was raspier, harsher than Felipe's. "Our kind's not good enough for you, eh, little brother?"

"My kind is human," Felipe said evenly. "Besides, she's not a girlfriend. She's in my protective custody."

"Does she have a name?" Rafe asked, looking back at Carrie.

His face was similar to Felipe's in shape, but because he was older, or maybe because he was thinner, his cheekbones looked angular, his nose sharp. He was dangerous-looking, like a wolf or an attack dog.

"She has one," Felipe said pleasantly. "But you don't need to know it. The fewer people who know her name, the fewer who can spread the word on the street that she was here, no?"

Carrie looked from Rafe to Felipe. "*She* doesn't like people talking about her as if she wasn't in the room, *if* you boys don't mind."

Rafe said something to Felipe in Spanish.

Felipe shook his head. "Stop," he said quietly.

Rafe turned again to Carrie. "Even though you are not one of our kind, I was pointing out your obvious physical attributes to my little brother," he said. "Sometimes he gets so caught up in being superhuman, he forgets that the people he's dealing with are mere flesh and blood."

Carrie looked at Felipe, but he was staring down at the floor. Even though this building was air-conditioned, he was still perspiring. His face was expressionless but his jaw was tightly clenched. Whether it was from his brother's harsh words or the pain from his bullet wound, Carrie couldn't tell.

As if he felt her eyes on him, Felipe glanced up. There was sadness in his eyes. He tried to force a smile, but failed miserably.

"I don't think I've ever seen him with his hair this long," Rafe continued. "He usually wears it well above his ears, you know? And I'm certain I've never seen him with his jacket off and trousers torn. What's the deal with my little brother? He under cover?"

"I don't know." Carrie stood up. "I'd like to leave," she said, lifting her chin and staring straight into Rafe's peculiar, lifeless eyes.

Felipe reached out and took her arm. Rafe, of course, didn't miss the move.

"But you're in 'protective custody,' no?" he said. "Maybe you don't think you need to be? Ah, but Felipe, he always knows what's best for everyone else. Felipe, he's always right. Except..." Rafe's gaze flickered back to the bandage on Felipe's leg, and all the blood that covered what was left of his tuxedo. "Maybe this time Felipe was a little *too* right, huh? And maybe someone with a gun doesn't like being wrong. Was it anyone I know, *niño?* One of our other brothers and sisters perhaps? Maybe you've betrayed one of them lately, the way you've betrayed me, huh?"

That one hurt. Even though Felipe's expression didn't change, his fingers tightened around her wrist, and Carrie knew that the barbs from Rafe's sarcastic comment had struck hard.

Still, when Felipe spoke, his voice was even. "You don't know the man who shot me," he said. "But you probably know *of* him."

Rafe laughed, but it was humorless. "I know of half a dozen men who'd probably like very much to shoot you or any one of the men in blue you work with," he said, "and that's without thinking very hard."

"This one's real trouble, man," Felipe said.

He spoke quietly, but there was something in his tone that made Rafe pause. He turned to the two men who were standing behind him and spoke to them in Spanish. They went out of the room, closing the door behind him.

"Tommy Walsh," Felipe said. He glanced at Carrie. "He wants us both dead."

"Walsh," Rafe said. His thin face became even more wary and aloof.

Carrie felt fear flicker in the pit of her stomach. Rafe's quiet response to Walsh's name told her more than any louder reaction could've done.

"I need help," Felipe said quietly. "I'm in deep, man. I've been shot, Walsh is after us and Richter's got a man in my department, ready to get rid of me the minute I resurface at the precinct.''

"So you come to me," Rafe said softly, sarcastically. "I'm touched."

"All I want is to get cleaned up," Felipe said. "A shower, and maybe some clean clothes for both me and..." He looked at Carrie. "Her."

Rafe smiled, a bitter twist of his lips that attempted to hide his anger. "You don't even trust *me* with her name, huh?"

"I'm sorry," Felipe said. "I don't."

Rafe's temper exploded. "You're not sorry, you self-righteous, holier-than-thou son of a—"

"You're wrong," Felipe interrupted him, his cool vanishing, too. His voice shook with passion and he pulled himself clumsily to his feet. "I spent more years sorry than you even have memories of. Sorry for *your* mistakes, sorry for *your* pain. Sorry for you, and sorry for myself, too, because your mistakes and your pain were mine to share. They were *my* burden, too. I *am* sorry I don't trust you, but I don't. That's one thing you taught me well, Raphael—that you were not to be fully trusted, *never* to be fully trusted."

"If you don't trust me," Rafe snarled, "why the hell did you bother to come here? How do you know I'm not going to run out and tip Walsh off that you and little Miss No-name are here?"

"I don't know that you're not going to," Felipe said. "I can only hope that you won't. I can only pray you'll remember everything I've done for you—"

"You kept me from hitting bottom on my own," Rafe countered hotly. "Because of you, it took me another three years to come clean."

"When some people hit bottom, they hit with enough force to kill themselves," Felipe said. "I knew you were going to hate me for doing it, but I loved you and I didn't want you to *die*." He shook his head in resignation and turned to Carrie. "Come on, we're getting out of here. He's not going to help."

"I don't hate you," Rafe said, suddenly quiet.

To Carrie's surprise, his eyes were filled with tears, tears and a depth of emotion that made his eyes look so much more like Felipe's. But then he blinked, and both the tears and the emotion were gone, leaving his eyes oddly flat again.

"My apartment's on the second floor," Rafe continued, his voice still quiet. "You can take a shower there. There're clothes in the closet. Help yourself. I'll have Highboy show you up."

And with that, Rafe turned and walked out of the room.

Raphael Salazar's apartment consisted of one small room with a tiny attached bathroom. He had a sofa bed with a small coffee table in front of it and a cheap television set and a VCR on a stand in front of that. There was nothing on the walls—no pictures, no photos, nothing to personalize the room.

A dresser stood in the corner, with shaving supplies and a brush and comb neatly arranged on top, a small mirror attached to the wall above it. Several days' worth of newspapers were on the coffee table, but they, too, were neatly stacked.

In the other corner was a makeshift kitchen area, with a tiny sink built into an equally tiny counter area. A small table and a pair of cheap kitchen chairs sat nearby. On top of the table was a hot plate and a plastic sugar bowl. Underneath the table was a small, square refrigerator.

There was one window, with bars both on the inside and the outside.

Felipe locked the door behind the man in the Bugs Bunny shirt—Rafe had called him Highboy. He limped to the window and pulled down the shade.

"So, you see? My brother Rafe's real," he said to Carrie. "Any chance you're starting to believe what I've told you about Walsh and Richter?"

Carrie could see herself in the mirror over the dresser. Her hair was tangled and limp. She had a smudge of blood—Felipe's blood—across her cheek. *Was* she starting to believe him? She didn't know what to think anymore.

Felipe sat down on one of the kitchen chairs. He didn't wait for her to answer. "Why don't you take a shower?" he suggested gently. "You'll feel better. It'll clear your head."

"We need to—*you* need to get your leg cleaned up," Carrie said. "You should go first."

His eyes were warm as he looked up at her. "Thanks," he said. Then he peered at his roughly bandaged leg and grimaced. "But it's going to take me a while to get undressed. So go ahead. Just don't use up all the hot water, okay?"

He started unfastening the mother-of-pearl buttons of his tuxedo shirt, and Carrie turned away. A shower seemed like an especially good idea—particularly since the alternative was to stand and watch Felipe strip down to his underwear. Or beyond.

Carrie quickly went into the bathroom.

It was as Spartan as the rest of the apartment. The white tile floor was spotless. The sink, tub and toilet were gleaming white porcelain. The shower curtain looked fairly new. It was clear plastic, and it hadn't yet been fogged up by mildew and age. The room was devoid of any personal items—with the exception of a copy of *Off Road Cycle* magazine on the top of the toilet tank. A small cabinet held clean white towels in a neatly folded stack.

There was no window for her to climb out of and escape.

Carrie wasn't quite sure whether to feel disappointed or relieved. Because the truth was, Rafe's reaction to the name Tommy Walsh *had* made her start to wonder if Felipe's story wasn't true.

Lord above, maybe Felipe *was* a cop.

Carrie locked the door securely behind her and quickly stripped off her clothes.

The shower felt good, and she washed her hair with Rafe's inexpensive shampoo, wondering if maybe everything Felipe Salazar had told her was the truth.

If that was the case, he'd saved her life more than once tonight. And with no thanks from her.

She came out of the shower and toweled herself dry. She didn't want to put her bloodstained dress back on, but she had no choice.

She also had no comb, so she ran her fingers through her wet hair, trying to untangle it. When she'd done the best she could, she put her hand on the doorknob.

Taking a deep breath, Carrie opened the door. She opened it slowly, then peeked around to see if Felipe had moved from his seat in the far corner of the room.

He had. He was standing in front of the tiny kitchen sink, his back to her. He'd undressed down to an expensive-looking pair of dark green and navy blue paisley silk boxer shorts and a white tank undershirt that contrasted with the rich darkness of his tanned skin. He was wearing more than he would have had she run into him on the beach. Still, he was in his underwear, and Carrie felt uncomfortable—possibly because she had dreamed about him wearing even less.

His body was as trim and athletic as she'd imagined. The sleek muscles in his shoulders and arms rippled as he supported his weight on the kitchen counter. The water was running, and he didn't hear her as she approached.

Without his pants on, she could clearly see the wound that the bullet had made on the side of his thigh, just under the edge of his shorts. He was lucky that the bullet hadn't hit an artery. The wound was still bleeding slightly, or maybe it was bleeding again from his attempts to clean threads of tuxedo fabric from the gash. Bright red blood trickled slowly down his leg.

As she watched, he reached into the sink to wring water and blood from a washcloth he was rinsing out. He swayed slightly and caught himself on the edge of the sink, closing his eyes and trying to breathe deeply.

"Why don't you sit down?" Carrie said. "I'll do that."

He opened his eyes and turned to look at her. "Ah," he said, "you're out of the shower."

"Sit down," she said again. She took the washcloth from his hands and finished rinsing it in the sink.

Felipe didn't move. He stood there, inches away from her, so close she could feel the heat from his body.

"So," she said, turning off the water and wringing the cloth out, "what on earth made you decide to be a detective in the vice squad? I figure you're vice, right? That's where organized crime fits in, doesn't it?"

She looked steadily up into the warmth of his brown eyes. He looked back searchingly, and then he smiled, a real genuine smile despite his pain. It softened his face and made him seem so much younger.

But he *was* young, Carrie realized. He probably wasn't much older than she was—twenty-five. He was twenty-six or twenty-seven at the most.

"You believe me." It was a statement, but his eyes were full of questions.

"God help me," Carrie said. "I think I'm starting to. But..." She shook her head, pulling away from the hypnotizing heat of his eyes, turning back to the sink.

"What?"

He touched her. It was just a light hand on her shoulder, just the gentlest of caresses.

"You have a question?" he asked. "I'll answer anything you want to know, if I can."

Carrie moved out of reach, crossing her arms in front of her, afraid of the way that touch made her feel. "I still can't believe anyone would want to kill *me*," she said. "I didn't even get a good look at that muscle man—you know, Tommy Walsh." She shook her head. "I probably wouldn't even be able to pick him out in a lineup."

"Probably," Felipe said. "Probably's not good enough for Tommy. He'd kill a blind man at a crime scene simply on the off chance that the man caught a whiff of his cologne. Promise me something, Caroline."

She looked up at him, and once again was sucked into the intensity of his gaze.

"Promise me you'll ask Rafe—or anyone else here—about Tommy Walsh," Felipe said. "Please don't leave until you hear what the word on the street is about him. Promise me you won't leave."

Carrie swallowed. He was so serious, so intense. His hair was slick with perspiration and several stray curls clung to the side of his handsome face. With his midnight eyes, he was willing her to agree.

"Promise me," he whispered again.

She nodded, not sure whether or not she was lying. "All right."

But he believed her and relief made him sag. She moved quickly beside him, holding him up.

"Come on," she said. "You better sit down."

"Part of my problem," Felipe said ruefully, "is that I've got a bullet where I sit down."

He did, too. Still have a bullet in his leg, that is. There was an entry wound, but no exit wound. That was bad. That was *really* bad, especially since he refused to go to the hospital. Carrie helped him into one of the kitchen chairs.

He swore softly in Spanish. The change in his position must've hurt like hell. Carrie knelt next to him.

"You're going to need to get that bullet out," she said, examining the back of his leg. "This already looks infected."

He nodded slowly. "Unfortunately, I can't do it myself."

"You need a doctor," Carrie said.

"That's going to have to wait," Felipe said.

"Until when?" Carrie asked. "Until after you get so sick you can't even stand, or until after you die?"

Felipe pushed himself up off the chair. "I need a shower," he said. "Then I'll figure out what to do."

"You'll need antibiotics, too," Carrie said. "Where are you going to get them?"

"I don't know." Painfully, he reached down to where he'd thrown his pants onto the floor, and dug through his pockets. He pulled out a key.

"Since you trust me," he said, handing her the key, "it's only fair that I trust you." He gestured to the key. "It's for the dead bolt on the apartment door."

Carrie glanced at the door, then back at the shiny key in her hand.

"You promised me you wouldn't leave," Felipe reminded her.

He turned, carrying his bloody clothes and his shoulder holster and gun with him to the bathroom. He pushed the door shut behind him, but didn't latch it.

Carrie heard the water turn on. Slowly, she sat down on the sofa.

Felipe needed a doctor. They both needed some kind of protection from this Tommy Walsh. And—if Felipe's story really was true—Felipe needed to figure out exactly who in the police department was on Lawrence Richter's payroll.

Carrie shook her head. It was too much. A few hours ago, her biggest problem had been how to ditch her date without hurting his feelings. Now she was neck-deep in intrigue and murder attempts... and undercover police detectives with charming smiles that could make her melt.

It was getting more and more difficult *not* to believe Felipe. Was his story really becoming more convincing, or was she simply falling victim to his persuasive eyes?

Still, if she truly were his hostage, he wouldn't have given her a key to the door. He wouldn't have risked the possibility of her running away.

A sharp knock on the door broke into her thoughts and made her jump up.

"Who's there?" she asked, aware once again that she was holding the key. She could actually unlock the door if she wanted to.

"Rafe," Felipe's brother's voice replied. "I've brought something for you to eat. Open up."

Carrie slipped the key into the dead bolt's lock, but it didn't fit. She tried again. No, it was definitely the wrong key. "They key doesn't work," she said.

"There are two keys," Rafe said impatiently. "One has a round head, the other is square. The round one opens the dead bolt. The square is for the bathroom door."

Carrie looked down at the key in her hand. The head was square. Felipe hadn't given her the key to unlock the apartment door after all.

"The food's outside the door," Rafe said, his voice already fading as he walked away.

So much for Felipe trusting her...

Carrie turned and looked at the bathroom door. It was ajar, and she could clearly hear the shower still running.

Lord, maybe she *was* his hostage. Maybe everything he'd told her was one great big lie.

Angrily, she marched to the bathroom door and pushed it open.

Felipe was in the shower, eyes closed, hands braced against the tile wall as he let the water stream down onto his head. She could see him clearly through the plastic shower curtain. He was naked, of course. He was very, *very* naked.

Which made sense, again of course, because he was in the shower.

The bathroom door slowly swung all the way open and hit the wall with a thud.

Felipe looked up and directly into Carrie's eyes.

For one heart-stopping moment, the rest of the world ceased to exist. Tommy Walsh and Lawrence Richter and all the car chases and gunfire and anger and mistrust vanished, swirling down the drain with the blood-tinged water. Carrie was all that was left behind—Carrie, and this incredible-looking man, with his seemingly perfect, gentle smile and kind brown eyes.

But he wasn't smiling now, and his eyes couldn't possibly be described as kind. Hot, yes. Intense, definitely. Passionate, absolutely.

He made no effort to cover himself. Clearly, he was comfortable with his body—and why shouldn't he be, with a body like that? He had muscular legs, narrow hips, a flat stomach with a full array of washboardlike muscles. His chest was wide, his shoulders were broad and his arms were powerful-looking.

His skin was smooth and slick with water, accentuating the planes and angles and curves of his muscles. He didn't have a tan line—either he sunbathed nude, or his skin was naturally a beautiful golden brown.

Felipe slicked his hair back out of his face and turned off the water. With one movement of his hand, he pushed the shower curtains open. Steam billowed into the tiny bathroom, following him as he stepped out of the tub, making him seem mystical and savage.

He reached for a towel and wrapped it around his waist, careful of his injured leg. "Is there a problem?" he asked in his gentle, musical accent.

For heaven's sake, she was standing there like a ninny, with her mouth hanging open, just staring at him as if she'd never seen a naked man before in her life.

She'd never seen one like Felipe, that was for sure.

"You gave me the wrong key," she said. Her voice came out sounding squeaky, not accusing or outraged the way she'd intended.

Water ran in tiny rivulets from his shoulders, down his neatly sculpted chest, up and down the ripples of his abdominal muscles and into the towel, knotted casually beneath his belly button. He had an exceptionally nice-looking belly button.

"You promised you wouldn't leave," Felipe said.

Carrie jerked her eyes up from where she'd been staring at his smooth, perfect stomach. "I didn't promise I wouldn't let your brother in," she said. "He brought up some food, and I couldn't unlock the door."

"You couldn't?" He sounded surprised.

"You knew perfectly well I couldn't," she said. He took another towel and began drying his dripping hair. "There were two keys—you purposely gave me the wrong one."

He was watching her. His eyes didn't give away either his guilt or his innocence. "My mistake," he said quietly.

A mistake? Carrie wasn't so sure. She couldn't believe this man ever made *any* mistakes.

Felipe had hung his torn and dirty tuxedo pants on the back of the bathroom door, along with his holster and gun. He reached into the pants pocket and took out another key.

"I'm sorry," he said, handing it to Carrie. "Please don't mistrust me because of this."

The key in her hand had a round head. It would unlock the dead bolt and let her out of Rafe's apartment.

"You're going to let me walk out of here?" she asked.

"You promised not to leave," he said. "You're a smart lady, Caroline. I don't think you will leave—not after you hear what my brother and his friends have to say about Tommy Walsh. And if you do decide you have to leave, I hope you'll be smart enough to go home to Montana."

"How did you know I'm from Montana?" she asked suspiciously.

He looped the second towel around his neck and sat gingerly on top of the closed toilet. He was hurting, but he still managed to smile at her. "After our first meeting at Sea Circus," he said, "I was...intrigued, shall we say? I went back—and not just to make sure you were all right, although I went back for that reason, too."

"If you're really a cop," Carrie said, searching his eyes for something, *any*thing that would convince her he was telling the truth, "why didn't you say something? Why didn't you introduce yourself to me?"

"I should have," he said simply. There were pages of meaning compressed into those three little words. His eyes caressed her face and Carrie had to look away. "I loved watching you with the dolphins," he added. "I've always wanted to swim with dolphins, but I think I'd draw the line at getting into the tank with the killer whales—what were their names? Biffy and Louise?"

She looked back up at him. "You really *were* there," she said. "Weren't you?"

Felipe nodded. "I came more than once," he said, "although I tried not to. I thought knowing me would be dangerous for you." He smiled ruefully. "Looks like I was right."

"Nothing at Sea Circus mentions that I'm from Montana," Carrie said. "Was that just a good guess?"

"No," he said. "Don't be angry, but I looked you up in the police computer. I also found out that you have the habit of driving too fast on I-75. Two speeding tickets in the course of one week. Eighty-one one day, seventy-nine the next." He shook his head, making tsking sounds. "Shame on you, Miss Brooks."

He was hiding a smile, but that smile finally slipped out. Carrie found herself smiling back at him.

"I have no excuse," she said, "and obviously I didn't learn my lesson, did I? I slowed down, but not by much."

"I took care of the tickets for you," Felipe said. "It was the least I could do after locking you in your trunk."

Carrie's smile faded. "Was that really necessary?" she asked. "I mean, assuming you really are a police detective, and assuming you really were under cover that night at Sea Circus. What do you really think would have happened if you hadn't locked me in the trunk of my car?"

Felipe sighed. "I *am* a police detective," he said, clearly disappointed that she still doubted him. "I *was* under cover that night. And if I hadn't put you in the trunk where you were safe, well, those men I was with? They were not very nice men. I would have had to hurt them. Or worse. Because I would not have let them hurt you.''

It was very hard not to believe him, not when he sat there, gazing up at her with that protective light in his eyes.

I would not have let them hurt you.

Carrie could almost believe it. She *wanted* to believe it.

"Talk to Rafe," Felipe said. "Talk to some of the other men who live here. Ask them about Tommy Walsh. Then come back and talk to me. Okay?"

Carrie nodded. Okay.

She turned and walked out of the bathroom. She could feel his eyes watching her as she crossed to the apartment door. She could feel him watching as she turned the key, unlocking the bolt. She glanced back once, then slipped out the door.

Felipe scrambled for the living room, searching for a clock. There was one on the VCR—it read 9:36 p.m.

Thank God.

The halfway house was locked up tight from 9:30 every night until 6:00 in the morning.

Carrie wouldn't be able to leave the building even if she wanted to—not without a great deal of trouble anyway. She certainly wouldn't be able to simply walk away.

And that was good, because Felipe couldn't let her leave. He would not let her get killed, even if that meant locking her up, holding her prisoner. Even if it meant that she would hate him.

Better that she hated him and stayed alive, than loved him and died.

Chapter 7

Carrie hadn't really noticed when she'd first come in, but now she realized the entire halfway house was as spotlessly clean and orderly as Rafe's apartment. The halls and stairway were swept and brightly lit, and the walls wore a fresh coat of paint.

She wandered down past a large common room and into the kitchen. Highboy was cleaning the stove, an apron tied carefully around his wide expanse.

Rafe was sitting at the kitchen table, drinking a diet cola straight from the can. He looked up as Carrie lingered in the doorway.

"Is he okay?" Rafe asked without greeting. They both knew who he was talking about. Felipe.

Carrie shook her head. "He's still got a bullet in his leg," she said. "Not only does it hurt him, but it's going to make him sick."

Rafe blinked. "I know what a bullet does, what it can do," he said. He turned to the man cleaning the stove, and spoke to him in Spanish.

The man nodded and left the room, squeezing past Carrie, who still stood in the doorway.

"Gracias," Rafe called after him. He looked at Carrie. "We have a former medical doctor in residence. He spent about four years in service in 'Nam. He'll know how to take care of a bullet wound. He owes me, big time. This will make us even."

"May I sit down?" Carrie asked.

Rafe shrugged. "It's a free country. Sit where you want."

Carrie came into the kitchen and sat down at the table across from him. The kitchen was as immaculate as the rest of the house—maybe even more so. From somewhere, maybe the common room down the hall, came the sound of canned TV laughter.

"This is a nice place," Carrie said.

Rafe laughed derisively. "That surprises you," he said. "No, don't deny it, I know it does. You think, ex-cons, recovering addicts and alcoholics, and you automatically think dump, right? Yeah." He laughed again. "The problem is, some of the time you're right. But not here." He sat forward, leaning toward her across the table, his flat brown eyes oddly alight. "One of the things you need to learn when you're an addict is self-respect. You think anyone who truly respects themselves would shoot themselves full of crap? No way. So how do you learn to respect yourself? One of the things you do is take pride in where you live. You *don't* live in a dump. You keep your place clean. And then you look around and you say, 'Hey, I live in this nice place, so maybe I'm worth something after all. What do you know?'"

Carrie didn't speak. She wasn't sure what to say. She could feel Rafe Salazar's eyes studying her.

"Forty-eight hours," he said suddenly.

She looked up at him. "Excuse me?"

"That's my prediction," he said with a wolfish grin. "My little brother's gonna get you into bed with him in the next forty-eight hours."

Carrie felt herself blush, but she held her chin up and looked him straight in the eye. "You're wrong," she said. "But wrong or right, I really don't think that it's any of your business."

"You look like one of those little blond angels we used to hang on our Christmas tree," Rafe mused. "Even when he was a kid, Felipe liked the little blond angels. He's not going to be able to resist you, angel. If you don't want him in your bed, you're gonna have to work hard at keeping your distance."

"Thanks for the tip," Carrie said dryly. "You have any additional words of wisdom to share with me about this Tommy Walsh guy?"

"Why's he after you?" Rafe asked.

Good question. "I was there when Felipe's cover was blown," Carrie said. "I think your brother had infiltrated some crime boss's organization—"

"Lawrence Richter," Rafe broke in, supplying the name.

"That's right," Carrie said. "Felipe says he has enough information to put both Walsh and Richter away."

"And you were there when Felipe's cover was blown?" Rafe repeated. "How much 'there'?"

Carrie made herself steadily meet his eyes as she confessed, "I, um, blew his cover."

Rafe didn't say anything for several long moments. He took a sip from his can of soda and put it carefully down on the table, turning it so that the label was directly in front of him.

"Well, angel," he finally said, "if I were you, I'd think about getting my personal effects and last will and testament in order."

Carrie had been holding her breath, but now she let it out in a ragged swoosh of air. "That bad, huh?"

"You have two options," Rafe said. "Either you change your identity and disappear, or . . . Walsh finds you and you die."

"Even though I'm not positive I could ID him?" Carrie asked.

"Walsh wasted a six-year-old for witnessing a hit," Rafe said. "He's got to do Felipe—he's got no choice, not if Felipe can put Richter in jail. But my little brother's a cop. Killing him's a capital offense. We're talking mandatory death sentence. You'd be able to tie Walsh to Felipe's death. Walsh probably doesn't like the idea of the electric chair, so he's got to do you, too."

"But Felipe's not dead," Carrie said.

"Yet," Rafe finished grimly. "I knew the *estúpido* sonuvabitch would get himself into something like this someday. I swear to God—" He looked up at Carrie, stopping abruptly. "There's something that you should know about my little brother."

Carrie waited for him to explain.

"He expects everybody to be the same kind of saint that he is," Rafe said. "It's impossible to live up to his expectations." He smiled, but it was humorless. "No doubt you'll disappoint him too, angel, when he finds out you're just human, a mere mortal like the rest of us."

"Can you really blame him for being disappointed and mistrustful of you?" Carrie asked Rafe quietly.

Her words struck home. She could see it in the tension in his face and shoulders, but Rafe shook his head. "He scorns me because I am an addict. A recovering addict, but an addict just the same. But you know what?" Rafe added. "Felipe, he's an addict, too. He's addicted to living on the edge. He's addicted to danger. Either that, or he's got some kind of sick death wish, no? What kind of man would try to bring Richter and Walsh down? What kind of man would put himself eyeball-deep in that kind of danger?"

"A brave man," Carrie answered. "A man who wants to help and protect innocent people."

As she spoke those words defending Felipe, Carrie realized that she believed him. She believed he was a cop. She believed what he'd said about Richter and Walsh. She believed everything Felipe had told her.

Rafe laughed and laughed. "Ah, angel, you've already bought into the saint story, huh?"

It was something of a relief, believing Felipe. She could rely on him to protect her from Tommy Walsh. She could quit fighting him, quit searching for a way to escape. She could let herself trust him. And she could stop worrying so much about the powerful attraction that sparked between them every time their eyes met....

"You're not so different from your brother," Carrie observed. "You help people, too."

"Felipe doesn't see it that way," Rafe said. "To him, I'm just a time bomb, ready to explode and start smoking crack again. He can't see past what I was."

"That's because you hurt and disappointed him when he was a child," Carrie said. "You can't expect him just to forget that."

"He'll never forget," Rafe said bitterly. "He'll never forgive me."

Exasperated, Carrie stood up, shoving her chair away from the table with a screech. "If you really want him to forgive you, you might try being a little nicer to him," she said sharply. "Good Lord, Felipe walks in here with a bullet in his leg, needing help, and you insult him and argue with him and are downright *mean* to him. Maybe *you're* the one who won't forgive and forget."

She pushed her chair back under the table and strode out of the room.

Rafe's harsh laughter followed her down the hall. "An angel for the saint," he said. "It's perfect. Did I say forty-eight hours? I'm gonna change that prediction to twenty-four."

Carrie ignored him, hurrying up the stairs.

Felipe's leg was throbbing, and he was so nauseated he was sure he must look green. But the bullet was out of his leg, thanks to a tall, heavyset man who called himself Doc Bird.

He'd given Felipe something to bite down on as he dug for the bullet. It had been a grueling two minutes, but only two minutes. One hundred and twenty seconds of hell. It could've been far worse.

Once more, Felipe was drenched with sweat. But he doubted he could stand up and take another shower. Besides, the stitches Doc Bird had put into his leg had come with instructions not to get them wet for at least a day if not two.

He pushed the hair out of his eyes and tried to focus on the clock on the VCR. It was nearly ten o'clock. Where was Caroline?

Another ten minutes, and pain or no pain, nausea or no nausea, he was going to go looking for her. Until then, he had to find something to distract himself.

He checked out the pile of newspapers on the coffee table. The top paper had a headline about St. Simone's newly appointed chief of police, a man named Earley.

Felipe knew him. He'd met him at least half a dozen times, maybe more. He was a little too conservative, a little too old-fashioned and probably exactly what the city needed in a police chief.

He picked up the paper, but the tiny print made his eyes swim and he threw it back on the table. Instead, he picked up the remote control and switched on the television.

The Fox affiliate carried a ten o'clock news program. Curious to see if the news had been released about his so-called connection to the Sandlot Murders, he switched to that station.

The program was just starting. The lead story concerned an outbreak of salmonella poisoning at a local nursing home. Three elderly people had already died, dozens more were ill.

Next came the story about newly appointed Chief Earley. Felipe was surprised. He'd been almost positive that the fact that he was suspected of committing the Sandlot Murders would've been leaked to the media. But there was no mention of it. Nothing at all.

There was a brief interview with Earley, then a background profile. The police chief had served in Vietnam as a demolitions expert. Felipe hadn't known that. Apparently Earley had worked clearing booby traps from the labyrinth of underground tunnels that Vietcong guerrillas hid in during the daytime. His was one of the most dangerous and terrifying jobs in the marines. It was not a job for the faint of heart or the claustrophobic, that was for sure.

Felipe heard a sound in the hallway, and pushed the mute button on the TV remote control. The apartment door swung open, and . . . thank you, Lord.

Caroline was standing there.

She came into the apartment, closing the door behind her

She seemed embarrassed, almost shy, and Felipe realized that he was wearing only his boxer shorts. He hadn't had the energy to make it over to Rafe's closet to find a pair of jeans or a T-shirt to put on.

Still, she crossed over to the sofa, looking down at him. "You look awful," she said.

He tried to smile. *"Gracias,"* he said. "I *feel* awful. But the bullet's out. My brother sent someone up, someone who I think was a doctor at one time."

Carrie nodded. "I know," she said. She knelt on the floor next to the sofa. "It must really hurt. I'm sorry."

"I'm not," Felipe said. He took a deep breath in and released it slowly. He found that now he *could* smile at her. "I don't mind the pain. In fact, I like it. It reminds me that I'm alive. And I really like being alive—particularly after an evening like this one."

Carrie smiled tentatively back at him. How beautiful she was. Felipe had to hold on tightly to the remote control to keep himself from reaching out and drawing her into his arms. What he would have given for one small, comforting embrace. Except there was no way on earth an embrace between them would have remained either small or comforting for long.

"I don't think you realize how close we both came to being killed tonight," Felipe said quietly, searching the depths of her sea green eyes.

But she didn't look away. She didn't turn her head. She didn't shut him out. Instead, she nodded. Yes.

"Yes, I do," she said. "I talked to your brother about Walsh."

"And ...?"

"I believe you," she said.

"About Walsh?"

"About everything."

Heat coursed through him at her words. She believed him. Even though he knew that he shouldn't, Felipe let go of the remote and reached for Carrie. He touched the side of her face and her skin was so smooth, so soft. And she didn't pull away.

He could see her pulse beating at the delicate base of her neck, he could see her chest rising and falling with each breath she took, he could see her lips, parted slightly and moistened with the tip of her tongue, and still she didn't pull away.

She looked the very way he felt—hypnotized.

Knowing quite well that he shouldn't, but unable to stop himself, he leaned forward to kiss her. How he wanted to kiss her! He truly didn't have a choice.

He brushed his lips against hers in the smallest, gentlest, most delicate of kisses.

Her eyelids fluttered, and she looked up at him. She looked scared to death, terrified, but she still didn't pull away.

So he kissed her again, knowing that he shouldn't, knowing absolutely that kissing this woman was a gigantic mistake. He liked her too much—*way* too much. He couldn't afford to have any kind of relationship with her. He couldn't bear the fact that just *knowing* him would put her in danger. And, maybe for the first time in his entire life, he knew that he wouldn't be able to keep the physical, sexual side of a relationship with Caroline from becoming entangled with the emotional. And that truly frightened him.

No, Caroline was not the only one who was scared to death. But he couldn't stop himself. And this time, she met him halfway. She reached up and threaded her arms around his neck and kissed him as if there were no tomorrow.

And maybe, just maybe, she was right.

But the danger they were in, the risk of impending death, wasn't the real reason Felipe pulled her even closer and deepened the kiss. He did it for one reason only—because he so desperately wanted to. He could no sooner resist Caroline Brooks than he could stop breathing.

Her mouth was so sweet, her lips so inviting. Her hair was like silk as he ran his fingers through it. And her soft, fragile body was neither entirely fragile nor entirely soft. She was slight and slender, yes, but still quite strong. He slid one hand down her back to the curve of her firm derriere and pulled her toward him.

Man, five minutes ago, he'd been lying here on the sofa, feeling like death warmed over, uncertain whether or not he'd even be able to stand. It was funny what desire could do to a man. Because now he knew without a doubt that he could stand. He could stand. He could walk. Man, he could run laps if he needed to.

His fingers found the edge of Caroline's dress, and the soft, smooth warmth of her thigh. Felipe heard himself groan, and she pulled back, alarmed.

"Did I hurt you?" she whispered, her voice husky. Her hair was tousled and her cheeks were flushed. It didn't take much imagination to picture her amid the rumpled sheets of a bed....

"Oh, yes," he said, barely hiding his smile. "You can't imagine my pain. Although it has nothing to do with my leg."

She blushed and laughed, then leaned forward to kiss him again.

And then the door burst open.

Felipe reacted. He found his gun almost instinctively, remembering he had thrown the holster over the back of the sofa. As he drew it out, he pulled himself off the sofa so that his body was shielding Carrie's.

"Jesus, it's only me," Rafe said. "Put that thing away, Superman. Lois Lane's still safe."

Felipe sagged with relief. It was only his brother. Relief turned sharply to annoyance. "Didn't our mother teach you to knock?" he asked, dragging himself back onto the sofa.

Rafe smiled humorlessly at his brother. He looked pointedly at Carrie, who was running her fingers through her disheveled hair. "Yeah," he said. "She also taught us not to play with fire—a rule you've obviously forgotten, little brother."

Felipe reached down to help Carrie onto the sofa next to him. He kept his arm behind her, his fingers lightly touching her shoulder. She glanced at him, and he nearly felt burned. Rafe was right. He *was* playing with fire. But what a way to go.

He looked up at Rafe. "Was there something you needed?"

Rafe looked at the television, which was still on, but muted. A commercial for a dishwashing liquid was showing.

"Were you watching the news—no, obviously not," Rafe said, answering his own question.

Felipe sat up a little straighter. "Why?" he asked.

Rafe glanced at him. "I think you know why," he said. He bent down and picked the remote control off the floor. As the commercial ended, he pressed the mute button.

"To recount a story just in," the news anchor said, looking seriously out from the television screen, "police sources have revealed that they are searching for a suspect in the controversial Sandlot Murders case."

A rather grainy picture of Felipe appeared at the top right of the screen, with the words Rogue Cop in jagged letters underneath.

"Police Detective Felipe Salazar," the anchor reported, her voice still solemn, "being labeled a rogue cop by the supervisors in his department..."

"Good Lord!" Carrie cried, leaning forward to look more closely at the screen. Felipe's hand fell away from her shoulder.

"...is wanted in connection with last week's double slaying in a downtown sandlot, next to the East 43rd Street Elementary School. Salazar, described in the official police statement as being a twenty-five-year-old Latino male, is six feet tall, one hundred seventy pounds, with dark hair and eyes. He is believed to be armed and extremely dangerous."

Caroline was staring at the television, clearly aghast. She looked up at Felipe, and he knew with a sinking heart that all her doubts about him had come flooding back.

"It's a frame," Felipe told her, but the news broadcast had once again caught her attention.

"We're going to the Fourth Precinct where we have a reporter standing by," the anchor said, reaching up to adjust a tiny speaker in her ear. "Hello, Walt, are you there?"

The picture switched to that of a man standing in the brightly lit lobby of the police station.

"This is Walter Myers reporting from downtown at the Fourth Precinct, where Felipe Salazar is a member of the police force," the man said, staring into the camera. "Newly appointed Police Chief Jack Earley will be arriving shortly to hold a press conference. We'll be breaking into regular programming to bring you that live report."

The camera followed Walter Myers down the corridor.

A man stepped into camera range. "Gentlemen, I'm going to have to ask you to leave," he said.

"That's Diego," Felipe said. His friend and former partner had gotten a haircut since he'd seen him last. But other than that, Jim Keegan looked the same. He was wearing his standard uniform—jeans and rumpled button-down shirt, with a loosened tie around his neck to make it look a little more businesslike.

Carrie glanced at him. "That's the man you called?"

"Yeah."

"And you are . . . ?" the reporter asked.

"Detective James Keegan," Jim replied patiently. "I'm afraid you're going to have to continue your news report outside, sir."

"His name's not Diego, it's James," Carrie said, her eyes still glued to the screen.

"Diego's Spanish for James," Rafe told her.

"Can you comment on the latest suspect in the Sandlot Murders?" the reporter asked Jim.

"No, I cannot," he replied firmly, herding them back to the door.

"Do you know Salazar?" the reporter asked.

"Yes, I do," Jim said.

"Do you believe he committed this crime?"

Jim was about to respond, then he glanced toward the camera. It was almost as if he'd decided to change his answer. "You never know," he told the reporter. "That's one thing I've learned in all my years on the force. You just never know."

The reporter looked into the camera. "Back to you, Mary."

The news anchor reappeared with another story, and Rafe reached over and turned off the television.

Carrie didn't move. "You don't seem surprised by this," she said tightly to Felipe.

"It's a setup," he said again. "A frame. And yes, you're right. I'm not surprised. I knew they were going to try to pin these murders on me."

She turned and looked at him. He could see anger in her eyes. Anger and hurt. "You knew," she said. "And you didn't tell me. This is really why you can't go to the police, isn't it? Because you're wanted for *murder.*"

"I didn't do it," Felipe said. How could she think that he would kill someone in cold blood? "I wouldn't kill anyone."

"Not anyone who didn't deserve it," Rafe cut in. "But a vigilante-style execution . . . ? Maybe."

"Stop it," Felipe said sharply. "You know damn well—"

"I only know you're a big fan of justice," Rafe retorted. "You'd send your own brother back to prison, two years hard labor. You're probably capable of delivering this kind of justice, no?"

Carrie was looking at Felipe as if he'd just been accused of slaying infants. "Even your friend, what's his name—Keegan—wouldn't stand up for you," she said.

Felipe reached for her hand. She didn't pull away fast enough, so he held it, wishing that she could somehow get inside his head and see for herself that he was telling the truth.

"Caroline, don't you see?" he said quietly, intensely. "This is why Walsh let us get away. Richter's man in the police department set up this frame, somehow making me look like a suspect in this murder case. They may not even have any evidence against me, I don't know. If they *do* have anything, it's trumped up or fake. But the case is never going to go to court, because as soon as they find me and bring me in, Walsh will be tipped off. He'll wait until I'm being transported and then he'll put a bullet in my head. Everyone will assume my death was some kind of mob counter-hit, and the case will be closed."

Carrie didn't look convinced. She was staring down at her hand, entrapped by Felipe's larger hand.

"I need you to leave," Rafe said. "Your being here is jeopardizing everything I've worked hard for—including my own freedom. I won't serve time for aiding and abetting. Not even for you, little brother."

Caroline pulled her hand free.

Felipe looked up at Rafe. "Don't you mean *especially* not for me?" he asked bitterly, then ran his hand across his face. "I'm sorry. I didn't mean that."

"Yes, you did," Rafe said. He sighed. "Look, I had one of my staff get rid of the car you drove over here. I can't risk giving you one of my vans, but I'm going to tell you where I keep the keys, do you follow?"

Felipe nodded.

"They're in the kitchen, top cabinet, left of the microwave. I'll give you seventy-two hours, then I'm going to report the van stolen," Rafe continued.

"Do you have a tape recorder I can borrow, too?" Felipe asked.

"There's a tape deck in the van," Rafe told him, "though this is hardly the time to be thinking about tunes, little brother."

Felipe ran a hand back through his hair. "No," he said, "I need to make a recording, to make a tape telling what I know about Richter and Walsh. You know. In case..."

Rafe nodded curtly. "I'll find you something," he said. "The bastard's gonna blow you away, least you can do is leave behind incriminating evidence, right?"

"Wrong," Felipe said. "It wouldn't be evidence. A taped statement wouldn't hold up in court. No, it would just be information to help the next guys nail Richter."

"You mean..." Rafe stared at him. "If you're dead, that's it? No case against Richter?"

"That's why he's so hot to waste me," Felipe said.

"Jesus," Rafe said. "You don't stand a chance."

Carrie was silent. She stared down sightlessly at the floor.

Rafe crossed to the closet and pulled out a pair of jeans and some worn-out black leather boots. "Here," he said, handing them to Felipe. He took a T-shirt and a clean pair of socks from his dresser and tossed them onto the sofa. He gestured toward Carrie. "I don't have anything in her size," he said. "But she can put a shirt on over that dress. And you, you probably need something to cover up that holster and gun," he added, crossing back to the closet.

He took out a black leather biker's jacket.

Felipe shook his head. "I can't take that," he said. "That's your jacket, man."

Rafe looked down at the jacket in his hands. When he looked up again, the lines in his face seemed deeper, the seat of his mouth even tighter than normal. "I don't have anything else to give you, Felipe," he said, for once all the sarcasm gone from his voice. "I *am* sorry that I can't let you stay. Do you have somewhere to go?"

Felipe nodded. "Yeah. I've got someplace in mind, someplace to lie low for a day or two until I feel like running again."

"Then what?"

"Then I find out who Richter's mysterious partner is," Felipe said. "Richter called him Captain Rat. I thought there was some connection to the wharf, the harbor authority, maybe the Coast Guard, but now I think this 'Rat' is a captain in the police department. Who else could have engineered this kind of a frame-up so quickly?"

Stiffly, gingerly, Felipe pulled on the jeans. They were a little loose—his brother was taller than he was—but they fitted just fine over his bandaged leg. He pulled the T-shirt over his head and slipped on his shoulder holster.

That little bit of movement exhausted him, and he had to stop and gather his strength. Only God could help them if Walsh came after them now.

He opened his eyes and found Caroline watching him, wariness still on her face. She looked away, unable to hold his gaze.

She didn't trust him, didn't believe him again.

They were back to square one.

Chapter 8

Carrie stood in the hallway with Rafe, waiting while Felipe limped into the kitchen. He was taking the keys to one of the halfway house's vans, with Rafe supposedly unaware.

She still couldn't believe the news report they'd just seen on the television.

The man she was with was indeed Felipe Salazar—that much had been established without a doubt. He *was* a detective with St. Simone's Fourth Precinct—that was true, too. And he could kiss exactly as she'd imagined in her dreams—better, in fact.

Good grief, one kiss, and she'd been ready... Well, she wasn't sure exactly *what* she'd been ready for, but she certainly hadn't been ready to find out that this handsome, charismatic man who could kiss like a dream was wanted for murder.

Felipe was wanted for *murder*.

He said he didn't do it. He said it was a setup, a frame. Carrie wanted to believe him, but she couldn't ignore the fact that if the man was a cold-blooded killer, he certainly wouldn't balk at lying.

Rafe was watching her, his flat, expressionless eyes studying her face.

"Do you believe Felipe?" she asked him.

He shrugged, holding his arms out wide. "I don't know," he said. "Used to be my brother couldn't even fib. He was the straightest kid you ever met, you know? He was the kind of kid who'd break something and then stick around to face the music. No running or hiding." He glanced toward the kitchen door, but there was no sign of Felipe. "But working under cover, he's had to learn to lie. I mean, when you think about it, an undercover cop does nothing *but* lie, huh?"

Carrie nodded.

"Do *you* believe him?" Rafe asked.

But Carrie didn't have a chance to answer. Felipe came out of the kitchen.

Part of her *did* believe him. When he told her he'd been set up, his words had been very persuasive. And the look in his eyes had begged her to trust him. She ought to trust him, considering the way they'd connected. And they had really connected—the proof was in that kiss they'd shared.

Hoo boy, what a kiss. . . .

But just because Felipe Salazar had the power to knock her socks off with a kiss didn't mean that she should simply trust him. And the truth was, her belief in him was based on instinct, on gut reaction alone. It had nothing to do with logic or provable facts.

And that scared her. How could she believe him when there was no proof to back his words? How could she trust him when all of the data implied that he was not to be trusted?

She couldn't. Despite her gut reaction, despite their obvious attraction, she couldn't let herself trust him. It was that simple.

"You get what you need?" Rafe asked Felipe, leading them to the front door.

Felipe nodded. His expression was almost as guarded as Rafe's. Carrie thought he was trying to hide the pain in his leg until he glanced at her. But with one look at his eyes, she could see that his pain wasn't from the bullet wound. It was from his disappointment. In her.

Rafe had stopped in the entry hall. He held a key, but he didn't attempt to unlock the front door.

Felipe looked incredible in those blue jeans and that black leather jacket, with his hair loose and flowing around his shoulders. It was different from the way he'd looked in his tuxedo, but no less commanding.

"Highboy's got the other key," Rafe explained. "Until he gets down here, we're locked in."

Locked in?

Felipe was studying the tips of his borrowed boots, his hands jammed deep into the pockets of his jeans as he leaned against the wall.

"Locked in?" Carrie asked.

Felipe still didn't look up, so she turned questioningly to his brother.

"Yeah," Rafe said. "That's the way the halfway house operates. Door doesn't open unless both guys who hold the keys can be talked into opening it. See, night can be the worst time for some of the addicts. I know it always was for me—still is sometimes. If the door is locked, and you can't get out of the house, you can't give in to the devil. We keep the door locked tight from 9:30 at night until 6:00 in the morning. It helps everyone stay clean. No one comes in or goes out unless it's an emergency. And it has to be one mother of an emergency."

The doors were locked after 9:30. Carrie looked at Felipe, who was still studying his boots as Highboy came down the stairs carrying the key.

Felipe had given her the key to get out of Rafe's apartment—but only after 9:30. She'd thought that he'd set her free, but she had still been a prisoner. She simply hadn't realized it at the time.

Highboy unlocked the top bolt; Rafe undid the bottom. The door swung open and Felipe and Carrie stepped outside.

Carrie's head was spinning. She took a deep breath, trying to clear it, but the night was warm and the air was tainted with the smell of trash.

"Raphael," Felipe said, turning back to his brother. "*Gracias.*" He held out his hand, but Rafe turned away.

"*Dejame,*" Rafe said flatly, closing the door in Felipe's face.

The hurt that flashed in Felipe's eyes was heartbreaking. But Carrie didn't have time to feel bad. If ever there was an opportunity to get away, it was right at this very moment.

She started down the sidewalk at a brisk pace, hoping Felipe wouldn't even notice that she was walking away. But he caught up with her before she'd gone ten yards. He took hold of her arm. "The van's parked in the alley," he said. "It's the other direction."

"That's real nice," Carrie said, "but I'm not going in the van with you."

"Yes," he said, "you are." His patience was wearing thin—she could hear it in his voice. He led her around the side of the house to the alley where the van was waiting.

"So I *am* your hostage," she said, steadily meeting his eyes and refusing to be seduced by the heat she could see there. "I have been all along, haven't I?"

"Caroline, you're not a hostage."

She looked pointedly down at his hand holding her arm. "Coulda fooled me," she said.

Something snapped. She could see it in his eyes, in the tenseness of his jaw.

"You believed me a half hour ago," he said tightly.

"You should have told me you were wanted for murder," she countered.

"I didn't really think they could pull off a frame-up this big—not until I saw it myself," he said. He laughed harshly. "Ah, the power of television. You'd rather believe what you see on the screen than believe me, no?"

"How can I believe you?" Carrie asked, "when I don't even know you?"

"You know me," Felipe said, his voice suddenly soft. His dark eyes glittered in the moonlight. "I think you know me quite well, in fact. Trust your heart, Caroline."

She closed her eyes, afraid of the hypnotizing power of his gaze, afraid of the magnetic pull of this man, afraid of the way his hold on her arm suddenly felt like a caress.

But then he let her go. "Okay," he said, still quietly. "You're free to go."

Carrie opened her eyes in surprise, and he dropped the keys to the van into her hand.

"There's one condition," he said. "You have to get on the interstate heading north. You have to go directly to your father's home in Montana, tell your father and your brothers everything that's happened here tonight, and then ask them to protect you. If you won't let me do it, you've got to let them."

"I'm just supposed to leave you here?" Carrie asked incredulously. "With a bullet wound in your leg?"

He shook his head. "I don't have time to argue with you," he said. "Especially not out here in the open like this, where anyone can see me. I've got an awful lot to do tonight. My first priority is to make sure you're safe. My second is to stay alive so that tomorrow I can get to my third priority—clearing my name. So kiss me goodbye and get the hell out of here."

Carrie looked from the keys in her hand, to the van, then back to Felipe. His number-one priority was her safety. In fact, he'd given up his one means of escape for her. Without the van, he'd be forced to take public transportation and risk being spotted by some vigilant citizen who'd seen the evening news. Of course, he could always travel by foot— although how far he'd get on his injured leg was uncertain.

He looked pale in the moonlight, and she could see that he was perspiring again. The pain from his bullet wound had to have been excruciating. He was just barely standing on his feet. How could she just drive away from him?

His eyes held no reproach, no recriminations. She could see only gentleness and warmth.

"Go," he whispered. "Godspeed, Caroline Brooks."

But Carrie didn't want to go. She wanted to stay. She didn't want to have to rely on her family for protection—not when she had the best possible protection right here in St. Simone.

Her feelings weren't scientific. They weren't based on fact or data or any kind of proof. For the first time in years, Carrie was rejecting the obvious and trusting her heart.

She took several steps forward, closing the gap between them, stood on her toes and kissed him.

She could taste his surprise. Nevertheless, he pulled her to him and kissed her, too. It was a long, slow, deep kiss, a sweet kiss, perhaps the sweetest she'd ever known.

He was kissing her goodbye, Carrie realized suddenly. He was giving her a kiss to last a lifetime, a kiss to remember him by.

He held her close, as if gathering his strength to push her away. "Don't stop for anything until you're out of state," he said, his voice husky.

She looked up at him and could actually see tears in his eyes.

"After you're out of Florida," he continued, "get rid of the van—leave it in some neighborhood just parked on the street. Then take a bus. Pay in cash and don't use your real name." He released her, digging into the back pocket of his jeans for his wallet. "I'm going to give you some money—"

"No," Carrie said. There were tears in her own eyes now. He was giving her the van *and* some money, too? She wiped at her eyes fiercely with the back of her hand.

Felipe shook his head. "Caroline, you're going to need—"

"Get in the van," she said, unlocking the passenger-side door. "I'm driving."

He stepped forward and touched the side of her face. "As much as I'd like to, I can't go to Montana with you."

"I'm not going to Montana," she said, then smiled at the hope that sprang into his eyes. He was trying to control it, trying not to allow himself to assume anything. "I'm safer with you," she added. "My brothers are lousy shots."

He nodded slowly, as if he was taking her words very seriously. "You've decided to believe me?" he said.

"Is there anything else that you've neglected to tell me?" she asked. "Any other sensational murders or maybe a kidnapped child or two in your basement? Or maybe you've been keeping secrets from me about your health. Any brain tumors or terminal illnesses you've been hiding?"

He smiled and shook his head. "Nothing of that great a magnitude."

"Then get in the van," she said, hoping to hell that she wasn't going to regret this.

Felipe sat low in the passenger seat of the cargo van so that no one could see him. He didn't like that he wasn't driving. In fact, he couldn't remember the last time he'd been in a car but not behind the wheel—excluding rides in Richter's limousine, of course.

He watched Carrie as she drove. She'd had to shift the driver's seat way up close to the steering wheel, but she drove the oversize vehicle with all the confidence and skill of an experienced truck driver.

This was a far cry from the little red sports car she'd had all those months ago at Sea Circus, when they'd first met. Still, someone who owned a precision automobile like Carrie's had to care about her car. And, in Felipe's experience, people who cared about their cars tended to know how to drive, and drive well. And usually fast. Her two speeding tickets verified that fact—although at the moment she was keeping their speed slightly below the limit. The time they'd save by going faster wasn't worth the risk of getting pulled over.

Carrie glanced over at him. He tried to smile, but the muscles in his face weren't working quite the way they should have been.

"You okay?" she asked, concern thickening her already husky voice, accentuating her slight Western drawl. She sounded a little bit—just a *little* bit—like Lauren Bacall trying to imitate John Wayne. On a woman of her less-than-imposing size, with all that silky blond hair and those enormous blue eyes, the effect was utterly charming.

"My leg hurts," Felipe admitted. *Hurts* was an enormous understatement. The damn thing throbbed steadily with a knifelike pain. And, as a bonus, he felt nauseated from the antibiotic Doc Bird had given him. He was supposed to take one of the capsules four times a day to keep his wound from becoming infected. Doc Bird had given him a ten-day supply of the medicine.

Ten days. He could only hope he lived that long.

Man, he was exhausted.

"Is there anything I can do?" Carrie asked quietly. She glanced at him again, and this time he managed to smile.

"You're doing it," he said.

"Where are we going?" she asked. "Besides south?"

"Sanibel Island," he told her. "Diego's in-laws own a beach house out there. It's empty at this time of year. We can hide there, at least overnight."

She nodded, her eyes carefully on the highway.

He took out the tape recorder that Rafe had given him. It was small and cheap and at least twenty-five years old. But it would get the job done.

"If you don't mind," Felipe said, "I'd like to record that information about Richter's operation."

"In case you're not around to do it in person," Carrie said, glancing over at him.

He nodded. "Yeah."

"But you will be," she said.

"Yes," he said with more certainty in his voice than he felt. "But I would hate not to make this tape, and then be wrong."

"Rafe thinks we don't stand a chance, doesn't he?"

We. Felipe liked the sound of that. She was on his side. "My brother is a pessimist," he said.

"But you're not," she answered back.

"We're still alive, aren't we?" he declared. "Against all odds, our hearts are still beating. Either we're lucky, or God's got a reason for keeping us around."

"God?" she said, turning to look at him in the darkness.

"Don't you believe in God?" he asked. "Some god, any god? Some force bigger than we are?"

She turned her head away from him as if she was embarrassed. "Gee, I don't know."

"Too bad," Felipe said, studying her profile as she drove. He adored the way her nose turned up very slightly at the end. "I've found believing is helpful in times like this."

She glanced back at him again. "I'm ... surprised," she said.

Felipe smiled. "That's good," he said. "I'd hate to be boring."

Caroline laughed, a low, husky sound that hit him low in the gut and spread all the way out to his fingers and toes. Man, bullet wound or not, he would have sold his soul right at that moment for a chance to finish what they'd started with a kiss back in Rafe's apartment. His borrowed blue jeans were getting tighter and more uncomfortable by the second. But at least it took his mind off the pain in his leg.

"Believe me," she said. "You're not boring." She looked over at him, but quickly focused on the road again, as if she could see his desire simmering in his eyes. She probably could. He wasn't very good at hiding that sort of thing. "Go on and make your tape," she added. "I'd like to know why someone's trying to kill you—and me."

Felipe looked down at the tape recorder, and ejected the tape that his brother had put inside. It needed to be rewound to the beginning, so he put it back in and pushed the rewind button. Then he pressed Record and Play and silently counted to five to let the leader run out.

"My name is Felipe Ricardo Salazar, and I am a police detective with the Fourth Precinct in St. Simone," he said, speaking clearly into the machine's built-in microphone, still watching Caroline as he talked. "Today is January 17, 11:45 p.m.

"Early August of last year, I went under cover to infiltrate Lawrence Richter's crime syndicate. Posing as Raoul Tomás Garcia Vasquez, I have spent the past five months winning both Tommy Walsh's and Lawrence Richter's confidence."

Felipe took a deep breath. "Two months ago, I learned of a scam that I believe Richter has been operating for nearly a decade here in Florida. He imports illegal aliens from Cuba and Haiti and other Caribbean islands, and even from as far away as Mexico, charging them exorbitant prices for a so-called safe passage and entry into the United States. After they arrive, having spent every penny of their life savings, they are told of other, equally exorbitant fees for forged green cards that will enable them to stay. Richter's men sign a contract with these people, trading their future wages for these coveted—and counterfeit, therefore worthless—green cards.''

Carrie drew in a sharp breath, again glancing over at Felipe.

"In short," he said, nodding grimly at her, "it's a form of indentured servitude, or should I say slavery? Richter currently has a work force of over twenty-two hundred illegal aliens—including children. Child labour laws don't apply to children who technically don't exist."

"That's awful," Carrie murmured.

"I've seen the below-poverty conditions that these people live in," Felipe continued, watching the impact his words had on her through the expressions on her face. "Most of them are housed in run-down buildings that Richter has bought in the worst neighborhoods in the city. These buildings have no running water, no electricity and no hope of ever being renovated. They are scheduled to be torn down, but Richter has orchestrated a series of delays in the legal proceedings surrounding their condemnation. It could literally be years before the buildings are destroyed, and by that time, Richter will have purchased—dirt cheap—other equally squalid buildings.

"Most of these apartment buildings are between Howard and Stern Streets, on First and Second Avenues." He sighed. "Although by the time you hear this tape, all the illegal tenants will probably have been moved.

"Garrett Hedford and Stuart Tiffler are two of Richter's men who use intimidation to keep the work force in line," he continued. "They also schedule the arrival of additional boatloads of people. In the past two months, I've seen ships arriving in both Miami and Fort Myers." Quickly, he rattled off the information on the ships' names and ports of call.

"I've seen copies of Richter's books," he said, shifting in his seat, trying to ease the endless throbbing in his leg. "He grosses over two hundred thousand dollars each *month* from these people, his *slaves*. I've witnessed him giving orders to both Hedford and Tiffler, as well as Tommy Walsh. I've witnessed the production of the counterfeit green cards, and their distribution to the illegal aliens. I've witnessed the signing of contracts, indenturing these people to Richter—although his name is not used. A corporate front, called L&R Co. is used, and it virtually cannot be traced to Lawrence Richter. At least not without me around. I've witnessed Richter transferring funds from the L&R account to his Swiss bank account."

"Felipe."

He turned off the tape recorder, looking up at Caroline. "Yes?"

"If you know all this," she asked, "what were you waiting for? You'd seen enough to put Richter away."

"His partner," he reminded her. "I found out that Richter wasn't working alone. The more I found out, the more I wanted to catch this other man, too." He smiled ruefully. "The more I found out, the more I realized I *had* to nail this guy. I'd guessed he was someone in St. Simone's government, someone who'd have access to my whereabouts after I went into protective custody while awaiting Richter's trial. I was the chief witness against Richter—the *only* witness. If I didn't bring a case against this other guy, too, this inside guy, I'd end up dead. I'm lucky I found out about this Captain Rat. If I hadn't, I probably never would have heard the bullet coming."

Caroline swallowed. "You say that so casually."

"It's my job," he replied.

"It's an awful job," she said.

"No, it's not," he returned gently.

"In my opinion it is," she said. She looked at him. "And I'm entitled to my own opinion."

Felipe leaned back against the headrest, just watching her. She believed him. Oh, she didn't believe him one hundred percent, but she believed him enough to stick around. And that was what counted.

Is there anything else that you've neglected to tell me? Her words echoed in his mind as he watched her drive.

Nothing of that great a magnitude.

But his answer had been a lie. And not just because there was something that he hadn't told her. It was true, there *was* something, but he couldn't possibly have told her about it, because he wasn't sure yet himself exactly what it was. It was difficult to pinpoint, harder even to define, these feelings, this *emotion* that seemed to swirl around him, enveloping him in a chaos both perfect and terrible whenever she looked in his direction, whenever he caught her eye.

What was it? He didn't know. Man, he didn't *want* to know.

But whatever it was, something told him it was of a far greater magnitude than he could ever imagine.

"I want to tell you . . . why I didn't come back and explain who I was and what I was doing that night at Sea Circus," Felipe said softly.

Carrie glanced at him, startled. He'd been quiet for so long, she was certain he'd been asleep.

"You know I went under cover as part of the Richter investigation back in August," he said. "One week I was pretending to be Carlos and running with some of the leaders of the most powerful gangs in St. Simone, and the next I was Raoul, driving a Jaguar and living in a penthouse at the Harbor's Gate. I had maybe three days between the two assignments. It . . . wasn't long enough."

"Long enough for what?" Carrie asked, looking over at him again. "It was certainly long enough for you to come and apologize."

He shifted in his seat. "It wasn't long enough for what I wanted," he said bluntly. "And I didn't think you deserved to be a one-night stand."

Carrie laughed, afraid to look at him, afraid of what she knew she'd see in his eyes. Desire. He'd stopped trying to hide it from her ever since they'd shared that kiss. "How gallant of you," she said. "You were saving me from my own lack of control, huh?"

"At the risk of sounding conceited," he said, "you would not have been able to resist me."

Coming from any other man's lips, his words would have been outrageous and disgustingly egomaniacal. But when Felipe said them, those words, combined with the rueful look in his eyes, were merely a statement of fact.

It was, however, no less disconcerting.

"Your brother thinks I'm going to sleep with you within the next twenty-four hours," Carrie said tightly. "But that's not why I'm here, and I intend to prove him wrong. In fact, I think we should ignore this . . . this . . . physical attraction until after you clear your name and Lawrence Richter and Tommy Walsh are in jail."

Felipe was silent. One mile, then two, sped by under their wheels before he spoke. "That's probably best," he agreed quietly.

It was. It was best. Still, Carrie couldn't help but remember the power of his kisses. If Rafe hadn't interrupted them, she very likely would have made love to Felipe right there on the sofa, injured leg and all. No, forget twenty-four hours. It would have been more like four hours. Four hours after they'd met—not counting the half hour or so at Sea Circus six months ago, and the dozens of dreams she'd had about him since then—and she would have had sex with this man. Did he have some special power over her specifically, she wondered, or did she experience this phenomenon with every woman he met?

"I'm sorry if Rafe offended you," Felipe said. He shook his head. "He had no business saying that to you." His dark eyes were lit with anger and embarrassment. "I *am* sorry, Caroline."

"It's okay," she said. "He was just trying to rattle me." She laughed. "It worked, too."

"I don't understand him," Felipe said, shaking his head again. He ran one hand across his forehead, applying pressure, as if he had a headache. "Sometimes I think I never will." He looked up at her. "It's not as if he didn't know that crack was addictive. It's not as if he didn't know it could kill him. So what the hell made him do it? What pushed him over the edge? And what kind of man cares more about getting a rush than he does about his life?"

"Rafe seems to think you get a similar rush from being an undercover cop," Carrie said.

His gaze sharpened. "You talked to him about me?"

"Only a little," Carrie said. "He wants you to forgive him."

"He sure as hell has a funny way of showing that," Felipe muttered. "And I *do* forgive him," he added. "I just don't trust him. How do I know he's going to stay clean? How can I be sure he won't start using again?"

All his frustration and anger and hurt—deep, deep hurt—showed on his face. He was speaking to her from his heart, sharing his darkest fears and innermost secrets with her.

She liked him, Carrie realized suddenly. There were so many sides to him, so much more than a handsome face, more than those exotic cheekbones and the long, curly hair.

Who would've guessed that such a powerful, independent, self-sufficient man would believe so firmly in the idea of a god? And in this day and age, when religion was a low priority in most people's busy lives?

Who would've guessed that talk of his brother could reduce him in part to the little boy that he'd once been, badly hurt, and afraid of being hurt again?

And who would've guessed that he'd let her see that pain, rather than try to conceal it from her?

Yeah, she liked him, despite the fact that he'd locked her in the trunk of her car, despite the fact that he'd put her life in jeopardy.

He was waiting for her to say something, watching her with those liquid eyes.

"Sometimes," Carrie said softly, her eyes on the highway, talking about more than Rafe—*much* more than Rafe, "you've just got to have faith."

Chapter 9

Carrie drove past the darkened beach house three times before Felipe nodded his head.

"Okay, no one's there," he said, his gentle Hispanic accent like velvet in the darkness. "Let's park over on the next block. I don't want to leave the van out front, or even in the driveway."

"Maybe I should drop you off," Carrie said, "so you don't have to walk that far."

He didn't say anything. He just looked at her, one eyebrow slightly raised.

"Bad idea?" she asked.

"Bad idea. I can't protect you if I'm here and you're a block away."

You can't protect either of us if you're too tired and in too much pain to walk, she wanted to say. But then she thought better of it, remembering the way he'd run after her when he'd stopped to make that phone call. He'd had a bullet in his leg, yet he'd still managed to chase her across the parking lot. And he'd caught her—with a flying tackle and total disregard for his injury.

Yes, dropping him off *was* a bad idea. If mobsters with guns wanted her dead, then maybe it was a good idea if Felipe Salazar stayed near her at all times, healthy or injured, awake or asleep.

Awake or...

The image of Felipe asleep next to her in the clean white sheets of a cozy double bed was a powerful one. His wavy black hair spread out across the snow-white pillow, his eyes closed, his long, dark eyelashes like fans against his tanned cheeks, his body relaxed but his muscles still hard as steel under silky smooth skin....

Thinking this way wasn't going to help her one bit. And sleeping with him would be rash and reckless—and possibly a knee-jerk reaction to the danger they were in. Yes, he was sexy as hell. Yes, he was sensitive and compassionate and he seemed to know exactly what she was thinking when he looked deeply into her eyes. Yes, he was quite possibly the most complicated, interesting and exciting man she'd ever met.

But imagine what would happen if—heaven forbid—she let herself fall in love with this man. Could she imagine them together, having breakfast every morning for the rest of their lives?

Actually, the image was not as difficult to conjure up as she'd thought. In fact, it was a nice picture, a comfortable picture. He'd be sitting at the kitchen table, drinking a glass of orange juice and eating a bowl of cereal. She'd be sitting across from him, spreading jam on her toast. He'd look up, meet her eyes and smile and...

Carrie shook her head, trying to dispel the warm feeling that had somehow invaded her body. So, okay, the thought of Felipe Salazar eating breakfast with her every morning wasn't such an alien one.

But imagine her taking him home to meet her father. Imagine Felipe Salazar in the mountains of Montana. Well, actually, that wasn't such an incongruous picture, either. She could imagine teaching him to ride a horse, imagine him loving it, imagine them riding up into that meadow above the house and sharing a picnic lunch spread out on a blanket. A picnic lunch and a whole lot more....

As for her dad, well, he'd be put off at first by Felipe's accent, by his long hair and the diamond stud he wore in his left ear. But her father was a fair man, and he'd quickly see that Felipe was everything he could want for his only daughter—

Good grief. What was she doing? One kiss, and she was daydreaming about happily-ever-after.

Happily-ever-after could end permanently and quite abruptly in a matter of days, considering the danger they were in. And even if it didn't, even if Walsh didn't find them and kill them...well, Felipe Salazar wasn't exactly the happily-ever-after kind.

Sure, he had a certain steadiness, a certain serenity about him that counteracted the risks he took. But he *did* take risks, and it was clear that he loved the danger and excitement. What had Rafe said? He'd said that Felipe was addicted to danger.

No, if she wanted to dream up some image to help keep her resolve to stay away from this man, all she had to do was picture his being led away from her in handcuffs. *That* was a much more likely scenario than any she'd imagined. Yes, she had no doubt that he would make love to her exquisitely. It would be desperately exciting, incredibly thrilling, considering both their adrenaline levels were already quite high. But the reality was, this man was wanted by the police. For murder.

He said he didn't commit the crime.

She wanted to believe him. She *did* believe him.

But what if she was wrong? What if he *was* a cold-blooded killer? What if he wanted her around only as a hostage, not for her protection? What if...?

Carrie parked the car and turned off the engine. He was watching her as if he could read her mind, as if he knew her every thought. She handed him the keys, which he pocketed.

Carrie cleared her throat. "Do we have a way to get into the house?" she asked.

"I know where a key is hidden," Felipe said, opening his door and swinging his legs out.

He winced as his feet hit the ground, and Carrie quickly got out of the van and went around the front to help him.

"I'm okay," he insisted. But he swayed slightly, and she slipped his arm around her shoulders.

He surely outweighed her by more than sixty pounds, and the leather jacket he was wearing added even more to that. But Carrie was strong. Besides, she didn't try to carry him; she merely offered support.

Slowly, they moved down the street and around the corner toward the beach house.

Carrie's head was tucked up almost underneath Felipe's arm, and her own arm went around his waist under his jacket. As they walked, his thigh brushed against hers.

She tried to ignore the heat that coursed through her. After all, it had been her idea to suppress the physical attraction they both obviously felt toward each other. And *he* seemed to have no trouble doing just that.

But then she stumbled slightly, and he reached for her to keep her from falling. The movement made his T-shirt go up, and all of a sudden her fingers were against the smoothness of his bare back. He inhaled sharply, and she quickly pulled her hand away.

"Sorry," she said, not certain which she was apologizing for—nearly tripping and taking him down with her, or touching him that way.

He didn't say a word, he just looked at her, the moonlight failing to fully light his face. His eyes were in shadows, not that she could have deciphered the mysteries in his hooded gaze even if they hadn't been. But one thing was very clear. He wasn't finding it easy to keep his distance from her. He was simply better at hiding it.

But he wasn't hiding it now. She could hear him breathing, smell his warm, masculine scent, feel his heart beating—racing, really—in his chest.

Her own pulse was pounding just as hard and fast. Soon they were going to be inside the beach house. Soon they'd be behind the closed door. Alone. Together. With the world and all of its threats and dangers and realities carefully shut outside.

She could do anything, *any*thing, and no one would ever know. Except . . . *she* would know. She could make love to this man whom she wanted to trust and believe in, and then hope beyond hope that he *wasn't* the man the police were looking for.

But if he was...

Carrie walked down the driveway around to the rear of the house with her arm still tightly encircling Felipe's waist. He stopped at the bottom of the stairs leading up to the back porch, pulling her more fully into his arms, turning what might have been called support into an undeniable embrace.

"Caroline," he said, his mouth a whisper away from hers. He touched her hair, moving it back from her face in the gentlest of caresses.

Carrie stood staring up into the darkness of his eyes, unable to move, unable to speak. He was going to kiss her. He was going to...

Instead, he released her, stepping away and using the stair railing for support.

"The key's under the flowerpot next to the back door," Felipe said, his voice husky. He cleared his throat. "We must remember not to turn on any lights inside. We don't want to catch the neighbors' attention."

As Carrie watched, he pulled himself up the stairs. He found the key exactly where he'd said it was and unlocked the door. Motioning for her to be quiet, he went inside first.

She followed him into the dark house and stood silently in the coolness. He stood several feet in front of her, his black jacket and jeans making him little more than a dark shape. He was listening intently, and Carrie found herself listening, too.

There was a clock somewhere in the room, and the sound of it ticking seemed thunderously loud. Outside the closed windows, the surf murmured, but other than that and the clock, the house was silent.

The air-conditioning unit came on with a hum, and Carrie nearly jumped out of her skin.

Felipe vanished, his dark shape moving out of the room they were in—the kitchen, Carrie saw as her eyes became more accustomed to the dark. But he reappeared a moment later.

"It's all right," he said, still whispering even though he had no need to. "There's no one here."

He opened one of the drawers and rummaged around, coming up with a box of matches. He lit one, and the tiny light seemed unnaturally bright.

The beach house was gorgeous—at least the kitchen was. The shiny finish of blond pine cabinets gleamed in the match's glow. White and blue Mexican tile made up the countertops and floor.

A candle stood on the windowsill, and as Carrie watched, Felipe lighted it. "Come," he said, leading the way into the living room, shielding the candle's flame with his hand.

The living room was as splendid as the kitchen. More so. A huge fan hung from a beamed cathedral ceiling. Big glass windows and sliding doors covered nearly one entire wall. A huge stone fireplace was in the corner. White wicker furniture had been grouped around the room, creating an airy, spacious feeling.

Perfect. The beach house, the candlelight—it was all incredibly romantic. In fact, she couldn't remember anything quite so utterly romantic. And she was here, alone, with the most charismatic, attractive, *irresistible* man she'd ever met.

Absolutely perfect.

But Felipe didn't stop in the living room. He led her down a hallway, toward a trio of bedrooms. He stopped outside of one of them. "Check to make sure the shades are pulled down," he said, still speaking softly in the hush of the quiet house.

Carrie went into the room and crossed toward the windows. She pulled first one and then the other shade down.

"Those windows face the neighbor's," Felipe said.

Carrie nodded, not daring to meet his gaze. Instead, she looked around.

This was the master bedroom. It was big, with the same high ceiling as the living room. A king-size bed with a heavy oak frame was set against one wall. There were two doors in the far wall. One led to an open walk-in closet that was nearly as big as her entire apartment. The other opened into an adjoining bathroom. Carrie could see the gleam of tile and mirrors, shiny and clean and new.

The other wall, the same wall that in the living room held all those windows, was covered by curtains. She was willing to bet there were sliding glass doors behind them, doors leading out onto a private deck, with maybe a hot tub overlooking the backyard, which was in fact the moonlight-kissed beach.

It was too much. It was all way too much.

She wasn't going to be able to resist him. She was going to turn around, and he would be watching her with those black velvet eyes. And then she would fall headlong, with no hope of landing on her feet, off the dizzying cliff of desire and need.

She turned to look at Felipe. He stood in the doorway holding out the candle, offering it to her.

Carrie crossed toward him and took it. Their fingers brushed, and she jerked her hand away as if she'd been burned.

Holding her gaze, he backed away from her into the hallway. "Good night," he said, and closed the door.

He was gone.

Carrie stood there for a moment, staring at the rich wood of the door.

He was gone.

Obviously, he'd taken seriously her request to keep their relationship platonic.

Carrie looked around the room—at that enormous bed, at the luxurious plush carpeting, at the rich fabric of the draperies.

It wouldn't have taken much effort on Felipe's part to change her mind. In fact, another one of his high-powered kisses would've surely done the trick.

But he hadn't tried. He'd respected her decision.

Carrie wasn't sure whether to feel happy or sad.

Happy, she told herself fiercely as she went into the bathroom. She was happy.

Happily, she washed her face. Happily, she brushed her teeth with her finger and some borrowed toothpaste. And happily, she climbed into that great big bed all by herself and blew out the candle.

And lay there.

* * *

Felipe stared at the ceiling, listening to the sounds of the house, wishing he could fall asleep.

From his bed, he heard the sound of water running as Caroline Brooks drew herself a bath. It was one in the morning. She'd been quiet for a while, but now she was up and moving around. He guessed she couldn't sleep, either.

It wasn't hard to imagine her lying back and soaking in that bathtub. He'd stayed here at this beach house before, slept in the master bedroom. He'd soaked in that tub himself.

He'd been alone at the time. Come to think of it, he'd never brought any of his lady friends here to Sanibel Island. He'd never wanted to share either the peaceful solitude when he was alone, or the friendly atmosphere that prevailed when Diego and Emily Keegan were also here.

True, he'd once or twice brought Jewel Hays and her little boy, Billy. But Jewel was like a sister to him. They were old friends, nothing more.

But Caroline...

He closed his eyes, remembering the taste of her, the feel of her in his arms, the touch of her fingers on his neck and in his hair. Truthfully, his wounded leg wasn't the only thing that was throbbing.

He could go to her. Right now. He could stand up and walk the few feet down the hall and into the master bedroom. He could push open the bathroom door and she would look up at him in the candlelight, her huge blue-green eyes wide with surprise.

He would move closer and look down at the graceful lines of her body through the clear, warm water of the tub. She would sit up, water falling off her in a sheet, her small, firm breasts like some delicious, exotic, mouth-watering fruit.

Please, he'd say. It would be all he'd have to say, and she'd hold out her arms to him. He'd slip off his boxer shorts and join her in the water...

Felipe's eyes opened. No, he wouldn't. He wasn't supposed to get his stitches wet—at least not with more than a quick shower. Certainly he wasn't supposed to soak them in a tub.

He smiled ruefully at his overactive imagination. Like hell she would hold out her arms to him and welcome him. Like hell she would urge him to make love to her. She'd told him in no uncertain terms that she didn't want their relationship to become sexual.

Sure, he could seduce her. He knew that was a fact from looking into her eyes earlier tonight. He could kiss her and ignite the rocket fuel of their mutual attraction, and the earsplitting roar would drown out her protests. He'd kiss her again, and those protests would fade away. It wouldn't take long before she'd help him undress her, before she'd undress him, all her reservations forgotten.

At least temporarily.

And therein lay the reason he didn't stand up and go into the master bedroom, he thought with another smile. Caroline had asked him specifically to back off. She'd said no, quite distinctly and directly to his unspoken question, to the look she'd surely seen in his eyes. No. And no didn't mean maybe. No didn't mean catch me later when I'm more vulnerable. No meant no.

In the other room, on the other side of the wall, came the sound of water swirling around and then the pipes thumped as the water was turned back on. Caroline was adding hot water to the tub. Too bad. Felipe could think of a dozen or so ways to warm her up. He shifted his position in the bed, trying desperately to get comfortable.

He couldn't blame her for wanting to keep her distance. Until just a few hours ago, she'd thought he was some kind of criminal, some gang leader named Carlos who ran with an ugly bunch of friends. And just when she finally believed that he was who he said he was, she found out that he was wanted for murder. No, he couldn't blame her.

Quite honestly, Felipe was amazed she'd come here with him. He was grateful and relieved that she had. Because as he'd watched that news broadcast, as he'd watched her face as *she'd* watched it, he had been certain that she would never trust him again. And if he hadn't talked her into going to Montana, he *would* have had to make her his prisoner, his hostage, just the way she feared. And God, what a mess *that* would have been. But no way was he going to let her walk around without protection. No way was he going to let Tommy Walsh kill her. No way. No *way*.

The savage rush, the intensity of his feelings, made him grip the bedsheet like a rope that kept him from falling into some terrible abyss. Dear God, what was wrong with him?

He tried to tell himself he'd feel the same about any woman, about any *person* who was in danger of being killed, who was a target for Tommy Walsh's bullets.

But that wasn't true.

Caroline Brooks was special. If she died, he'd more than mourn the loss of a human life. He'd grieve deeply for himself, for his own loss. And he would miss her desperately, even though he'd only known her for a short time.

She fit. In his arms, she fit perfectly. And she fit in his heart. *His* heart? Heaven help him, he realized with a sudden flash of icy fear, it wasn't his heart anymore. Sure, it still beat in his chest, but it was hers. She had stolen it. She'd stolen it all those months ago during that night at Sea Circus. Why else had he gone back all those times to watch her from a distance? Why had he told Diego and Emily about her? Why had she haunted his dreams for months?

No, he tried to tell himself. That had been attraction. Nothing more. Attraction, simple lust. Well, maybe not simple. But it was entirely sexual. Wasn't it? Just a case of raw sexual attraction. Just as this . . . this . . . odd feeling in his chest was nothing more than a case of being overtired. Or it was heartburn, from the antibiotic. Sure. That was probably it.

He closed his eyes, willing himself to sleep. In the morning, in the light of day, he'd feel better. He'd be back on track.

From the other room he heard the sound of water going down the drain. With sudden clarity, he could picture Caroline Brooks, stepping from the bathtub, reaching for a towel, her lithe body wet and shivering with cold and . . .

Felipe stared at the ceiling, listening to the sounds of the house, wishing he could fall asleep.

Chapter 10

A car pulled into the driveway, and Felipe was instantly awake and reaching for his gun.

He sat up and threw the sheet from his legs before the engine was turned off.

It was morning. Daylight seeped in around the shades. He hit the well-polished floorboards running, his mind racing even faster. Hide. They had to hide. But where? He remembered a crawl space underneath the house with an access door on the floor of the closet in the master bedroom. *Yes.*

Felipe ignored the sudden pain in his injured leg as he scooped his jeans, his shirt and his holster off the chair he'd thrown them over the night before, and snatched his boots from the floor.

He could hear the sound of a car door—one car door—as he moved swiftly and silently down the hall toward the master bedroom and Caroline.

He could hear the sound of footsteps—one set of footsteps—on the back porch as he pushed the bedroom door open.

Caroline was fast asleep, sprawled diagonally across the king-size bed. She'd kicked one tanned leg free from the sheets and her face was partially hidden under a cloud of golden hair. Her arms were spread wide as if she were embracing the world. She was wearing blue cotton high-cut panties and an old white tank top she must've found in one of Emily's father's dresser drawers.

His body began to tighten, an instant reaction to her state of dishabille, or maybe just a reaction to her presence. But he had no time to consider this, no time to do more than get them out of there, to keep them safely hidden from whoever was coming inside.

Felipe jammed his gun into the holster that was over his shoulder. With one hand, he swept Caroline's hair back from her face. The other he clamped firmly down over her mouth.

She woke up immediately. Her eyes were wide as she stared at him for a moment, a scream at the back of her throat securely stopped by his hand.

"It's okay," he whispered. "It's me. Someone's outside—they're coming in."

Instant understanding filled her eyes and he helped her sit up. She untangled herself from the sheets as he searched in vain for her clothes. Damn, he couldn't find them. Where had she put her dress and sandals?

But then there was no time. As a key turned in the back door, there was no time for anything but hiding.

Still carrying his own clothes, Felipe took Carrie's hand and tugged her toward the big walk-in closet. Motioning for her to be silent, he pulled back the carpet, revealing the access to the crawl space. He pulled up the inset brass ring, and the small trapdoor opened with a squeak.

"Go on," he whispered to Caroline. "It's a crawl space. It's not deep—it's less than three feet down. Just climb in."

But she didn't move. She stared down into the darkness, her eyes wider than ever, her hair a golden tangle around her face. She heard the back door open, and she turned, glancing over her shoulder toward the sound, then looked at Felipe.

He threw his clothes and holster into the crawl space, keeping his gun in his hand.

"Quickly," he urged. "I'll be right behind you."

Wordlessly, she shook her head.

The back door closed behind whoever had come inside.

Felipe grabbed Caroline around the waist and pulled her down with him into the crawl space.

It was dark and damp and tight and hot and filled with cobwebs and other things he didn't want to think about. He closed the access door over their heads, taking care to flip the carpet back over it.

And then it was *really* dark.

There was barely enough room for him to lie on his side without his shoulder brushing the support beams for the floor above. Gingerly, Felipe shifted around, one arm still encircling Caroline's waist, the gun in his other hand pointed up through the blackness at where he knew the access door to be. Carrie's back was against his chest, her head tightly nestled below his chin. He could feel her heart pounding and hear her ragged breathing in the pitch darkness.

And then he could hear footsteps.

In his arms, Caroline held her breath as if she was afraid whoever was up there might be able to hear her.

She was terrified. Her entire body was trembling. But she tried to stop herself from shaking, entwining her smooth legs with his as if to anchor herself. It didn't help.

It certainly didn't help him.

Her round little bottom was pressed intimately up against him, and now his thigh was wedged firmly between her legs. His left hand was up underneath her shirt, and his thumb rested against the swell of her breast.

Felipe felt many trickles of sweat begin their journeys. One traveled down his back, others slid past his ear, another rolled down his collarbone.

The footsteps moved across the floor again. Whoever was up there was not overhead. The sound was coming from the other side of the house—where the kitchen and living room were located.

Caroline seemed to realize that, too, and she let herself breathe again. She took short, fast breaths as if she were running a marathon—or as if she were nearing sexual release.

That particular image was nearly too much for Felipe to bear. He tried to concentrate on the concentric waves of pain that were radiating from his wounded leg rather than his growing arousal.

But it was no use. Despite the imminent danger, despite his pain, he couldn't stop himself from being turned on. Afraid of offending Caroline, knowing his silk boxers did little to hide his state, he tried to loosen his hold on her and back away from her just an inch or two.

But she wouldn't let him go. "No,' she breathed almost inaudibly in the silence, turning her head toward him. "Felipe, please, stay with me!"

There was such desperation in her voice, such fear—and such total trust that his presence could make it all okay. He stopped trying to pull away.

"I'm here, sweetheart," he whispered. He was experiencing a jumble of emotions he could barely recognize. Protectiveness—he felt fierce, almost savage protectiveness. And he felt possessiveness, yes, there was plenty of that, too. Only God could help Tommy Walsh, or whoever else tried to take this woman away from him. And gluing everything together was sort of an odd tenderness, making all these powerful emotions stick like a painful lump high up in his chest, making his eyes burn and his heart hurt.

And the really loco part of it was, despite the fact that he wanted her so badly, these things he was feeling had absolutely nothing to do with sex, with the desire that was making his blood boil.

Above their heads the telephone rang.

The footsteps moved rapidly toward the kitchen.

In the total darkness of the crawl space, Felipe strained to listen.

"Hello?" a faint voice said. "No, who's callin'?"

Female. Southern belle accent. Anywhere from thirty to sixty years old. Not Tommy Walsh. Not a threat.

"No, I'm sorry," the voice said. "The Marshalls aren't here right now. They'll be down in February. I can take a message and call the daughter if you wish. She and her husband are in and out all the time." There was a pause, and then the gentle tinkling of a delicate laugh. "No, no. I live next door. I'm just over to water the plants. Uh-huh. That's right.'' Another laugh. ''Bye now.''

Felipe lowered his gun to the floor, suddenly aware how much his arm ached from holding it up for so long. He let himself relax slightly, twisting his head to get the kinks out of his neck.

But in his arms, Caroline still shook.

''Hey,'' he said softly, putting the safety on his gun. He set it down, away from them on the hard dirt floor and wrapped his other arm around her. Maybe in her fear she hadn't heard the phone conversation; maybe it hadn't sunk in. ''It's all right— we're all right. We're not in any danger. Even if she sees the unmade beds, even if she calls the police, we'll still have time to get away.''

Carrie took in a deep breath and tried to let it slowly out of her mouth. But that still didn't stop her trembling. ''It's so dark,'' she whispered, her husky voice cutting through the pitch black. ''I can't see anything.''

''But that's good,'' Felipe said soothingly. ''If we can't see anything, than no one can see us, right?''

''No,'' she said. Her voice sounded choked, unnatural, her breath still coming in sobs. God in heaven, was she crying? Felipe reached up and felt the tears on her face. She *was*. She was crying. His heart lurched.

''Caroline,'' he whispered, his voice nearly cracking with his concern. ''*Cara*, my God, are you hurt? What's wrong?''

''I'm okay,'' she whispered. But it sounded as if she was trying to convince herself as well as him. ''It's okay. See, I'm claustrophobic, but I'm okay.''

Claustrophobic?

Man, to a claustrophobic, the past ten minutes had to have been a total nightmare, a living hell. And she was still living it. Squeezed tightly together in a narrow crawl space, without any light...

''My God,'' he said, hardly aware he was speaking aloud. ''My *God*—''

''Shh,'' she said, turning toward him, trying to comfort *him*. ''It's all right. I'm all right. It's okay, because you're with me. I'm not alone. Really, it's not so bad.''

Not so bad? She was still trembling. He could feel her heart drumming in her chest. And she couldn't stop the tears that were flowing down her face, wetting his neck.

And, oh, God, give him strength! At Sea Circus, he'd locked Caroline in the trunk of her car. He'd locked her in the tiny, dark airless trunk of her little sports car, all by herself.

Felipe felt sick. His stomach churned and tears burned his eyes. Two hours. She'd been in there for two hours, she'd told him. He knew 911 calls were often dangerously backed up, but *two hours!* What he'd done to her was tantamount to torture.

"Oh, Caroline," he whispered raggedly, holding her tightly. "I'm so sorry."

The footsteps upstairs had been silent for a while. From outside the house, Felipe heard the sound of a car engine. The voice, the neighbor, had left.

He found his gun in the darkness, then moved toward the access door. He was careful to bring Caroline with him, careful to keep as much of his body in contact with hers as he possibly could, aware that such obvious proof of his presence helped her.

With a heave, he pushed the trapdoor open, and light— brilliant, glorious, golden light flooded down on top of them.

Caroline scrambled toward the light, and Felipe helped her up and out. Gathering his clothes and holster from where he'd thrown them, he climbed stiffly after her.

She lay on the floor of the master bedroom. Her eyes were closed and her hair had tumbled forward to hide her face.

Felipe holstered his gun and tossed aside the pile of clothes he'd been holding. He knelt next to her and brushed her hair back from her face.

"I'm sorry," he said again. "At Sea Circus, when I put you in your trunk... God help me, I had no idea."

She opened her startlingly sea green eyes and looked directly up at him. "I know that," she said, still breathing hard. "How could you have known? Besides, you did what you had to do to save me."

He was miserable, and he realized that every bit of his misery showed clearly on his face. No wonder she had been so angry with him at Schroedinger's restaurant. No wonder she was adamant about keeping her distance. "How you must hate me," he said.

She pushed herself up off the floor. Reaching out with one hand, she touched the side of his face. "No," she said quietly. She took a deep breath in, then let it slowly out. "No, I don't."

The tears that were in Felipe's eyes threatened to overflow. He reached up, pressing her hand tightly to his cheek. "I'd never do anything to hurt you," he said. "Please believe that."

She nodded, her own eyes luminous. Her face was smudged with dirt, and her tears had made clean tracks through it. Still, she looked beautiful. Lord, the torment he'd put her through...

She tried to smile and actually succeeded. "That was a heck of a way to wake up," she said. "A hand over my mouth to scare me to death, and then a trip to my own personal hell. Tomorrow you might try something a little lower key—maybe like this."

And then she kissed him.

She kissed *him*.

It started out feather light, the gentlest of butterfly kisses.

Felipe pulled back, surprised and even embarrassed. Had she really kissed him? Or maybe he'd kissed her, and maybe—certainly—he shouldn't have.

But she leaned forward again, and this time there was no mistaking. She *did* kiss him.

Her mouth was warm and soft, her lips opening under his, pliant and willing and...oh, *yes*.

He pulled her against him, turning his head to kiss her deeper, harder, longer. She molded her body against his and wrapped her arms around him.

Dizzy with desire, Felipe sank down onto the floor, pulling her with him. Their legs intertwined, and this time, he let himself truly enjoy the sensation of her smooth, silky skin against his. He kissed her again and again, exploring her mouth with his tongue, taking his time, content just to kiss her for hours and hours.

But then she moved against him, the softness of her belly against him. Her legs tightened around his thigh and he heard himself groan.

Her heart was beating as fast and hard as it had been down in the crawl space—faster, even. She tugged at him, and he rolled over so that he was on top of her.

This was not a case of him seducing her. This was not a case of him taking advantage . . . or was it?

Felipe pulled back. "Caroline," he said, shaking his head, unable to speak.

She looked up at him, fire in her sea green eyes. He reached for her hand, pulling her so that she was sitting up. Confusion and then trepidation replaced the fire in her eyes.

"You don't want to . . . ?" she whispered.

"*You* don't want to," he replied, hardly believing he was saying those words, hardly believing he was denying himself what would surely be a first-class trip to heaven. "You told me that yesterday, *cara*, remember?"

She looked at the obvious sign of his arousal. He couldn't hide it, so he didn't bother to try. He could feel her eyes studying him, searching his face. He looked back at her, steadily meeting her gaze.

"Is it okay if I changed my mind?" she asked softly, and his heart leaped.

"Oh, yes," he said huskily. "It's very okay."

"I changed my mind," she said.

He wanted to touch her. But right at this moment, it was enough to look, knowing that soon, very soon, he would be touching her.

For the first time, he let himself really see her in that ridiculous excuse for a shirt. The thin material was nearly transparent as it hung loosely on her slight frame. The armholes dipped down almost to her waist, revealing the soft, round sides of her breasts. Her nipples were dark, tight points that the shirt did little to conceal. It was sexy as hell and her smile told him that she knew it. She liked knowing that she turned him on. That was good, because he couldn't have hidden his attraction to her even if he had wanted to.

She was beautiful, and she was to be his. That knowledge made his body nearly hum with desire.

"Do you have any protection?" she asked. "A condom?"

"I keep one in my wallet." He smiled. "I kept it there in hopes that I'd meet up with you."

She laughed. "I know that's supposed to be romantic," she said, her eyes dancing with amusement. "But, really, Felipe, that's *such* a total crock of—"

"Do you know for sure it's not true?" he countered, his eyes sliding down her body, across those perfect breasts, down her shapely legs then up again to meet her eyes. "I've met you in my dreams quite often these past six months, Caroline Brooks."

Her smile faded, leaving only heat in her eyes. She moistened her lips with a nervous flick of her tongue. "Why don't you call me Carrie?" she asked.

"Because Caroline is more beautiful," he said. "It suits you."

She rolled her eyes. "Ease up on the B.S., Salazar," she said, "or I might change my mind again."

He watched her steadily. "It's not bull," he said serenely. "And, you know, if you change your mind again, that's okay, too."

She smiled at his words, but then stopped as she realized he wasn't kidding. It *was* okay. *Every*thing was okay.

"There is more to the way I feel about you than sex," Felipe said quietly. His words were true but purposely vague. He couldn't get more specific. He was afraid to delve more deeply into his own feelings. But even though it scared him—both the words he spoke and the feelings that prompted those words—she had the right to know.

She looked down, away from him, and he was struck by how sweet, how young and innocent she looked. She was only twenty-five—that was his age, too, he realized. But she was still young and he was not. He'd grown up a lot faster, a lot harder. They came from different neighborhoods, he and Caroline. The mountains of her father's ranch couldn't be compared to the rough, unforgiving city streets where he'd spent his childhood—what little of it he'd had. He'd been twenty-five for the past fifteen years. She'd been twenty-five only since last October 16—at least that was what had been listed on her driver's license.

But then she glanced up at him from underneath her long eyelashes and smiled. It was a smile that promised paradise, a dazzling contrast to her seeming shyness moments before. She was full of surprises, full of contradictions, a living kaleidoscope of mercurial energy and emotion. He liked that. He liked *her*.

He leaned forward to kiss her and she met him halfway.

The explosion of passion was nearly instantaneous. He heard her moan as he pulled her, hard, against him. As he kissed her again, he felt her hands in his hair, on his back, touching, caressing, drawing him yet closer.

They were back exactly where they'd been several minutes earlier. Only this time, when Caroline pulled him down on top of her, she opened her legs, pressing the heat of her most intimate self against him.

Oh, *yes*.

The pain in his leg no longer existed. St. Simone and Lawrence Richter and Tommy Walsh and this whole damned mess they were in no longer existed. The world—the entire *universe*—no longer existed.

There was only Caroline.

Felipe rolled over onto his back, pulling her along so that she was straddling him. She kissed him, her tongue dancing with his, mimicking the movement of their bodies as she slowly, sensuously moved on top of him. Her hair fell around his face, a curtain of gold, as his hands cupped her buttocks, fixing her more tightly against him. Only the silk of his shorts and the cotton of her panties kept him from entering her.

"Oh, Caroline," he breathed. "This is . . ." He couldn't find the words. But he didn't have to.

She stopped kissing him long enough to gaze down into his eyes and he knew that whatever it was he was feeling— this euphoria, this sense of perfection, of completeness—she was feeling it, too.

He found the edge of her shirt and pushed it up and over her head. Her breasts were small and round and perfectly proportioned to the rest of her body. He covered them with his hands, groaning at the pleasure of touching her soft flesh. She moaned, too, pressing herself forward.

With one swift move, he flipped her onto her back, moving to touch one taut, pink nipple with his lips. Gently, so gently, he kissed her, then touched her lightly with his tongue.

Her skin smelled fresh and clean and ever so slightly of sun block. Yes, now more than ever, he would associate that scent with paradise.

Felipe could feel his pulse racing. He tried to bring it under control, to slow down his breathing and ease this feeling of an imminent explosion that tightened his throat and his gut and made him ache even lower. He wanted to rip off her panties and his boxer shorts and plunge himself deep inside her.

Instead, he forced himself to move deliberately, unhurriedly. He drew languid circles around her nipple with his tongue while his hands swept slowly up and down her tanned, flat stomach to the edge of her panties and then up and across her other breast. She touched him the same way, too, almost reverently, as if she couldn't believe she was finally getting her heart's desire.

Her fingers felt cool and delicate against the burning heat of his skin. Could she feel his heartbeat? he wondered. Did she know that the gentleness of her touch had the power to make him tremble? As he drew her more fully into his mouth, pulling, sucking, laving her with his tongue, she gripped his shoulders with a strength that surprised him. She arched her back, wanting more. Her response nearly did him in, nearly pushed him over the edge.

By sheer willpower, he managed to hang on to his sanity and his control. He closed his eyes, counting slowly to ten. When he opened them, she was watching him. She smiled and his heart nearly burst. If it wasn't one part of him ready to explode, it was another.

She pushed his hair back from his face in a gentle, loving caress. It warmed him and he smiled back at her, whispering words of endearment in Spanish—words he wouldn't have dared say to her in a language she could understand.

He broke away from the spell her ocean-colored eyes had cast over him, gazing down at her beautiful body, clad only in those blue panties.

She was tanned all over, he realized. At least on the top. She did have a tan line where she'd worn bathing-suit bottoms, and another line of shading where she'd worn shorts, but her breasts had the same perfect, golden tan as her shoulders and arms and stomach.

More contradictions. Somehow he couldn't imagine Caroline driving south down the coast from St. Simone to hang out at Tamiami Beach, the area's only topless sunbathing spot. Still, she'd obviously spent some time—quite a bit of time—in the sun without her top on.

"Nice tan," he murmured, and she blushed. More contradictions. But then he lowered his mouth to her other breast, and she forgot her embarrassment. He felt her hands in his hair as she ran her fingers through his dark curls. He ran his hand down her stomach again, and when he would've stopped short of her panties, she lifted her hips, pressing herself up and into his hand. She couldn't have been any clearer about what she wanted if she'd announced it through a megaphone.

So he slipped his hand beneath the elastic waistband of her panties, lifting his head to gaze into her eyes as he touched first the nest of her curls and then her soft heat. The light of pleasure on her face was sinfully delicious as he explored her most intimately.

This would be enough, he realized. Even though he was straining against his shorts, even though he wanted to be inside this woman more than he'd ever wanted anything in his life, simply giving her pleasure would truly be enough.

She closed her eyes, moving against him as he stroked her harder, deeper.

He murmured to her in Spanish, telling her of the strange sensations in his heart, urging her on, right there, right now, as he held her in his arms.

But Caroline had an entirely different idea.

She reached for him, encircling his shaft with her hand right through the silk of his shorts. "This is what I want," he whispered. She moved her hand along his length and he bit back a cry of pleasure.

She reached for the waistband of his boxers, pulling them down, freeing him from their restraint. And then she was touching him, her fingers against his hardness, and once again he fought for self-control.

But she wasn't going to let him get it back.

She sat up, pulling away from him, getting up on her knees to drag his shorts down his legs, careful to lift them over the bandage that covered his stitches, touching him all the while. Feverishly, he reached for his jeans, for the wallet that was still in the back pocket, and for the condom that was stored there.

His hands shook as he tore open the foil package. She pushed off her panties—how beautiful she was!—then quickly helped him cover himself. Helped? Not really. She stroked him, squeezed him, caressed him as he blindly tried to put on the damned condom.

All of his English had left him, every single blasted word of it. He tried to tell her that he wanted to make love to her this first time in the traditional way. The first time, the man should be on top, giving the pleasure.

But she didn't understand. She murmured something to him about his leg, something about not wanting him to hurt himself, something he didn't understand because he wasn't hurting—he was feeling absolutely no pain. She kissed him, still straddling him, moving her hips so that she touched him with her moistness and heat. Oh, man, at this rate, he'd be finished in seven seconds. Felipe lifted her up, about to turn her and lay her down on her back, wincing when all at once the pain from his leg cut through. And, then, "No."

The single word penetrated and he froze.

No?

He looked into her eyes through the fog of desire, and she shook her head.

Yes, that was definitely a no.

Stopping like this was going to kill him, but if she'd changed her mind, then he'd stop. He was holding his breath, he realized, and he let it out with a long, ragged sigh, trying desperately to regain his equilibrium. What had happened? Had he done something wrong?

Slowly he lowered her back down, but instead of moving away from him, she moved toward him. With one smooth thrust, she unsheathed him.

Oh, *yes.*

It was a lot like being thrown a surprise birthday party. He was caught totally off guard, but instantly able to adjust to the shock. And just as quickly, he understood what she had been saying no to. She wanted to be on top.

It went against the grain of everything he believed about making love to a woman. The man gave and took the pleasure. The man was in control.

And he was not in control here.

But as she moved on top of him, as she rode him, her eyes half-closed with pleasure, her long, blond hair loose around her shoulders, covering all but the tantalizing tips of her breasts, Felipe realized an awful truth.

When it came to making love to Caroline Brooks, he would never truly be in control.

The only consolation was that she was not in control, either.

He moved his hips, thrusting up to meet her downward movement, driving himself deep into her. Her eyes widened, then shut tightly, and she threw her head back, crying out her pleasure at the sensation.

He was lost, swept away by passion and pleasure and an ache in his heart he was beginning to fear would never let up.

Time blurred, and he pulled her down to kiss him as they moved together. *Together.* He wasn't making love to Caroline, he was making love *with* her. The thought exploded in his head as clearly as the flash of light from fireworks. Suddenly, all of his previous beliefs about making love seemed old-fashioned and obsolete. Because as sure as he was born, he'd never in his life felt anything even remotely like what he was feeling right now. It was delicious ecstasy, wild abandon, pure pleasure. And he was sharing it with Caroline. It was dizzying, consuming, terrifying. Could he actually feel this way for more than the briefest moment and not disintegrate?

And still they moved together.

She pulled away from his kiss to sit up, still atop him, and the movement sent him plunging harder and deeper into her again and again. Her head went back and she clutched at his arms, and feeling something close to disbelief, Felipe fell over the side of a cliff.

He felt the last shred of his ragged control dissolve as his body took full command. He exploded with a violent rush as, for the only time since he'd first made love at age sixteen, he finished before his lover.

He heard the hoarse sound of his voice crying out her name, heard her answering cry, felt her shudder of pleasure as she, too, found her release.

His ears were ringing as she slumped on top of him, her hair covering his face. He closed his eyes, breathing in the sweet scent of her shampoo, feeling their two hearts racing, pounding a syncopated tattoo.

His breathing slowed, and his pulse finally returned to near normal. But the dizzying, consuming emotions that had been let loose in his mind and in his heart at their coupling wouldn't fade away.

Perhaps they never would.

That thought scared him to death.

What could it mean? Why was he feeling this way?

They swirled around him like a tornado, those almost palpable emotions, forming a pattern of words that repeated over and over in his mind.

Te amo. Te adoro.

I love you.

His eyes opened and he stared at the ceiling through a haze of golden hair.

He was in love with Caroline Brooks.

No. He couldn't be. He wouldn't let himself be. It was not possible. Not now. Especially not now. But not later, either. There was no room in his life for such a thing.

And there was no room in *her* life for both him and the danger he would bring with him. How many gang members, mobsters and crime lords had he angered over the past few years? How many contracts were there on his life right now? And how many people wouldn't think twice about ripping the life from an innocent young woman, simply to get back at the undercover police detective who had given them their due?

No.

If he cared about her at all, after this was over and he knew that she was safe, he would walk away. And if he loved her, he'd run.

Te amo. Te adoro.

No. It wasn't true. And even if it was, he couldn't tell her. He'd never tell her.

Never.

Chapter 11

"I'm sorry," Felipe said quietly, his mouth up against her ear.

Carrie turned her head to look at him, pushing her hair back off her face.

He gazed up at her, his dark eyes mysterious and unreadable.

"Sorry?" she asked.

She could have sworn she saw a flash of embarrassment in those eyes. He looked away from her, but then forced his gaze back up, steadily meeting her inquisitive stare.

He moistened his lips. "I, uh..." he said, then he cleared his throat. "Usually... I'm not so... inconsiderate. Usually... I allow my partner to... reach, uh, satisfaction first."

Carrie felt herself start to smile as the meaning of his words penetrated. She couldn't hide a laugh. "Are you *apologizing* for the way you just made love to me?" she asked, her voice dripping with disbelief.

He *was* embarrassed. He closed his eyes briefly, then nodded his head.

Carrie couldn't keep from laughing. "Mister, are you telling me that this is just an off day—that you've done that even *better?*"

"I came before you," he said. He wasn't laughing.

"Was it a race?" she asked. "And were you trying to let me win?"

Unblinkingly serious, he gazed up at her. "It's important to me," he said. And then he blushed slightly, looking away, unable to meet her eyes. "This hasn't happened since... It hasn't happened ever."

Carrie's heart flip-flopped in her chest. The tinge of red across his high cheekbones was utterly charming, despite the slightly archaic and macho tinge to his words.

He was still inside her and she didn't move off him. She didn't want to. The glow from the perfection of their joining still surrounded her. She nestled her head on his shoulder, careful that her hair didn't fall across his face, marveling at how well they fit together, even now, even after.

He stroked her back almost absentmindedly, his fingers trailing lightly from her neck to her derriere and up again.

"Do you know," she murmured, lifting her chin so that her breath touched his ear, "what it felt like to me just now?"

His hand stopped moving. He swallowed, then shook his head once slightly. He'd closed his eyes, but he was listening to her very carefully, absorbing each of her words.

"Do you know," she asked, stopping for a moment to brush her lips lightly along the line of his jaw, "what a turn-on it is when the man you're making love to loses control like that?"

Again, he shook his head.

"It's unlike anything you can imagine," she said, her voice husky with the memory and the emotion. "At the risk of feeding your ego, I've never been made love to like that before. *And* as far as I'm concerned, we were together. You started first. Big deal. I was a millisecond behind you. Who's counting?"

He opened his eyes and turned his head to look at her. "You're very sweet," he said, pressing a kiss to her forehead.

"You don't believe me?" Carrie shook her head, feeling impatience rising in her. Impatience, and something else.

Hurt? How could he not think that the love they'd just shared was anything but sensational? "I can't believe we're arguing about this. Can you honestly tell me that that entire experience gets stamped *rejected* because of one minute detail that didn't happen exactly the way you'd planned? Or are you telling me that the whole thing was lousy—and if that's the case, I better take a good long look at my sex life, because if *that* was lousy, I've been missing something all these years!"

"Caroline—"

"And if that's the case, we're on very different wavelengths, Detective, with you thinking that was lousy sex, and me thinking…" She took a deep breath and let it slowly out. "And me thinking it's never been so perfect, so complete," she finished miserably.

She rolled off him, wishing she could crawl away and hide. How had this happened? Two minutes ago, she'd been laughing, euphoric. Then this man whom she thought she was finally beginning to know and understand, this man who had been so amazingly in tune with her every want and need as he'd made love to her, this man had mutated into some kind of rigid caveman who needed to follow an extremely macho set of rules when making love. She began to search almost frantically for her clothes.

Felipe caught her arm. "Please," he said. "I was being stupid." He pulled her close to him and cradled her in his arms. "I was being *really* stupid. You were right. I was … stupid."

"Damn straight you were," Carrie muttered.

He gently moved her chin so that she was facing him. "I was frightened," he murmured. "The power of the feelings… It still frightens me. Forgive me, Caroline."

And then he kissed her.

He may have voiced some very old-fashioned ideas about male and female roles in bed, but his apology sounded sincere, and he could kiss like no one else in the world.

Most men that Carrie had known had kissed her for a reason. To placate or apologize. To get on her good side. To get her into bed.

But even though Felipe had just apologized to her, his kiss was very separate from his words. He kissed her purely for the sake of kissing her, for the pleasure of her mouth against his.

He kissed her slowly, lazily, his tongue sweeping possessively into her mouth, claiming her, staking out his territory.

Carrie heard herself sigh, felt herself melt, felt the world tilt and disappear. Maybe having a lover who could be an absolute caveman at times *wasn't* such a terrible thing. She laced her fingers up through his long, gorgeous hair, slanting her head to grant him easier access to her mouth.

He drew in a breath and murmured to her in Spanish. She couldn't understand the words, but his voice sounded like poetry in the hush of the quiet room. And still he kissed her.

She felt dizzying heat pooling in her stomach. Was it really possible that she wanted him again? Already?

He lifted his head, supporting his upper body with one elbow as he looked down at her. "I love kissing you," he said.

Carrie's heart pounded in her chest. For a moment, when he'd started that sentence, she had been so sure he was about to tell her something else. *I love you.* But how could she expect him to say that? He barely knew her.

They were undeniably compatible—especially physically. They'd certainly proved that. And despite Felipe's momentary slip revealing his old-fashioned beliefs, she honestly liked him more and more with each passing moment. Heck, she liked him more *because* of his slip. Before she'd seen that side of him, he'd been too damn perfect. She liked him better because now she knew that he was human and that he had his weaknesses and doubts.

He was stroking her, his strong, warm hand sliding up her hip and over the curve of her waist. His eyes were hooded as he looked at her. Carrie felt the tips of her breasts harden into tight little beads under the weight of his gaze. He glanced into her eyes and smiled.

"Do you really go out to Tamiami Beach?" he asked.

Tamiami...? Where...? The nude beach, Carrie remembered. No, not nude, topless. He was referring to her nearly allover tan. She felt her face heat with a blush.

"No," she said, shaking her head. "No. I...do a lot of research work out on my boat, all by myself." Did he really want to hear the entire story? He was listening, waiting for her to continue, so she did.

"I always used to just wear my bathing suit, but one day I was out doing some work along the coast near one of the swamps, and I forgot to bring my suit or even a change of clothes. I was bringing in a sampling of the marine life that had died as a result of an oil spill, and I ended up with tar all over my T-shirt." An angry alligator had surprised her near an illegal garbage dump and she'd tripped in her haste to get back into her boat. "It was hotter than hell that day, and the sun was heating the tar on my shirt. Obviously, it wouldn't rinse out, and I was actually afraid it was going to burn me. My options were to take off the shirt, or turn and head for home. I figured if I were a man, I'd have had my shirt off hours earlier, so...I took off the shirt and put in five more hours of work. And got a great tan."

She smiled up into his eyes. "I also got a...certain sense of liberation. Ever since then, when I'm alone on my boat, I go topless. No one knows but me. And now you."

He leaned forward to touch the peak of her breast with the tip of his tongue. "The thought of you working like this is...stimulating," he murmured. "Someday, will you let me come and help?" But then he shook his head, as if he thought better of his words. "Or maybe that's not such a good idea," he added. "It would be too distracting, at least for me."

He pulled back from her, no longer meeting her eyes. He ran his fingers through his hair, rubbed his forehead as if he had a headache. She could see the sudden tension in his neck and shoulders. Even the well-defined muscles in his arms seemed tighter. He hadn't moved an inch, but mentally he was stepping back, away from her. Was he doing that because he thought she wanted him to? Did he think she still wanted him to keep his distance?

"I'd love for you to come out on my boat someday," Carrie said quietly, trying to read his reaction.

But Felipe shook his head, still looking away from her. "We don't have someday, *cara*," he said just as quietly. "We only have right here and right now." He looked up at her then. The deep sadness was back in his eyes.

"Walsh and Richter aren't going to be looking for us forever," Carrie said. "And you're going to prove that you didn't kill those men in the sandlot—"

"Even then," he said, interrupting her. "Even if this ends and we're both still alive..." He took a deep breath. "I can't make you any promises, Caroline. I probably should have told you this before we made love, but... I can't fall in love with you."

His words filled her with a disappointment that was a great deal stronger than she'd expected. And his words proved how deceptive good sex could be. She'd interpreted his caresses, his sighs, those long looks he gave her, and especially the way he'd clung to her and called out her name, as a measure of his feelings. In truth, those things were merely a measure of *what* he was feeling. Physical sensations, not love in any way, shape or form.

But what the heck, she told herself, she hadn't *really* thought Felipe Salazar would fall in love with her, had she?

Yes. The word rose in her throat like a bubble that had to break free.

No, she told herself harshly. No, she hadn't. And it was good he'd told her this, because now that she knew, she'd make damn sure she wouldn't fall in love with him.

She forced her mouth into a smile. "Well, that's fine," she said to Felipe. "Because I have no intention of falling in love with you, either. You know, I don't even really trust you entirely."

Now, why the hell had she said that? She saw the flash of hurt leap into his eyes, and knew that her words had stung. She *knew* that his innocence was a sticky subject for Felipe, that he wanted her to trust him.

But what she'd said was true, she told herself. For all she knew, he really had killed those men. Or maybe he hadn't actually pulled the trigger himself. Maybe he was just involved in some other awful way. She had seen no proof that he wasn't involved. She only had his word.

You said it because you wanted to hurt him. You said it because you want him to fall in love with you, because you've already fallen in love with him.

"You must trust me on some level," Felipe said, "or you wouldn't have made love to me."

Carrie lifted her arms over her head and stretched, pretending desperately to be casual and noncommittal while her brain and her heart were going in twenty different directions. He followed her movement with heat in his eyes, like a cat watching a bird and ready to pounce. Was it desire or anger glowing there?

"I trusted that sex with you would be great," she said, keeping her voice light. Inside, she felt heavier than lead. She *wasn't* in love with him. She *wasn't*... "I wasn't wrong, was I?" She pushed herself off the floor and stood. "I'm going to take a shower, maybe take another soak in that tub." She stopped at the bathroom door, looking back at him. "Too bad you can't get your stitches wet for another day or so."

Then it was all desire that flared in his eyes. "Maybe I can—"

"You told me nothing but a quick shower until tomorrow," Carrie said, pretending that she actually *wanted* him to shower with her, pretending that his admission that he didn't love her, would *never* love her, was something that she took casually in stride, pretending that her heart wasn't breaking. "And if you get in the shower with me, it won't be quick. You better wait out here."

He smiled at her, a smile that held a promise of paradise. But no, he'd said he couldn't promise her anything. Nothing but sexual pleasure anyway, and certainly not paradise. Paradise was more than pure, raw sex. Paradise was murmured words of love, promises of forever. He wasn't even going to pretend to give her that.

Carrie supposed she should be grateful that he wasn't trying to deceive her. At least he'd been up-front and honest about his feelings—or lack of feelings in this case.

He was so utterly handsome, lying there on the floor buck naked, his long, muscular legs stretched out in front of him. His hips were narrow, leading up to his equally narrow waist and the washboard muscles of his stomach. He didn't have much hair on his chest. He didn't need it; it would have hidden the near perfection of his pecs and other steel-hard muscles. His skin was smooth and golden brown, his nipples a darker shade of that same delicious color. A line of dark hair started at his belly button and spread downward toward the thick thatch of black curls between his legs and . . .

He was fully aroused.

She did that to him, Carrie knew. With her talk of showering together, her stories of working on her boat without a top, and with the way she'd just looked at him—as if she were starving and he was a five-course gourmet meal. . . .

He was more than willing to let himself make love to her. *Make* love, yet not love her. He wouldn't let himself love her.

It didn't seem fair.

It *wasn't* fair.

Carrie went into the bathroom and turned on the shower. Stepping under the rush of water, she closed her eyes.

He *could* be a killer, she reminded herself. Maybe if she repeated that over and over, she'd stop loving him. Maybe she should take precautions against further hurt and take care not to make love to Felipe again.

Yeah, right. And maybe alligators could fly.

Rafe's prediction had come true, she realized ruefully. Less than twenty-four hours had passed since she'd sat with Felipe's brother in the kitchen of the halfway house, and sure enough, she'd gone and slept with Felipe. Slept with. It was a funny expression, considering neither of them had ever had the slightest intention of sleeping. Gone to bed with? That wasn't true, either, since they'd made love on the plush carpeting on the bedroom floor. Made love to. Only half-true—her half, not his. Still, a half truth was better than none, wasn't it?

Any predictions for the next twenty-four hours? she wondered as she turned her face up to the stream of water.

Where was Rafe when she needed him? Too bad he hadn't warned her she was going to fall in love with his little brother. Of course, if he'd as much as suggested the possibility, she would've laughed that off, too.

The water falling on her face hid her tears. As long as she stood there in the shower, Carrie could pretend that she wasn't crying.

Predictions for the next twenty-four hours? She had one that she knew so damn well to be true, it would make Nostradamus look like a cheap carnival palm reader.

Sometime in the next twenty-four hours or less—and probably many, many hours less—she was going to make love again to that man, that beautiful, exciting, charismatic, dangerous man that she'd so foolishly, and against all her better judgment, fallen in love with.

Chapter 12

Untangling her wet hair with a brush she'd found in the bathroom, and dressed in a too-big pair of cutoffs and a man's dress shirt that nearly covered the legs of the shorts, Carrie walked down the hall toward the living room. Felipe was nowhere in sight.

She stood looking out through the big glass doors at the turquoise blue ocean. The private beach was deserted and picture postcard perfect. She could see why someone would want to build a beach house on this spot. The sun reflecting off the white sand filtered in through the tinted glass of the windows, illuminating the living room with an unearthly golden light.

A sound from behind her made her turn around.

Felipe stood in the doorway that led to the kitchen. His hair, too, was wet from his own quick shower, and he ran his fingers through the tight curls, loosening them and letting the air dry them. His eyes were gentle, so soft and serene as he looked at her. There was no sign of the fire that had threatened to consume her only an hour or so earlier. But then his gaze traveled down her body, grazing her breasts, taking in the fact that she wasn't wearing a bra underneath her shirt, reminding her that both her bra and panties were hanging in the bathroom, drying. His eyes caressed the length of her legs, lingering, heating her with just a look.

The fire was still there, Carrie realized as he glanced back into her eyes. He was just very, very good at keeping it hidden.

"Are you hungry?" he asked, his soft accent like velvet in the quiet room.

Carrie's stomach clenched with a sudden rush of desire, and inwardly she kicked herself for her body's blatant reaction to this man. Hungry? Yes, sir, but not for food.

He was wearing only a pair of dark blue, knee-length shorts. A size or more too large, they hung low around his waist. He looked as if he were on vacation at the beach, as if he'd just come in from a morning of swimming in the surf. His muscles rippled as he gave his hair one last shake dry. Carrie remembered the feel of those arms around her, the incredible smoothness of his skin. She wanted to touch him again, but he stayed in the doorway all the way across the room.

"There wasn't much in the kitchen," Felipe said, "but I found some frozen vegetables and a bag of rice. The rice should be done in about five minutes. The vegetables are already hot."

He was going to play it normal, pretend that nothing between them had changed. He was going to be polite and friendly and keep his distance until the heat between them got too intense, until they ended up making love again. He wasn't going to hold her in his arms just for the sake of holding her, for the sake of closeness and comfort and warmth. And, oh, how she needed that right now.

To Carrie's horror, she felt her eyes fill with tears. Why? Why was she crying now? She never cried—well, hardly ever. And she was *damned* if she was going to cry in front of Felipe again. Fiercely blinking, she quickly turned away from him, pretending to study the view of the ocean. The blues of the water and the sky blurred together and she blinked even harder, forcing back her tears.

"Are you all right?" There was concern in his warm voice, and she heard him start to limp toward her. Heaven help her if he got too close. She'd end up crying in his arms, and that was the *last* thing she wanted. She wanted him to hold her, but not out of pity.

She took a deep breath and turned to face him, forcing her mouth into a smile. He wasn't fooled—she could see that from his eyes, but he stopped on the other side of the couch that bisected the room.

"The thought of rice and vegetables always gets me choked up," she said breezily.

He smiled at her words, but the concern didn't leave his eyes. No doubt he'd figured out that she'd fallen in love with him. No doubt it was a common occurrence. Every woman he'd ever slept with probably fell in love with him. And no doubt the concern in his eyes came from his imagining all the grief she was going to give him—the jealous phone calls, the tears, the desperate visits to him at work....

Except that he was a suspected murderer on the run. And *she* wasn't like all the other women he'd ever known. She had backbone. She had grit. She had pride.

"What happens now?" she asked, holding her chin high, letting him see that her eyes were dry as she walked past him into the kitchen. It was a big room, with cabinets and tiled counters lining the walls, a center island with a sink in the middle of the room, and a huge, round, butcher-block-style table off to the side in a breakfast nook. Windows and skylights were everywhere, letting in the sunshine, but the trees and shrubs outside provided a screen for privacy. No one could see inside.

"We'll have lunch." He followed her.

"That's not what I meant." There were two pots on the pristine white stove and the fragrant smell of basmati rice filled the air.

"We'll stay here another night," he said, crossing to the stove and turning off the burners.

Another night here at the beach house, alone in the candlelight. Heat rushed through Carrie at the thought of Felipe with her in that king-size bed...but tonight was too far away. She didn't want to wait until tonight. Man, she was shameless.

But here and now was all she had. He'd told her that himself.

"And then what?" she asked. Her voice sounded husky, so she cleared her throat again.

"Then I try to contact Diego," Felipe said. He leaned forward, bracing his arms against the back of one of the chairs that surrounded the big wooden table, taking the weight off his injured leg. The muscles in his arms and shoulders tightened and stood out. "Hopefully, he'll be able to tell me something new, something that will tip me off as to who in the police department set this frame up."

"And if he can't?"

"If he can't, we find someplace else to hide while I figure out a way to get past the security system in Richter's mansion and—"

Shocked, Carrie's mouth dropped open. "That's incredibly dangerous." As she stared across the room at him, she remembered Rafe's words. *Felipe, he's an addict, too. He's addicted to danger.* "It's crazy."

"This whole thing is crazy," he countered.

"You're planning to go—no, *break into*— the house of a man who wants you dead?" She started to pace. If Felipe went into Richter's house, did he really stand a chance of coming out alive?

"I'll go there if necessary," he said, his eyes following her as she moved back and forth across the cool tile floor. "But I'll have to do it soon. If I wait too long, Richter and Walsh will be expecting me to show up. Right now, they know I've been shot because of all the blood in that car. They'll expect me to lie low, to recuperate." He smiled tightly. "They're probably hoping I'll die from infection."

Carrie stopped pacing. "How *is* your leg?"

"Better."

"Honestly?"

"Well, it's not getting any worse."

"Are you really going to be ready to leave here tomorrow?" Carrie asked.

"I have to be," Felipe said. "We can't stay here much longer. It's only a matter of time before someone finds the van and the police connect it to us."

"I could go out and drive it farther away from this house," Carrie suggested.

"Without me? Bad idea, remember?" he said, softening his words with a gentle smile.

Bad idea. It wasn't as bad an idea as falling in love with him. Falling in love with Felipe Salazar was about the worst idea she'd had in all of her twenty-five years.

Carrie crossed her arms and looked down at the floor. "It seems all my ideas are bad ones these days," she said.

He was silent for a very, *very* long time. In fact, he didn't speak until she glanced up at him. His expressive eyes held real sadness and disappointment.

"Caroline," he said, "are you having regrets? About making love to me?"

She couldn't hold his gaze. "I don't know what I'm feeling," she admitted.

"I never meant to take advantage of you—or of our situation," he said quietly. "Although I guess I must have—"

"Oh, cut the macho attitude," Carrie said, exasperated. "How do you know I didn't take advantage of *you?* How do you know I didn't intend to seduce you?"

"Are you saying you worked out a plan to seduce me while we were down in that crawl space?" he said. "Nice try, but..." He shook his head. "I don't buy it."

He was smiling, and despite the heaviness in her heart, that smile was contagious. Carrie found herself smiling back.

"With your wounded leg, you couldn't exactly run away from me," she observed, putting her hairbrush down on a wicker telephone stand.

"I *did* run," he said with a broader smile that exposed his straight white teeth. "Last night. And it was *after* you, if I remember correctly."

His smile faded as he gazed at her. Carrie looked down at the floor, suddenly embarrassed by his scrutiny. She could feel his eyes studying her, watching, trying to read her mind. "I didn't want you to have any regrets," he said softly. "I'm sorry."

Her lips were dry. She moistened them with her tongue, feeling his eyes follow the slight movement. "I don't regret making love to you," she whispered. "How can I regret something that I'm dying to do again?"

She turned to look at him and found he'd silently closed the gap between them. He was standing only inches away, yet not touching her.

"Maybe you were right," he mused, gazing into her eyes. "Maybe you did seduce me this morning. Because I think you are about to seduce me again, no?"

"What about lunch?" she breathed, lost in the whirl of heat in his eyes as he moved even closer but still didn't touch her.

"Lunch can wait," he said, watching her mouth.

He was waiting for her, Carrie realized. He was waiting for her to make the first move, to touch him, to kiss him. To seduce him.

But he didn't love her. He liked her, and he lusted after her, but he didn't love her. He said he wasn't going to let himself fall in love with her, either. Not now, not ever. That hurt. To think that he could control his emotions as easily as he controlled his body and—

But he'd lost control. When they made love this morning, Felipe had *lost control.* Who was to say the same wouldn't happen to the tight rein he held on his emotions?

Carrie wanted him to love her. It was crazy. For all she knew, he was going to spend the rest of his life in a maximum security penitentiary or—God help her—on death row for the crime of first-degree murder. For all she knew, he *had* pulled the trigger two times, sending bullets into the heads of those mobsters. Oh, she didn't *think* he was guilty. Naturally, she didn't want to believe him capable of such a thing. But she didn't truly *know.* There were no hard facts or any proof to placate the scientist that she was. And her faith in Felipe wouldn't help him in a court of law.

Yeah, she was probably certifiable for wanting this man to fall in love with her. But she wanted it. And she was *damned* if she was going to sit back and just give up, just settle for his here and now.

At the very least, she was going to give him something to remember her by—and quite vividly—for the rest of his life.

The rays of light streaming in through the windows gave Felipe a golden glow. He looked otherworldly with his long, dark hair curling around his broad shoulders, his muscular chest gleaming and smooth. Carrie wondered if that same light accentuated her pale hair and lightly tanned skin. She wondered if she looked even half as exotic, half as sexy as he did. She sure *felt* sexy as he watched her, desire churning in his eyes.

But if she *was* going to seduce him, if she *was* going to try to loosen the hold he had on his emotions, she had to move fast before she chickened out.

With one swift movement, she pulled her shirt over her head.

His quick smile and quiet laugh told her he hadn't been expecting her to do that. That was good. She wanted to keep him off-balance.

He gazed at her silently but his eyes spoke volumes as they caressed her breasts and the curve of her smooth, tanned shoulders. She truly felt beautiful when he looked at her that way. Beautiful and sexy and powerful and capable of damn near anything. There wasn't a chance in hell she'd chicken out now. She'd set the wheels in motion, and now she'd see it through.

But he didn't reach for her. Instead, he jammed his hands hard into the front pockets of his shorts as if not touching her was a difficult task. She knew, suddenly, what he was doing. She knew why he wasn't touching her.

No regrets.

This time, he was making damn sure that it was clear *she* initiated their lovemaking. Of course, she could still regret it afterward, but this way, his own sense of guilt would be much lighter.

She could smell his clean, fresh, masculine scent. His nostrils flared, and she knew he could smell her, too. He could surely smell the faint, herbal scent of the shampoo she'd used to wash her hair, the tangy sweetness of the sun lotion she'd found in the bathroom and used in place of a moisturizer, and the fresh mint toothpaste she'd used to clean her teeth.

Felipe's eyes followed her fingers to the button of her shorts. She undid it slowly. *Very* slowly. Then she pulled the zipper down slowly. *Very* slowly. The look on his face was incredible. Every muscle in his body was tight with tension as he waited. Carrie knew he was keeping himself from reaching out and speeding the process along.

Watching him, she pushed the shorts off her hips and they fell to the floor with a soft rustle. He inhaled sharply, a reaction to her lack of underwear. She stepped out of the shorts totally naked. Except, of course, for the slight blush that heated her cheeks. Damn her fair skin anyway.

Still, she held her chin high, steadily meeting his gaze. The heat in his eyes was fast approaching a nuclear meltdown. Still, he kept his hands in his pockets. Still, he didn't move.

"We could have lunch first," she whispered, unable to hide her smile. "Are you sure you're not hungry?"

He wet his lips. "Not for rice," he countered. His gaze dropped to the golden brown curls between her legs, then back to her face.

His message couldn't have been more clear.

The sudden rush of heat that shot through her caught her off guard. She swayed toward him, and at that same moment, she saw his control snap.

He reached for her, *lunged* for her, taking her into his arms and carrying her over to that huge, wooden table.

His hands and his mouth were everywhere, touching, kissing, suckling, licking. The sensation of his tongue in her belly button made her cry out, her voice echoing through the quiet of the house. She tried to sit up, but he held her firmly in place, using his tongue to try to drive her as deliriously insane as she'd driven him.

She writhed in pleasure, and her arm knocked a sugar bowl onto the kitchen floor with a crash. But she didn't care. She didn't care about anything except that she was making love to this man whom she adored.

She tried to reach for the button that fastened his shorts. He obliged by moving closer. Her hand fumbled with the button, and he reached down, wrapping her fingers tightly around him.

He undid the button himself, and the zipper, and then his shorts were sliding off. From somewhere, maybe out of thin air—and she wouldn't have been surprised if he were capable of such magic—maybe from the depths of his wallet, he procured a condom.

And then he was on top of her, inside her, filling he
completely with each urgent thrust. He groaned as he kisse
her, and she moved with him, in a rhythm of love as old a
time.

You're going to love me, Carrie told him with her eyes
her hands, her body. I'm going to make you love me.

But she couldn't talk, couldn't form words let alone sen
tences. She could only grip his shoulders more tightly an
moan her pleasure.

Felipe pulled back to look at her. His eyes were wild an
tinged with shock. He spoke to her. His words were i
Spanish, but his meaning was clear. Now. *Now.*

Now, like this morning, he was unable to hold back. Nov
like this morning, *she* had driven him to a place of wil
abandonment, a place where he had absolutely no contro

That knowledge sent her soaring, rockets of pleasur
bursting through her as her body tightened and clenched i
a culmination too intense to be real. But it *was* real. Wave
of hot and cold rushed through her, colors exploded in he
head as she wrapped her legs around Felipe and tried t
draw him closer, even closer to her.

She heard him cry out her name, and then something els
in Spanish as he exploded, thrusting harder and deeper ir
side her.

And then it was over. Carrie closed her eyes as Felipe l
his head fall forward next to hers. He rolled off her so as n
to squash her, but then quickly gathered her into his arr
in a tender embrace. Oh, how she loved him.

Together they lay there on the kitchen table.

Carrie started to laugh.

They were *lying* on the kitchen table. They'd just mac
love on the kitchen *table.* Heaven help them if they were ev
invited back to this beach house for dinner. Carrie wou
never make it through the meal without breaking into hy
terical laughter.

"You must be thinking what I'm thinking," Felipe saic
kissing the top of her head.

"Dinner here," Carrie said. "With the Marshalls."

"That's what I'm thinking," he said with a laugh.

"I wonder if they'll know," Carrie mused. "Just from...I don't know, the aura, the cosmic waves of sex that will ripple forth from this table from now on."

"Hmm," Felipe said, cupping her breast with his hand.

"Or maybe," Carrie said, "the Marshalls do exactly what we just did on this table all the time."

Felipe laughed, tipping her face up so he could kiss her on the mouth. "Maybe not," he said.

Carrie gazed up into his eyes. "That was *great* sex," she said. "Are we in agreement?"

He didn't answer—not right away. Finally, he nodded. "Yes," he said. "We're in agreement."

Chapter 13

Great sex.

Caroline's words echoed in Felipe's head.

Great sex. Was that all it really was to her?

She was curled up on the other end of the long couch, her head resting on a throw pillow, her eyes tightly closed. She looked like an angel as she slept, with her lips slightly parted, her long eyelashes fanned out against her smooth cheeks, her hair a tangle of unearthly gold around her face. She was enveloped in what was probably Jim Keegan's old white terry-cloth robe. If she stood up with it on, it would trail behind her like the train of a wedding gown.

A wedding gown. Now that would be a vision to behold: Caroline, resplendent in a white gown, her long, blond hair elegantly arranged up off her shoulders, a whisper-thin veil covering but not hiding her beautiful smile.

The groom would be a lucky man, his destiny a life of laughter and love, sweet kisses and sleepy blue-green eyes smiling up at him after wonderful, endless, sinfully delicious nights of loving.

Felipe's destiny, on the other hand, promised a procession of cold and lonely nights, stakeouts and time spent under cover with another identity, another name and no real future. Of course, he'd still have Caroline's blue-green eyes smiling at him—they'd haunt his dreams for the rest of his days.

Suddenly chilled and feeling desperately alone, Felipe stretched his leg down the couch toward Carrie, wanting their connection to remain unbroken for as long as it possibly could.

He slipped his foot under her robe, touching the warmth of her leg with his toes. She smiled and opened her turquoise eyes, and a hand appeared from beneath the mound of white terry cloth. She rested it gently on his leg, stroking him slightly as she closed her eyes again.

Great sex.

It had been incredibly great sex. In fact, that was the way Felipe had always preferred to think of it in the privacy of his own mind. He spoke to his lovers of "making love," but love never really entered into it—at least not more than the rather general love he had for all beautiful women. Sure, he'd imagined himself in love a time or two back when he was a teenager. But either it hadn't lasted or he'd been spurned and his broken heart had quickly healed. So quickly, in fact, that he'd soon come to doubt the truth of what he'd felt.

But this thing he'd been feeling lately, this lump of emotion that was lodged in his chest was unlike anything he'd ever felt before.

Maybe it wasn't love, he told himself. Maybe he was mistaken.

Caroline sighed and opened her eyes again. "What time is it?" she murmured.

He didn't need to glance at the clock on the wall. He could tell by the angle of the sun on the horizon. "Nearly six."

She yawned and stretched, her legs entwining with his on the couch, her arms reaching for the high, beamed ceiling.

Caroline folded her hands behind her head, elbows in the air, and looked down the couch at him. With one foot, she played with the edge of his shorts. "What does 'tay-yamo' mean?"

Her question made him freeze. Even his heart seemed to stop beating for a few solid seconds.

"What did you say?" he said.

"Tay-yamo," she said again.

Te amo.

I love you.

He kept his shock carefully hidden from her curious gaze.

"You said it more than once," Caroline said. She lowered her arms and began fiddling with the belt of the robe, aware of his sudden complete silence and clearly uncertain how to interpret it. "You remember, back when we *weren't* having lunch. Remember, the kitchen table . . . ?"

Her smile was half shy, half wicked and utterly charming.

"I remember the kitchen table." He would always remember the kitchen table. In fact, he would probably be thinking of it, ninety-five years old and on his deathbed. That is, if he lived that long.

"I was just wondering if . . ." She looked at him from underneath her long lashes. She wasn't being coy or trying to act cute. Her nervous shyness was as real as the sweet blush that often tinged her cheeks. It totally contradicted the woman who had brazenly and openly tempted him in the kitchen this noon, but that wasn't a shock. She was a nest of contradictions and surprises. He expected it by now.

She took a deep breath. "I was wondering if Tay-yamo was someone's name. Like an old girlfriend. Or maybe a not-so-old girlfriend . . . ?"

Felipe shook his head. "It's not a name," he said.

"Then what does it mean?" she asked. She said it again, practicing the unfamiliar Spanish words. "Tay-yamo. Am I saying it right?"

Te amo.

I love you.

Felipe could only nod. Had he really told her that he loved her?

"What does it mean?" she asked again.

He cleared his throat. "It's . . . rather difficult to translate."

He'd told her he loved her as they made love. He closed his eyes, and he could hear the echo of his voice calling out those words. *Te amo*. Yes, he'd really said it.

Worse than the shock of realizing he'd slipped, of realizing it was only chance that he'd said those words in a language Caroline didn't understand, worse than that was the sudden glaring knowledge that those words he'd cried were true.

He loved her.

She tucked her legs back underneath her robe, moving away from his foot. The sudden loss of her warmth, of the sensation of the closeness was too much for Felipe. He reached forward and pulled her so that she was sitting toboggan-style between his legs, her back against his chest. He wrapped his arms around her, holding her tightly.

He couldn't deny it anymore. He loved her.

He was doomed.

"Tay-yamo," she said again, and his heart clenched. She didn't know what she was saying, and she probably wouldn't say it if she *did* know what it meant. "You really can't translate it, huh?"

He shook his head. No.

How ironic that the tables had turned on him so absolutely. Here he'd gone and fallen in love, and *she'd* had "great sex."

"Tay-yamo. You were...exuberant when you first shouted it," she mused, that same wicked light in her eyes. "Is it kind of like, I don't know...yabba dabba do?"

Felipe laughed, holding her closer, loving her, wishing with all his heart that she loved him, too. But if she did, man, what a mess that would be. A double heartbreak instead of a single one. Because he was going to leave her when this was over. He *had* to leave her. He wouldn't risk putting her in danger. It would be easier for her, much easier, if she simply didn't fall in love with him, if she simply continued to consider their relationship a source of friendship and "great sex."

"Yes," he told her, pulling up her chin and kissing her soft lips. "It's *exactly* like yabba dabba do."

* * *

Felipe woke up at nine-thirty with Caroline in his arms.

Morning sunlight was streaming in around the edges of the shades and curtains in the master bedroom, and had been for quite some time.

He'd never slept so late before.

But it didn't surprise him. These past few days had been full of firsts.

Take, for example, the fact that he was lying here with the woman that he loved in his arms. Loved. That was a very big first.

Caroline was still fast asleep. He smiled despite the tension in his stomach and shoulders that his thoughts had created. She slept fiercely, her eyes tightly closed and her fists clenched, as if she was fighting to stay asleep.

He'd kept her up late last night. But then she'd woken him up at dawn.... She was as insatiable as he.

They'd stumbled around in the gray half-light, searching the master bedroom for condoms. They'd used up the one he'd carried in his wallet, *and* the others his brother had slipped him before they'd left the halfway house.

Felipe had been prepared to improvise, or heaven help him, even risk it—now *there* was another first—when Carrie had dug up a nearly full box. They were Jim's, and they'd been buried—hidden—way, way back underneath the sink.

Felipe was going to take every single one with him when they left. Jim wouldn't need them for a while—his wife, Emily, was five months pregnant.

He looked down at Caroline again, studying the pattern of freckles that splashed across her nose and cheeks, imagining her pregnant with his child. The want that rose in him was so intense he had to close his eyes and breathe deeply until it faded.

The baby would look like him, dark hair, dark eyes. He would be big—all of the Salazar babies were big—maybe even too big for Caroline to deliver safely. She was so tiny that the thought of her heavy with child and in possible physical danger because of it, because of *him*, was nearly overwhelming. If he got her pregnant, he'd spend nine months terrified that she would somehow be hurt...or worse.

Another reason not to tell her that he loved her. Another reason to walk away and never let her know the way she made his heart sing.

But—and it was time for yet another first—Felipe was starting to wonder if, when the time came, he'd actually have the strength to leave her.

Jim Keegan was married. Of course, he spent most of the time worried to hell about Emily. And Jim took precautions, too. He had a state-of-the-art security system and a dog the size of a small horse trained never to leave their yard. When he worked late at night, patrol cars would drive past his house, occasionally checking in with his wife. Felipe had stopped by himself, many times, as a favor to his old friend.

All that worry, all those precautions, and Jim only worked straightforward homicide. He rarely went under cover. His job was known to be far less dangerous than Felipe's.

Infiltrating street gangs and organized crime, which was what Felipe was so very, very good at, included a certain risk of retaliation or revenge. If he stayed with Caroline, if he let himself live the kind of life he longed for with her, he'd never be free from worry. His concentration would be off, and he'd probably get himself killed. Or *her* killed. And God help him, if anything happened to her, he'd never forgive himself.

No. When the time came, Felipe would find the strength to leave Caroline. Somehow, he'd manage to do it.

His leg started to ache, and he closed his eyes. Caroline snuggled against him, and he held her tighter, breathing in the sweet, familiar scent of paradise.

It wasn't going to be easy. God, even if *she* was the one who turned and walked away, it wouldn't be easy. Easier, but not easy.

Nothing would ever be easy again.

The bloodstains hadn't quite washed out of Carrie's dress, but the blue-flowered pattern managed to hide them, at least at a distant inspection. Now that the dress was clean and dry, she'd put it back on. Despite the stains, it fit far better than anything else she'd found in this house of tall people.

She stripped the sheets from the beds they'd used and put them and their dirty towels in a laundry basket. She left a note on top, apologizing for not taking the time to wash the linens.

Felipe was in the kitchen, washing up the pots and dishes. He'd been oddly quiet all morning, a strange shadow darkening his eyes. Whether it was the thought of leaving the sanctuary of the beach house or something else, Carrie didn't know. But he was tense—more so than usual—and seemed lost in his thoughts.

Making love in a bed had seemed almost anticlimactic after the kitchen table. Still, it had been...lovely. He'd made love to her slowly, so exquisitely slowly. She could have sworn she'd seen love in his eyes, but she was probably mistaken. It was more likely only a reflection of the candlelight.

She sighed. Felipe glanced up at her and she forced her mouth into a smile.

"Ready to go?" he asked, wiping his hands on a dish towel, then hanging it on a hook near the sink. He walked toward her.

"No," she said.

He pushed her hair back from her face so very gently. "Neither am I," he said. "But we have to."

He was wearing the jeans, T-shirt and jacket he'd borrowed from his brother Rafe. He'd pulled his hair into a ponytail and his face looked sterner and harder without the softening effect of his long, dark curls. But his eyes were soft and his lips were even softer as he leaned forward to kiss her.

"Where are we going?" Carrie asked.

The shadow came back, flitting quickly across his gaze, and he looked away, toward the door that would lead them out of the house. "To a friend's," he said vaguely. "I have to get my hair cut. I need to look as different as I possibly can."

Carrie reached up and touched his ponytail. "Cut short?" she asked, unable to hide her disappointment.

He smiled, amusement in his dark eyes. "What? You like it long like this?"

"Yes," she said, freeing his hair from the ponytail and running her fingers through it. "It's...sexy."

"Hmmm," he said, closing his eyes, letting her know he enjoyed her touch. "I'm sorry. I won't get it cut too short." He looked at her and smiled. "The police have two kinds of pictures of me—some are with my hair long, like this. The others are with it cut short. You know, I always wore my hair really short until about two years ago." He looked down at his clothes and made a face. "And this is not my normal wardrobe. I always wore designer suits and ties."

Carrie laughed. She just couldn't picture it. Although he had worn that tuxedo with a certain ease and familiarity.... "I'll believe that when you show me the pictures."

He stepped slightly away from her, putting the rubber band back in his hair. "Time to go."

Carrie watched him open the kitchen door. She didn't want to walk through it, afraid of whatever might be waiting for them in the harsh world outside. She stalled. "What if the van's not there? What if it's been towed?"

"We're not taking the van."

"We're not?"

Clasping her hand, he led her out the door onto the back porch. He locked the door and slipped the key back under the flowerpot. "We're taking Diego's bike."

His...*bike?*

Carrie followed Felipe down the stairs and around the house to a detached garage. He pulled up the garage door, and there it was. A big, shiny, chrome-and-black Harley-Davidson motorcycle. Diego's bike. Of course.

"Do you really know how to ride that thing?" Carrie asked.

Felipe wheeled it out into the sunlight, then closed the garage door.

He glanced at her and smiled. "Yes."

"I've never ridden one before," she said.

"Think of it as riding a horse with a powerful engine and a narrower saddle," he said. "You did ride horses in Montana, right?"

"Of course."

He smiled at the faintly insulted tone in her voice. "You know how when you let your horse run, really run, you feel it inside? You move together, you even think together—"

She interrupted him. "You ride?"

"My uncle Manny works at the racetrack," he said. "I still sometimes go over there and pick up a few extra dollars exercising the horses that are boarded in their stables."

"I don't really know that much about you, do I?" she said.

The shadow came flitting back into his eyes. He shook his head. "No, you don't."

"I mean, I had no idea ... Are you a good rider?"

"*I* think so. But I'm better at riding one of these," he said, turning away from her and slapping the seat of the motorcycle.

He swung one long leg over the bike, straddled the monster and slipped a key into the ignition.

"Climb on behind me," he said, handing her own of the helmets that had been hanging on the bike's handlebars. "Put your arms around my waist and hold on tight. Lean when I lean, move with me, okay? And careful where you put your legs and feet. The engine gets pretty hot."

She nodded, about to put the helmet on, when he suddenly pulled her tightly to him and kissed her on the mouth. It was a passionate kiss, filled with deep yearning and need, yet it was still sweetly, achingly tender.

Carrie's knees felt weak and her bones turned to jelly. When he released her, she nearly fell over. He put the helmet on her head, strapping it securely under her chin.

He started the motorcycle with a roar, wincing as he jarred his injured leg. The motor turned and caught. "Climb on," he shouted, strapping on his own helmet.

She wasn't too happy about getting on the motorcycle, but after a kiss like that, she'd probably follow him damn near anywhere.

Carrie took a deep breath, then swung her leg over the seat. The dress she was wearing wasn't exactly made for riding astride. She tried to secure it underneath her, then locked her arms around Felipe's waist.

As he drove slowly down the driveway, she looked back over her shoulder at the beach house, wishing they could have stayed there forever.

Chapter 14

St. Simone hadn't changed one bit during the two days they'd been away. The sun still shone endlessly down from a perfect blue sky, warming the cracked sidewalks and the tiny one- and two-bedroom houses that lined the street. This was the part of town that the tourists never came to visit.

It wasn't dangerous like the neighborhood Rafe's half-way house had been in. It was just quietly depressing. These were beach shacks, and on the water they might even have been charming or picturesque. But here, the ocean was more than a mile away. Here, they were just bleak, cheaply constructed boxes that were crumbling around their financially strapped owners.

Felipe pulled the motorcycle up to the curb and braced his feet on either side as they came to a stop. He cut the engine and the sudden silence was a blessing.

Carrie lifted the visor of her helmet and looked around. Whoever this friend was that Felipe was planning to visit, he didn't have much money. It wasn't Jim Keegan, that was for sure. Carrie couldn't picture the daughter of the people who owned that house on Sanibel Island living on this particular street.

Felipe took off his helmet and turned slightly to face her. "We should go inside quickly," he said. "The fewer people who see us, the better."

She climbed stiffly off the motorcycle, and he led the way toward a tiny yellow house. A rusty wire fence surrounded the postage stamp-size yard, and the gate squeaked as he pushed it open. But the yard was clean, the garden filled with beautiful flowers and the house was well kept, with a fresh coat of paint.

Felipe limped up the steps to a small landing and knocked on the screen door.

The inner door swung open and a small, freckled face looked out through the screen.

"Daddy!" a young voice cried, pushing the screen door wide. A little boy launched himself into Felipe's arms.

Daddy?

Carrie stared at Felipe in shock as the door banged shut. He met her eyes for only the briefest of moments over the top of a bright red head. His expression was unreadable.

"Oh my God," another voice said from the darkness behind the screen. "Get inside here, *fast!*"

Felipe's friend wasn't a he. His friend was a *she*.

She was tall, almost as tall as Felipe, with elegant, almost classical features, green eyes and long, wavy red hair. She was obviously the little boy's mother—the same little boy who'd called Felipe Daddy.

Good Lord, was this woman Felipe's *wife?* Carrie stared in shock, realizing that she'd never actually asked Felipe if he was married.

The green-eyed woman pushed open the screen door and pulled Felipe and the boy into the house, leaving Carrie out in the cold—only figuratively, of course, since the sun was beating warmly down on her head.

Still holding the child, Felipe pushed the screen back open. He took Carrie's arm and dragged her inside, shutting both doors tightly behind her.

Green-eyes looked at her with a mixture of curiosity and hostility. Carrie couldn't blame her. *She'd* be hostile, too, if *her* husband brought his lover home.

"What are you doing here?" Green-eyes asked Felipe. Her voice had the warm sugar-and-spice accent of the Deep South. "Everyone's looking for you. Jim Keegan was by just a few hours ago."

Felipe closed his eyes. "Damn. If only I'd known..."

The young woman was strikingly pretty, with long, pale, slender arms and legs. She was wearing a denim skirt and an off-white tank top with a gently scooped neckline. Her outfit wasn't necessarily feminine, but on her, it looked as delicate as lace. She looked like a dancer, tall and graceful. Next to her, Carrie felt like one of the seven dwarfs.

"I'm sorry," Felipe said. "I know this is awkward. But I didn't know where else to go."

"Phil, so help me God, if you screw up my life—"

"Billy, excuse your mother and me for a moment, please," Felipe said. The little boy slid down out of his arms. He gazed curiously at Carrie as he walked past her and sat down on the living room couch.

Felipe stepped closer to Green-eyes, touching her shoulder, speaking to her in a low, soft voice. Carrie couldn't make out the words, but his tone was soothing, almost seductive.

It was misery, watching him talk to her like that. Carrie stared at the worn floorboards of the living room floor, but she couldn't block the sound of his voice.

I don't really know that much about you, do I?

No, you don't.

Damn straight she didn't. She felt like a fool. She glanced up to find the little redhead watching her. She imagined she could see scorn and disgust in the youngster's eyes.

Carrie heard the answering murmur of Green-eyes's Southern accent, and her attention was drawn back to the other side of the room, where she and Felipe were having their own version of summit peace talks.

Was he touching her face? Had he kept that comforting hand on her shoulder, sliding it down her arm in a gentle, sensuous caress? Was she, right this very moment, lifting her face to his for a kiss.

Carrie couldn't keep from looking over at Felipe. She couldn't stop herself. But as soon as she did, she wished desperately that she hadn't. Because Felipe *was* touching the redheaded woman. He was pushing Green-eyes's wavy hair back from her face. Carrie's heart shriveled inside her as she remembered that he'd touched her that same way mere hours before.

How *could* he have? How could he make love to her the way he had, with his wife and child here in this little house, waiting for him to come home?

Felipe glanced up to find Carrie staring, and she quickly looked away, knowing all her hurt and jealousy were showing in her eyes.

"All right," Green-eyes said, walking across the living room and sitting on the couch next to Little Redhead. "So introduce me to your friend, why don't you?"

"Caroline," Felipe said, moving toward the couch, "meet Jewel and Billy." He didn't sit down but rather stood beside them. It was a charming family portrait. Carrie's head was spinning.

She searched the boy's face for any sign of Felipe's features, any similarities the child might have to his father.

She couldn't see a single one. The red hair, green eyes and freckles came directly from his mother. The nose was entirely the child's own, as was his chin and mouth.

"Daddy, I saw you on the news," Billy said. His small face suddenly looked pinched and nervous. "They say you're a bad man."

"Billy, hush," Green-eyes—Jewel—whispered. Her name suited her.

"No, that's okay," Felipe said. He knelt next to the boy. "You must be pretty upset, huh?"

Billy nodded.

"It's not true," Felipe said. "All that stuff they're saying on TV and in the papers. Someone made a mistake, and I'm being blamed for something that I didn't do."

"You didn't kill those guys?" the boy asked.

"No," Felipe said, "I didn't. And you know I'd never lie to you."

"I know," Billy said. He pressed his lips tightly together and stared down at his hands.

"I'm going to get it all worked out," Felipe said. "Don't worry, okay?"

"Okay." But it was said grudgingly.

"Feel any better?"

Billy shook his head.

Carrie's heart was in her throat. Felipe was gentle with the child, full of soft words and reassurances. It wasn't hard to imagine him talking to her in that same soothing tone. But there wasn't much he could say to make *her* feel any better, either.

"I'm sorry," Felipe murmured, pulling the little boy into his arms. "I wish I could wave a magic wand and make it all disappear, but I can't. I need time. Can you give me some time, Billy? Another week, maybe?"

Billy nodded, on the verge of tears. He wriggled free from Felipe's arms and ran out of the room.

Felipe started after him, but Jewel stood up and stopped him with a hand on his arm. "Let him go," she said. "He doesn't like to cry in front of anyone these days. He's a big boy, nearly seven. He's got enough to worry about—at least spare him the embarrassment."

Felipe looked as if he was about to cry, too. "I'm sorry," he said to Jewel.

"Whoever you're investigating," she said, "you sure got them scared, huh?"

"Yeah," Felipe laughed humorlessly. "We've got them shaking in their shoes, don't we, Caroline?"

She said nothing. What could she say? All she wanted to do was leave. Walk out the door, away from Felipe Salazar, away from his lies and deceit—except he'd never told her that he *wasn't* married. She'd stupidly never asked.

"It said on the news that you'd been shot," Jewel said, pushing her hair back behind her ear. "Are you all right?"

"I'm sore," Felipe said shortly. "I should stay off my leg for another week, but I don't have another week. I don't have enough time."

Jewel smiled wryly. "I know the feeling well. Come on into the kitchen. You can have something to eat while I cut your hair."

Now was Carrie's chance. She'd just stand up and let herself out the same door they'd come in.

Except Felipe took her arm and pulled her with him into the tiny kitchen.

"I need a bathing suit," he said to Jewel as he gently pushed Carrie down into a chair. "And one for Caroline, too." He took out his wallet and handed her a hundred-dollar bill. "Will you run down to Swim City and buy them for me? Caroline's a size five, and I'm still a medium. Get us something funky and young-looking. Something college kids would wear."

"Can I take a spin on that bike you drove up on?" Jewel asked. She filled a spray bottle with warm water from the sink, then dragged one of the kitchen chairs into the middle of the room.

"Sure." Felipe sat down in the chair, and Jewel wrapped a towel around his neck.

"Then it's no problem. I tell you, Phil, it kills me to cut this gorgeous hair off," Jewel said, wetting down his long curls.

"I don't need a bathing suit," Carrie said, finally finding her voice. Her numbness and disbelief were slowly being replaced by anger. That was good. Anger didn't hurt quite so much.

"You need to get out of that dress," Felipe said to her as Jewel combed his wet hair, parting it neatly on the side. "The police have probably issued a description of what you were wearing by now. And besides, we're going down to the beach. If you don't have a bathing suit, you'll stand out."

"*You* might be going to the beach," Carrie said. "But I'm not. I'm out of here."

"Don't be ridiculous—"

"Ridiculous?" she said. "*Ridiculous? This* is ridiculous, Detective. Sitting here like this..."

Jewel took a long, sharp-looking pair of scissors and began cutting Felipe's hair at cheekbone length. Long, dark curls fell on the beige linoleum floor. She glanced up at Carrie. "You got a problem with my kitchen? I admit it *is* kinda ugly...."

Carrie leaned forward. "I hate to break it to you, sister, but *Phil* here has been unfaithful."

Jewel just kept cutting his hair. "Why, you bad boy, you," she said to him.

"Caroline," Felipe started to say, but she ignored him.

"Don't you care?" Carrie asked Jewel.

Jewel smiled, quickly cutting the hair around Felipe's ears even shorter. "Nope."

"Well, *I* do," Carrie said coolly. "And I'm leaving."

Her chair squeaked as she pushed it back from the table and headed out of the room.

Felipe stood up. "Caroline, wait..."

Jewel put the scissors down. "It seems like this is a good time for me to get those things you wanted from the store."

Carrie spun back to face Felipe as he scrambled after her into the living room and followed her toward the front door. "And by the way," she said, "I have regrets. *Big* regrets. I regret the day I first laid eyes on you."

Felipe had done it. He'd gone and made Caroline ready and willing to walk away from him. Except he hadn't expected her to be quite this angry, quite this upset, quite this willing to walk right *now*.

He had had no idea that she would be so...jealous. *Jealous?* She *was.* She was jealous of Jewel. My God, maybe she cared about him more than she'd let on.

"And," she continued, "I *definitely* regret ever being so foolish as to make love to you, you two-timing *snake!*"

Felipe had been called quite a number of things in his life, but "two-timing snake" wasn't one of them. Out on the street, he heard the roar of Diego's bike as Jewel rode away.

He laughed—he couldn't help it. It was a combination of her words and the giddy way he felt, knowing she was *jealous.*

"Oh, you think it's funny?" she said. "Fine. I'm leaving, and this time you can't stop me."

Felipe stopped laughing. She was dead serious, and the thought of her walking away now was instantly sobering.

"No," he said. "No, it's not— Caroline, I've misled you."

"Damn straight you did, you *bastard.*"

"No," he said, pushing his freshly cut hair up and out of his eyes. "I've misled you by letting you believe I have any kind of relationship besides friendship with Jewel."

"No relationship?" she said. "Right. Your *friendship* created a son?"

"He's not my son," he said, talking low and fast as he followed her the last few steps to the door. "He calls me Daddy because he doesn't have anyone else to call that, and because I love him as if he were my son."

Carrie stopped with her hand on the doorknob. She wouldn't look at him, but he knew she was listening. It was a good thing she was listening because there was no way he would let her leave.

"I met Jewel when she was seventeen," Felipe said, talking quickly, quietly. "Billy was nearly three. She'd just come out of rehab, and her uncle was trying to hook her on crack again so he could resume his role as her pimp."

"Lord," Carrie breathed, finally looking up at him. Her eyes were wide and so blue.

"I helped put her uncle in jail," he told Caroline evenly. "She and I became friends. That's all it's ever been—friendship. I've never slept with her—I've never wanted to. I love her, but I'm not in love with her. Do you understand that?"

Caroline's eyes were brimming with tears, but she kept her head turned away. She never wanted him to see her cry. She was so tough, so independent, and at the same time, so damn fragile. She nodded her head. She understood.

"You must think I'm a fool," she said. "A jealous fool."

Jealous. She *was* jealous. Why did that make him so happy? It should worry him, make him wonder if maybe she cared about him too much. "I don't think you're a fool," he said gently.

"Well, that makes one of us," she said and went back into the kitchen.

Felipe briefly closed his eyes. She wasn't going to leave. Not yet anyway.

* * *

"You lovebirds get things ironed out?" Jewel asked Carrie as they sat in the kitchen.

Jewel had returned from the store and finished cutting Felipe's hair. Now Felipe had gone to find Billy, to say goodbye to the little boy.

Carrie was wearing the bathing suit that Jewel had bought at Swim City. It was a bikini of extremely minute dimensions, in a neon orange-and-black zebra-stripe print. Supposedly it made her look like a college student. Over it, she wore a filmy gauze beach cover-up and a pair of overalls dug out of the back of Jewel's closet. The long pants would make riding the motorcycle easier, and help keep her warm if they were out all night.

Carrie shrugged. "It's not love," she said.

"I don't sleep with guys I don't love," Jewel said. She took a sip from the glass of iced tea that sat on the table in front of her. "Not anymore." She looked at Carrie. "And I don't think you do, either."

Carrie was silent, tracing a design on the table with the condensation from her glass.

"How could you not be in love with that man?" Jewel asked.

Carrie looked up into the brilliant green of the younger woman's eyes. "Are you?" she asked.

Jewel laughed. "No," she said. "Well...I used to have a crush on Phil back when we first met, but that was a long time ago." She looked at Carrie from out of the corner of her eye. "However, he *is* the best-looking man on earth."

Carrie had to smile. "Amen to that. But that haircut you gave him makes him look about eighteen years old. I feel like a cradle robber."

"Just push his hair out of his face," Jewel said. "It's only when it's in his eyes that he looks young."

"You're good at cutting hair," Carrie said.

"Thanks," Jewel said almost shyly. "It started out as a temporary career. I'm actually going to school over at the state university. I'm majoring in business, with a minor in Spanish. Although, I like cutting hair so much, I just might stay with it. With the business degree, maybe someday I can own my own salon.''

''You speak Spanish?'' Carrie asked, leaning forward.

''Nearly like a native of Puerto Rico, or so Mrs. Salazar tells me,'' Jewel said. Her tone was tongue-in-cheek, but there was some pride there, too.

''Do you know what 'Tay-yamo' means?'' Carrie asked.

Jewel nearly dropped her glass of iced tea. She put it carefully down in front of her. ''Did Phil say that to you?'' she asked, bemused.

Carrie nodded. ''When I asked him what it meant, he told me it was too hard to translate.''

Jewel laughed. ''For Phil, yeah, it'd be really hard to translate. He's got a problem with that particular verb.''

''Okay, we better roll,'' Felipe said, coming into the kitchen. ''We've already been here to long.''

With his hair cut so that it fell forward past his eyes almost to the tip of his nose, he *did* look much younger. With the combination of his hairstyle and the boldly patterned knee-length bathing suit, the extralarge T-shirt and the cheap beach sandals he was wearing, he looked like he might even pass for a high school student. Provided, of course, that his shirt stayed on to cover the hard, well-developed muscles in his chest and shoulders, and his hair stayed in his face, hiding the mature leanness of his cheeks.

He touched Carrie lightly on the shoulder. His hand was warm through the fabric of her cover-up.

Carrie was still embarrassed about her jealous reaction to Jewel. He'd made it more than clear that she had no claim to his heart. He'd told her that he could only give her here and now, and he may very well have meant their time at the beach house. Come to think of it, that poignant kiss he'd given her before they left, that could very well have been a kiss goodbye.

It was probably over—at least, that part of their relationship was over—yet Carrie had acted like a jealous, spurned lover. Of course, her reaction hadn't been all jealousy. She'd been outraged at the thought that Felipe could make love to her with such little regard for his wife. She'd been shocked and appalled and angry that she had misjudged him so thoroughly. The man she thought she knew wouldn't cheat on his wife. He wouldn't have gotten married in the first place, but if he had, he'd be sure to keep his marriage vows.

Of course, Jewel *wasn't* Felipe's wife. Jewel wasn't even his lover, present *or* past.

So now what?

Carrie had let him see her jealousy and hurt, and now he probably knew that she'd been stupid enough to fall in love with him. He'd probably treat her with the same kindness and gentle compassion he'd shown little Billy.

Terrific.

"We were discussing the translation of interesting Spanish phrases," Jewel said to Felipe. "*Te amo,* for instance."

His hand dropped from Carrie's shoulder. She glanced up to find his gaze fixed on Jewel, his expression suddenly shuttered.

Jewel laughed. "I've always felt that *'te amo'* is one of those things that needs to be explained by the person who says it. The meaning is defined by the situation in which it's spoken." She leaned toward Carrie. "I can't tell you what Felipe meant when he said it. Only he can tell you that."

Chapter 15

"Why exactly are we going to the beach?" Carrie asked as she slipped the motorcycle helmet on her head. Felipe helped her on with a big, unwieldy backpack that held the rest of their clothes and a few beach towels.

"We're going to meet Diego," Felipe said, putting on his own helmet. "He and I used to eat an early dinner at the same sandwich stand on the beach every Wednesday night back when we were partners. I'm hoping that since it's Wednesday he'll show up. I need to talk to him."

"And you're sure that this Diego's not really some gorgeous woman?" Carrie said dryly. "Because if he is, I want to be prepared to go into another jealous snit. I *know* how much you must *love* that."

Felipe grabbed her around the waist and pulled her tightly to him. "I *do* love it when you're jealous," he murmured. If they hadn't been wearing the helmets, he would have kissed her. Instead, he just smiled into her eyes and ran his hands down her back, pulling her hips in closer to him. "But no, Diego's not a woman. You saw him on TV, on that news report, remember?"

Carrie nodded. She remembered. "I'm really sorry about before," she said softly. "Seriously, Felipe, I won't behave

like that again. I know I don't own you. I know I never will.
If I forget, just . . . remind me.''

She'd been so quick to believe the worst of him. Of
course, little Billy had called him Daddy, and she'd simply
followed that to its obvious conclusion.

The truth was, she was ready to doubt Felipe Salazar. Was
he a killer? She didn't think so. But if the least little bit of
evidence showed up that worked against him, she'd probably start to doubt his innocence again.

And yet she loved him. It was a strange and powerful
emotion, to be able to overlook the fact that this man *was*
wanted by the police for murder.

Felipe started the motorcycle, and Carrie climbed on behind him, wrapping her arms around his waist. He drove
slowly toward the beach, careful never to exceed the leisurely speed limit of the side streets.

They approached a patrol car, and Carrie tensed. But
Felipe didn't slow, didn't even seem to notice. He was utterly cool, and they passed with no problem. The police officer didn't even glance in their direction.

And then they were at the beach. Felipe parked the motorcycle and they walked toward the food stand.

It was odd, being out in the open. They were in plain sight
of anyone who happened to drive by. Except they were surrounded by dozens and dozens of people who looked just
like them. Shaggy-haired young men in bright, funky bathing suits and dark glasses. Young women of all shapes and
sizes, with all styles and colors of swimsuits, with all lengths
and shades of hair. They milled around the sandwich stand.
They sat on their towels on the nearby sand, or perched on
top of the picnic tables that were scattered across that part
of the beach.

It was the perfect place to hide. They were daringly hidden in plain view. No one would think to look for them here.

Except, hopefully, for Jim "Diego" Keegan.

Felipe found an empty picnic table in the shade, near a
pay phone. Taking Carrie's hand, he pulled her toward it.
He sat on top, not on the bench, and assumed the same relaxed slouch as the other kids. Carrie sat next to him.

"You look tense," he murmured. "Loosen up. And take off your overalls and shirt. You're the only one out here still dressed."

She stood up and slipped out of her pants. She rolled them up and set them next to her on the table. The gauze shirt she unbuttoned, but left on.

"Relax," Felipe said into her ear. "No one's going to look for us here."

She tried to loosen her shoulders, but it didn't seem to help. Felipe looped an arm around her neck, pulling her close. And then he kissed her.

It wasn't a little, polite, out-in-public kind of kiss. It was a huge, devouring, explore-the-tonsils, bone-melting kiss.

He released her, melted bones and all, keeping that possessive arm around her neck. She sagged against him, glad he was holding her up.

No one was watching. No one in this crowd of students had even noticed Felipe kissing her as if the world were coming to an end.

"Much better," he said with a flash of his straight white teeth. "Now you have that same hormone-glazed expression in your eyes that the other kids have."

"I do *not*," she said, insult tingeing her voice, knowing he was right. She pinched him in the side.

He squirmed away, laughing, but still watching the parking lot. "Do, too. You know, you look about sixteen in that bathing suit. It's real heart-attack material."

"Well, *you* look barely old enough to vote, so that makes us even," she said.

He took her hand, lacing his fingers with hers. "I wish I'd known you when you were sixteen," he said, stopping his keen perusal of the parking lot to look searchingly into her eyes. "You were probably one of those really smart, sexy girls. I bet you had every guy in high school following you around."

Carrie laughed. "I was a total nerd. No one followed me anywhere."

"I would have," Felipe said.

She glanced at him. "You would've scared me to death." She laughed. "You *still* scare me to death."

He looked out across the parking lot, squinting into the sunlight as he searched for Jim Keegan's car. "Really?"

Yes, really. Carrie was scared that the part of her heart that Felipe had invaded would never be the same after he left. She was scared that she'd never meet a man who could stand up to her memories of this one. She was scared that she'd love him forever, long after he was gone, long after he'd forgotten her.

And most of all, she was scared that she was wrong about him, that he *had* been involved in the Sandlot Murders.

She didn't answer him. Instead, she looked around in the late-afternoon light at the long, frothy line of water that pulsed and murmured at the edge of the sparkling white expanse of sand.

"I love the beach," she said. "You know, I was eighteen before I ever set eyes on the ocean, but I still loved it. I loved the pictures and the movies and TV shows. 'Hawaii Five-O-' repeats. 'Miami Vice.' 'Flipper.' Especially 'Flipper.' Sandy and Bud, remember them? So I came out to Florida to go to college and see the ocean. Mostly to see the ocean."

Felipe was listening to her carefully. He was also looking around, watching the cars that came and went in the parking lot, and gazing at the people passing by on the sidewalk. But every time he glanced at her, she knew from looking into his eyes that he was paying attention to every word she spoke. It was a nice feeling, knowing that someone was honestly listening to her.

"Everyone back home laughed at me because I wanted to be a marine biologist," Carrie told him. "Everyone told me that ranchers' daughters from Montana just didn't become marine biologists."

"Why not?" he asked.

She smiled and reached up to push his hair back from his face. "That's what I asked, too. Why not?" She shrugged. "No one had a good enough answer, so here I am. A marine biologist from Montana."

Felipe took her face between his hands and kissed her. His mouth was so sweet, his lips so gentle. Carrie's heart lodged in her throat, aching with love for him.

He still held her face after he kissed her, gazing deeply into her eyes.

Suddenly shy, and afraid that her feelings would show, Carrie pulled away. She looked down at her toes.

"Does that help with our cover?" she asked. "Does it make us seem more like college students when you kiss me?"

"That's not why I kissed you," Felipe said. "I kissed you because I wanted to. Because around you, Caroline, I have absolutely no control."

She looked up at him. He wasn't smiling or teasing. His face was dead serious as he gazed at the parking lot.

"No control," he murmured, the muscles working in his jaw.

Carrie gazed at him. No control. Over his body? Or over his emotions?

Hope formed in her stomach like a fragile butterfly. Maybe she *could* make him love her. Maybe...

Felipe was aware he'd given too much away.

Caroline sat next to him, lost in her own thoughts. How long 'til she figured out the control he'd spoken of losing had to do with his heart rather than his hormones?

Of course, her jealousy earlier today had revealed to him that her feelings for him were more than merely casual. And sooner or later, she was going to run into someone who was going to translate *te amo* for her, and then she'd know.

He loved her.

What would happen if he told her? *I love you, but we can't be together because I'd fear for your safety.*

She'd laugh and talk him into ignoring his fears. She'd convince him he was suffering from an overactive imagination.

And then one day, someone like Tommy Walsh would follow him home. And then the next day, Caroline would be dead.

No, he couldn't tell her. He couldn't take that risk.

She shifted slightly and leaned her head against his shoulder. Felipe slipped his arm around her waist, amazed as he always was at how perfectly they fit together.

She rested her hand on his knee, and he felt the sharp stab of desire. Tonight. Tonight she'd be in his arms again.

But they had no place to stay, nowhere to go. God only knows where they'd spend the night. Maybe they could get a room in a cheap motel by paying with cash and signing false names in the registry. But it would mean standing under the watchful eye of the desk clerk as he registered, hoping the guy hadn't seen the papers or the television news.

Of course, his haircut made him look quite a bit different—

Next to them, the public telephone began to ring.

Felipe was up on his feet in an instant. He answered it before it had completed the first ring.

"Yes?"

"Who's the blonde?"

It was Diego—Jim Keegan.

"Oh, man," Felipe said, relief rushing through him. "You don't know how good it is to hear your voice."

"Likewise," Diego said. "I drove by and saw you, but just as I was about to stop, I got this sense that I was being trailed. I don't know. Emily says when she got pregnant, I got paranoid. Maybe she's right. Still, I thought it would be smart to be cautious, you know?"

"Where are you calling from?" Felipe asked, glancing back at Caroline. She was watching him, trying to listen from her seat on the picnic table.

"I'm at a pay phone downtown," Jim Keegan said. "We got us a friendly line, Phil. No taps, no one listening in. So spill it. I know you didn't kill those guys in the sandlot. I got a truckload of questions. Let's start with the girl." He laughed, and Felipe had to smile at the familiar, husky sound. "I drive by, and I see you giving this great-looking blonde mouth-to-mouth. Who is she?"

"Her name is Caroline Brooks," Felipe said, glancing again at the great-looking blonde in question and lowering his voice so she wouldn't hear him. "Do you remember the lady I locked in the trunk of her car at Sea Circus?"

"You're kidding," Jim said. "You used to talk about her so much, Emily was convinced you'd be sending out wedding invitations within the year. How long have you been seeing her? What's going on? Is she helping you hide?"

"I never went back to introduce myself," Felipe admitted. "I haven't been seeing her at all." He told Jim what had happened at Schroedinger's restaurant, how by sheer chance, Caroline had been there that evening, how she had unwittingly blown his cover.

His friend was silent for a moment. "Then she's the same woman you left the restaurant with," he said. "That's why her name sounded familiar. We still don't have a picture of her, but the PR department is working on getting one to release to the press—along with a statement, my friend, that calls her your 'hostage.'"

Felipe swore softly.

"Apparently, the boyfriend's getting ready to tape an impassioned plea to *you,* trying to convince you to let the girl go. It'll be carried by all the local stations—"

"*Boy*friend?" Felipe said.

"Uh-oh," Jim said. "She didn't tell you she has a boyfriend?"

"No." Felipe turned his back to Caroline, afraid that the sudden jealousy that was making his stomach churn would show in his eyes. *Boyfriend?*

"Some ad exec. His name is—hang on a sec." Felipe could hear the sound of pages being turned as Jim skimmed his notes for the man's name. "Robert Penfield. The Third. Lah-di-dah. Big bucks, no brains. The guy's a real load, Phil. He's been doing the circuit of news programs and talk shows, milking the situation. Apparently, he was at the restaurant, when you quote, unquote 'kidnapped' Caroline—"

You two-timing snake... That's what Caroline had called him when she'd thought he was involved with Jewel, too. No way would she have been so vehement if she'd been doing some two-timing of her own, if she'd been hiding a boyfriend from him.

"He's not her boyfriend, this Penfield guy," Felipe said with sudden certainty. "A dinner date, maybe." He turned back to look at Caroline. "Do you know someone named Robert Penfield?" he said to her.

She stared at him blankly.

"The Third . . . ?"

Recognition dawned in her eyes. "I was having dinner with him at Schroedinger's."

"Have you been out with him before?"

"No," she said. "I only met him that afternoon."

"I was right," Felipe said to Jim. "He was her dinner date."

"He's been implying that she's his fiancée," Jim said.

"She didn't even recognize his name at first," Felipe said.

"Maybe that's simply a testament to the overwhelming power you have over women," Jim teased. "When you're around, old what's-his-name's forgotten."

"You got anything else for me, man?" Felipe asked. "Any *good* news?"

"Only bad," Jim said. "*Really* bad."

Felipe braced himself.

"The police just released the ballistics report to the press," Jim continued. "Your police-issue handgun fired the bullets that killed Tony Mareidas and Steve Dupree out in that sandlot."

"Oh, *man.*" Felipe closed his eyes. This *was* bad news.

"Was your gun ever taken from you in the past few weeks?" Jim asked. "Was it ever missing for any length of time?"

"No."

"Maybe while you were asleep? Or, um, otherwise preoccupied perhaps . . . ?"

"No. I sleep with it under my pillow," Felipe said. "And I've been sleeping alone." Except for the past few nights, and hopefully again tonight. . . .

"Then I'm right," Jim said. "Richter's got a man inside the St. Simone Police Force—and it's someone with enough rank and power to falsify a ballistics report."

"A captain," Felipe said.

"That's what I figured, too," Jim said.

Felipe told him about the mysterious Captain Rat, Richter's partner. "Last week I got a glimpse of Richter's personal schedule on his computer," Felipe said. "He's got a date to meet with this Captain Rat tomorrow at 3:30."

"Where?"

Felipe laughed humorlessly. "That's the catch. I don't know where."

A fourteen- or fifteen-year-old kid hovered nearby, waiting to use the pay phone. Felipe turned and gave him a steady look, and within moments, the boy nervously walked away.

"Okay, look," Jim was saying, "I'll go and do some more checking around. The bitch about this Richter investigation is that I don't know who the hell knows about it, and who is clueless. And I don't want to ask—I don't want anyone to know that *I* know. Damn, it's complicated. And meanwhile, no one's asking me if *I* know, because they don't want *me* to know what *they* know." He swore disgustedly. "Phil, I'm honestly thinking of just bringing it all out into the light."

"Not yet, man," Felipe said. "Don't do that yet. Until I know who the man on the inside is, I can't risk coming in. And without me, you've got nothing."

"I got nothing now," Jim said. "Maybe it's time to shake the hornet's nest, see who gets mad."

"Not yet," Felipe said again. "Maybe in a few days—"

"I'm worried about you, Phil."

"I'll get by," Felipe said with a quiet confidence that wasn't feigned. At least not entirely. "Don't do something that will put you—and Emily—in danger."

Jim Keegan was silent, and Felipe quickly told him about the tape he'd made and left in Rafe's van. "Just in case," he added.

Jim was still silent. Then, finally, he spoke. "Maybe you should just lie low," he said. "Stay out of sight. Let me nose around a bit more. I've checked out all but two of the police captains, all but Captain Swick and Captain Patterson. Personally, I find it hard to believe Patterson could ever be involved with Richter. He's such a straight arrow. Swick, on the other hand..."

"He's never liked me," Felipe said. "I've overheard him using... derogatory language in reference to... my cultural background, shall we say?"

"He's a bigot," Jim stated bluntly. "But that doesn't automatically make him a criminal."

"He lives down near the water, doesn't he?" Felipe asked. Come to think of it, Donald Swick lived in a very nice house right on the Gulf—a house way too big and expensive for a man who'd been on the police force all his working life.

"Yeah, over on Casa del Sol Avenue," Jim said. "His wife's out of town. He's been putting in quite a few extra hours, working with Chief Earley, trying to track you down. The media's been eating it up. Captain Swick and Chief Earley, the modern Untouchables."

"Man, I got a feeling about Swick," Felipe said. "I'm going to check him out."

"Let me," Jim said. "You stay hidden."

"No, I've got to do *some*thing," Felipe said. "You look into Patterson. I'll check out Swick's house."

"Phil at least find a safe place for Caroline and leave her there."

It was Felipe's turn to be silent. "Can you guarantee that wherever I put her, Tommy Walsh won't find her?" he finally said. "And can you guarantee that if I do find a safe place, she'll stay put?" He shook his head, even though Jim couldn't possibly see him over the telephone line. "No, she's staying with me, Diego. That way I'll *know* she's safe."

For once, Jim didn't argue. He just chuckled quietly. "It happened, huh, Felipe? You finally met your match."

"No—" The word wasn't even out of his mouth before Felipe recognized it was a lie. Diego was right. Caroline was the only woman he wanted, the only woman he'd ever want. After he said goodbye to her, he might as well enter a monastery.

"Oh good, and we're in denial, too." Jim's chuckle got louder. "You poor bastard, you don't stand a chance."

In his native language, Felipe soundly and quietly cursed out his best friend.

But Jim kept on laughing. "Just ask her to marry you and get it over with," he said. "You'll be surprised how much better you'll feel when you just give up the fight."

"I can't, man," Felipe said. "It's not possible. You *know* it's not possible."

"Rule number one," Jim said. "Nothing is impossible. Don't forget that. The first step is to wipe the street clean with Richter's face, bring down his whole organization, including this sonuvabitch on the force. After that, you can work things out with Caroline."

"Sure," Felipe said. Sure, he'd work things out by walking out. It was the only way.

After Jim had been transferred to homicide, Felipe had gotten used to working alone. He found that he *liked* working alone; he liked *being* alone. But the thought of being without Caroline made him feel achingly lonely. He'd never been lonely before, but now he knew he'd never be anything *but* lonely again.

"Remember, if you need transportation, the key to my car is on the right front wheel, where I always leave it. The car's in the lot at the precinct," Jim said. "I'm going to call you at this number same time tomorrow. Try to be here."

"I'll be here," Felipe said. "Or..." He didn't finish the sentence, but they both knew how it ended. He'd be there, or he'd be dead.

Chapter 16

"Whose house is this?" Carrie whispered.

"Don Swick," Felipe said. "He's a captain on the police force."

Carrie nodded. "Nice place," she said.

It was. It was very nice.

It had beachfront, in a section of town where beachfront didn't come cheap. Big and rambling, the single-level house sprawled across a well-manicured lawn with plenty of bushes and shrubbery to keep them hidden.

"You think this Captain Swick is your Captain Rat?" Carrie asked.

Felipe nodded. "Shh," he said, pressing one finger lightly to her lips.

It was hard to be quiet. Carrie was understandably nervous. This was the first time she'd ever broken into a police captain's house. It was the first time she'd broken into *any*-one's house.

But Felipe seemed to know what he was doing. He used a tiny penlight he'd taken from the beach house to examine what looked like the access box to a complex security system.

With a Swiss Army knife Carrie didn't even realize he had been carrying, Felipe set to work. She watched for a moment, then he murmured, "Keep an eye on the street, *cara*. Tell me if a car is coming."

Carrie nodded.

She was scared to death. She was scared that this Captain Swick *was* Richter's partner and that they'd be in danger if they went into his house. And she was scared that he wasn't, that they'd break into his house and still be no closer to clearing Felipe's name.

"Got it," he said quietly.

Carrie turned to see the door swing open.

Gun drawn, Felipe went inside first. He flashed the same penlight around an enormous kitchen. It was nearly twice as big as the kitchen at the beach house.

Carrie shut the door behind them, then followed Felipe out of the kitchen and down a long, carpeted hallway. They passed a dining room and a living room, both vast and quiet and dark and filled with expensive furniture.

It was creepy being in someone else's house like this. True, the beach house had been someone else's, too, but they'd been there with Jim Keegan's unspoken blessing. Here, there wasn't even a hint of an invitation from the owners.

Carrie followed Felipe into an enormous master bedroom suite. His penlight flashed around the room, revealing an unmade bed, clothes draped over the back of several easy chairs, laundry overflowing a hamper. The shades in the windows were all pulled completely down, as if Swick hadn't bothered to open them in the morning.

Felipe went over to the lamp on one of the bedside tables and switched on the light.

There were Chinese food cartons on a TV tray, along with a half-eaten bag of chips and the TV remote control. Books and papers were piled on the half of the bed that Swick hadn't slept in.

"He better clean this up before his wife gets home, huh?" Felipe murmured. "Man, what a mess."

"Where do we start?" Carrie asked.

"We're looking for a calendar or a date book or anything that might mention some kind of meeting tomorrow," Felipe said. "We're looking for any mention of Richter's name, or Walsh, or Mareidas and Dupree—"

"Who?"

"The men who were killed in the sandlot."

"Oh." Carrie nodded. "How about any mention of the company that's a front for Richter's illegal businesses?"

"L&R Co.," Felipe said. "Good thinking. You'd make a good cop."

"No thanks," Carrie said dryly. "This is not my idea of fun."

"You'd rather jump into a tank with a pair of killer whales, right?" Felipe teased.

"I'd take Biffy and Louise over Lawrence Richter and Tommy Walsh *any* day," Carrie said.

"To each his—or her—own," Felipe said with a smile. "Will you be all right in here by yourself? I'd like to go look for Swick's office. He must have a desk or something, where he keeps a calendar."

"I'll be fine," Carrie said, already flipping through the papers on the bed. She looked up. "Don't go far, though."

"I won't," he said. He moved toward her and kissed her, then disappeared into the darkness of the hall.

Swick's office was a disaster area. His desk was covered by a mountain of papers and files and scraps of envelopes and napkins with notes scribbled on them. Cardboard file boxes were everywhere, even on top of a state-of-the-art stereo system, even on top of a large-screen TV.

Felipe pulled down the shades and closed the curtains and switched on the desk lamp. Well aware of the time, well aware that they couldn't risk staying here too much longer, he grimly set to work, searching for something, *any*thing that would link Swick to Richter's organization.

Swick had a file on his desk for every case he'd worked on in the past—God, it must be the past three years. They seemed to be in no particular order, neither chronological nor alphabetical.

Underneath a two-and-a-half-year-old arson case, Felipe found a desk calendar. It was mounted on a heavy marble stand, and there was a page devoted to each day of the week.

It was open to the page dated January 3, which was more than two weeks ago, and probably the last date Swick had unearthed the calendar in this mess.

Quickly, Felipe flipped to January 20. Tomorrow's date. The date of Richter's meeting with his Captain Rat. There was something written on the calendar.

"Golf," it said. There was no mention of the time or location.

Was it some kind of code, or did it actually mean the game of golf? And if so, there were dozens of golf courses in St. Simone, dozens of possibilities for the game's—and the meeting's—location. Assuming, of course, that Swick was the Captain Rat he was looking for. Assuming that "golf" didn't mean simply golf.

One by one, Felipe opened the drawers of Swick's desk. They were as disorganized as the rest of the room. He quickly rummaged through them, but they appeared to be filled with files and papers even older than the ones on top of the police captain's desk.

He reached down to pull out the lower left drawer but it wouldn't open. He pulled harder, thinking it had jammed, but it still didn't budge. It was locked.

Using a letter opener he'd seen in the top center desk drawer, Felipe tried to jimmy the lock. He slipped the piece of metal in between the drawer and the frame, finally using it as a wedge and the butt of his gun as a hammer to splinter the wood and break the drawer open.

Pay dirt.

A manila envelope at the bottom of the drawer had "Salazar" scribbled across it in black marker.

Felipe took out the envelope and opened it.

An unmarked cassette tape fell into his hands. It was the only thing in the envelope, but Felipe was willing to bet it was all he needed. He quickly cleared the file boxes off the stereo, then popped the cassette into the tape player and turned the power on.

He hit the play button.

There were several moments of silence, then Lawrence Richter's voice came on, smooth and clearly recognizable.

"I've got a problem," he said. "A discipline problem."

"Tony and Steve," said Tommy Walsh's voice. "You want 'em snuffed. That's no problem."

"This is very difficult for me," Richter said. "Alfonse Mareidas has been a friend for a long time."

"Al knew his kid was as good as dead when word came through about the deal he and Dupree were making with the D.A.," Walsh said flatly. "If that had gone through, it would've taken down your entire westside operation. It wouldn't have touched you, but it would've been a mess. Al can't blame you for what you have to do."

"What *you* have to do," Richter said quietly.

"Of course," Walsh said.

"Make it quick and painless," Richter told him. "For Al's sake. But make a statement."

"With pleasure," Walsh said. "Consider Mareidas and Dupree permanently out of the picture."

"Have Julia send flowers to their families," Richter said, and the tape ended.

Yes.

Yes!

This tape was all the evidence Felipe needed to pin the Sandlot Murders on Richter and Walsh, and to clear his name. Now all he had to do was prove Donald Swick was Richter's Captain Rat. That was, unfortunately, easier said than done.

Felipe rewound the cassette tape and took it out of the tape player.

"Felipe!" He looked sharply to see Caroline standing in the doorway. "There's a car pulling into the driveway," she said, her eyes wide. "I saw lights, and—"

He stood up, stashing the tape in the back pocket of his jeans. "Let's get out of here," he said.

"I didn't find anything," she said as they ran down the hallway toward the kitchen door. "I didn't finish looking but—"

"I found a tape," Felipe told her. "A recording of Richter and Walsh planning the Sandlot Murders."

"My *God,*" Carrie breathed.

Felipe saw it a fraction of a second too late. A backup laser alarm had come on, probably since the other system had been off-line longer than fifteen or so minutes. Caroline was in front of him, and she reached to pull the door open before he could stop her.

The opening door interrupted the laser beam and all hell broke loose. The alarm shrieked, a high-pitched, keening sound that attempted to shatter their eardrums and announce an attempted break-in to the surrounding square mile.

Felipe grabbed Caroline's hand and pulled her out the door.

Car headlights flashed in his face, blinding him.

"Freeze!" bellowed a voice over the alarm. Swick. It was Swick.

Felipe didn't stop running.

"I said freeze!"

Shielding Caroline with his body, he took her with him as he dived for the bushes.

The booming sound of a gun being fired drowned out for a moment the relentless sound of the alarm.

Then, "God, Chief, you might've hit the girl!" Swick cried.

"Radio for backup," Chief Earley's voice rasped. "We got that son of a bitch cornered now."

Branches and vines slapped at Felipe's arms and legs as he and Caroline scrambled down the slight incline separating Swick's property from his neighbor's yard.

Lights were going on all over the neighborhood.

Felipe tried to stick to the darkness at the edges of the yards. He could hear Caroline breathing hard. He could almost smell her fear. Or maybe it was his own fear he could smell. *Madre de Dios,* she could've been shot. She *still* could be shot.

"Can you swim?" she asked him, straining for air as they hit a stretch of darkened lawn and ran full out.

"Yes," he huffed. He could hear police sirens in the distance, lots of sirens, drawing closer. Man, maybe they *were* cornered....

"Let's head for the water," Caroline gasped. "For the ocean. The tide should be pulling toward the south. We can swim down the coast."

Hope burst like a flare inside him.

"Te amo," he cried. "I *love* you! Caroline, that's brilliant!"

Cutting hard to the left, they ran west, toward the Gulf. Felipe's leg was throbbing, drumming with pain again, but he ignored it. It didn't matter. Nothing else mattered. He could only think of getting Caroline to safety.

Around them, the sound of sirens was growing louder and louder.

Felipe could smell the ocean, see the glimmer of the surf in the darkness. They were close. They were so close. One more road to cross, one more neatly manicured yard and then they'd hit the beach....

With a squeal of tires, a police car pulled onto the street and braked to a stop, cutting them off from the ocean and escape.

Felipe jerked Caroline down with him, hard, into the darkness of some bushes. He could feel her heart racing, hear her ragged breathing.

"I'm in position," the police officer said. "There's no sign of anyone out here. Shall I move on?"

"Stay where you are," the radio speaker crackled. "Keep your weapon loaded and ready. Suspect is armed and dangerous. Repeat, armed and dangerous."

"What now?" Caroline breathed into his ear.

Felipe shifted his weight off his injured leg. "I'm going to surrender," he whispered.

"No!"

"While this guy is busy with me," he said, ignoring her vehement protest, "I want you to sneak across the street and make it down to the water. Are you sure you're a strong enough swimmer?"

"I won't do it," she said tightly. "I won't let you turn yourself in. You said yourself you won't stay alive more than a day in protective custody—"

He kissed her. "I'll find a way," he said. "I'll beat the odds."

"Felipe—"

"Caroline, I won't have them shooting at you!"

"And I won't let you sacrifice yourself for me!"

"Your safety is my priority," he hissed. "Don't make this harder than it has to be."

"If you give yourself up, mister," Caroline said, her head at that determined angle, chin held high, "I'm going in with you. We're sticking together."

She wasn't going to give in. She wouldn't back down.

Felipe swore silently. He was going to have to find another way.

She touched him gently on the face, a whisper of a caress on his cheek. Her blue-green eyes were colorless in the darkness. She looked otherworldly, angelic.

When she spoke, her voice was little more than a whisper. "*Te amo,* too, you know."

Chapter 17

Carrie kept running, holding tightly to Felipe's hand, splashing through the swampy underbrush.

They'd managed to creep away from the police car, crawling back the way they'd come. Carrie had hoped that they would make it to the water by cutting across the road farther down. But other police cars had arrived, their bright headlights slicing through the darkness, lighting both the street and the surrounding yards, herding the fugitives back, away from the ocean.

Dear Lord, let them reach the water.

Then Felipe froze, holding out an arm to stop her, listening hard in the darkness.

Sirens. She could hear sirens and shouting, and...

Dogs. Oh, God, *dogs*. Someone had brought dogs, trained to track by scent alone. They were baying and barking frantically in the distance.

Felipe was drenched with sweat and limping again. His leg had to be hurting. Hers ached from fatigue, and she didn't have a three-day-old bullet wound making things worse.

"Come on," he said, his voice hoarse, and somehow, *some*how, he started running again.

They didn't make it more than fifty yards before they came up against a twelve-foot-high chain-link fence.

The dogs were getting closer, and Carrie could also hear the throbbing of a helicopter in the distance. She swore. A helicopter with a searchlight would be able to pick them out of the water, no problem.

If they ever made it into the water.

Felipe was thinking the same thing. "When we hit the ocean, we'll have to be ready to swim underwater," he said.

When? *If* was more like it. Carrie could smell the tang of the salt air, but the ocean was somewhere on the other side of this fence that was more than twice her height.

They moved along the fence. It stretched out seemingly forever into the darkness.

Carrie was all turned around. She'd lost her sense of direction. She had no idea where they were, except that the ocean was out of their reach. For all she knew, they'd been running in circles.

"Caroline," Felipe gasped, "do you have the access code to Sea Circus's security system?"

What? "Yeah," she said. "Why?"

And then it hit her. This fence was the fence that surrounded the perimeter of Sea Circus. Lord, she had no clue they'd come this far. If they kept going, kept following the fence, they'd hit one of the park's three entrances. She could punch in the code, open the gates and they'd be inside. There must be a hundred places to hide in the marine park. And the dogs wouldn't be allowed inside—they'd frighten and endanger the wildlife.

And then, there it was, the entrance, one hundred yards farther along the fence. They'd have to cross part of a parking lot to get there, but the lights were out, and in the darkness they wouldn't be seen. At this part of the park, a huge wooden barrier was behind the chain-link security fence. Once they were inside, no one would be able to see them.

A police car passed on the street, going seventy miles an hour, heading up toward Swick's house.

Felipe ran across the lot, bent nearly double. Carrie followed close behind.

She pushed the numbers of the alarm override into the control panel. It flashed green. Thank the Lord! She entered the numbers to unlock the gate, and it swung open with a soft *whoosh*.

Quickly they went in through the open gate, and Carrie keyed in the numbers to close the gate and reactivate the alarm system. The light flashed yellow, then red, then yellow, then red.

What the hell . . . ?

Then all over the park, bright spotlights came on, and sirens began to wail as the alarm went off.

"I did it right!" Carrie cried. "I *know* I did it right! Someone must've changed the access code!"

Felipe grabbed her hand, and again they were running, this time across the brightly lit marine park.

He was heading toward the fence that separated the park from the beach below. He was trying to reach the ocean and the escape it promised, despite the threat of helicopters and their searchlights.

But they weren't even halfway there when Carrie saw a police car skid onto the beach, tires sending showers of sand behind it. Felipe saw it, too, and swerved to the left, going deeper into the park.

All around them, outside the fence, police cars were pulling up, tires squealing. Felipe went around the side of the main aquarium tank and stopped for breath, holding Carrie tightly against him.

"You've got to hide," he said. "This is it, Caroline. They've got me. Let me at least save you—"

"We've been through this once already," Carrie said sharply. "Nothing's changed."

"Yes, it has," he said. "They know where we are. We're trapped."

"You hide with me," she said, "or I don't hide at all."

His hand was shaking as he pushed his hair back from his face. "Dammit, Caroline—"

"I know a place they'll never think to look," she said.

Taking his hand, she pulled him along with her faster and faster across the park. And then she stopped—directly in front of the killer whale tank.

*   *   *

The killer whale tank.

Caroline wanted them to hide in the killer whale tank.

Felipe would've laughed if he had had the time.

Outside the park, Felipe could hear the sound of the police, lots and *lots* of police, so many that he could hear them over the shrieking of the alarm. They were getting ready to come inside. There wasn't any time left.

"This is nuts," he said.

"No, it's not," Carrie said. "There's a place in the tank that can't be seen even from inside the downstairs underwater viewing room. It's a place that's covered by the planks of a walkway. We can stay at the surface, holding on to the edge of the tank. No one will ever find us."

"Except the killer whales," Felipe said, letting her pull him into a door marked Park Personnel Only.

"Move slowly and calmly inside the tank, and everything will be fine," Carrie said, leading him up a set of stairs and through a control room that contained sound equipment and a microphone for the marine show. A small window overlooked the tank. The counter in front of it was covered with piles of cassette tapes. "Biffy and Louise are very gentle."

"Caroline—"

"Trust me," she said, squeezing his hand. "It's your turn to trust *me*."

She pulled him out onto the boardwalk that ran along the edge of the tank. It was slick with water from the waves and foam splashing up onto it. Felipe's eyes widened at the sight of these two enormous beasts who were leaping out of the water, jaws open and big teeth bared.

Gentle? These creatures were *gentle?*

"They're just upset by the noise," Carrie said. "Come on." Sitting down, she dangled her feet in the water, then slipped over the side and into the tank.

Felipe heard the main gate burst open.

Carrie was watching him, holding out her hand to him.

Trust me.

She'd trusted him when he pulled her down into that crawl space at the beach house. She'd trusted him with her life ever since that fateful meeting at the restaurant. If she said the killer whales were gentle, then the killer whales were gentle.

Felipe took the cassette tape from his pocket and held it up so that Caroline could see it. "I can't take this into the water," he said. "I'm going to hide it."

She smiled. "In plain view," she said.

"That's right," he said.

"Hurry."

He hurried. Back inside the control room, he put his tape toward the far end of the counter, on the bottom of one of the piles of tapes.

Caroline was still waiting for him at the edge of the pool. Behind her, the killer whales belly flopped into the water, creating a maelstrom.

"Quickly," she said.

Felipe went into the water, boots and backpack and all. The water was cold, colder than he expected. And his clothes and boots weighed him down.

At least the alarms were muffled under the water. Yet to a marine animal used to quiet stillness, they must have been terribly loud and confusing.

Carrie swam in front of him and he opened his eyes and followed her. With her long, blond hair floating around her, she looked like some sea creature, a mermaid or sea sprite, luring him down to his death.

But that wasn't true. She was luring him *away* from his death and—

Felipe came face-to-face with a killer whale and froze. It opened its mouth as if to snap him in two, yet still he couldn't move. His lungs were bursting from lack of oxygen as he stared at its beady little eye.

And then, suddenly, Caroline was there, next to him.

She touched the *Orca,* gave it some kind of signal, then took Felipe's hand and pulled him toward the surface, safely underneath the boardwalk.

Felipe grabbed the side of the tank and drew in a deep, clean breath, gasping and filling his lungs again and again with precious air. Caroline was there next to him, holding him, pushing his wet hair back from his face, murmuring words of encouragement.

But no sooner had he started to catch his breath than the water in the tank started sloshing around again. Waves slapped him in the face.

"What's going on . . . ?" he gasped.

Carrie pressed her mouth against his ear. "I told Biffy to keep on jumping into the air," she said. "It's one of the moves we've trained them to do. It's featured in the Sea Circus show. It makes them look very ferocious."

"They don't need to *try* to look ferocious," Felipe muttered, shivering as the cool night breeze hit his wet head and face. He looked up at the boardwalk. It wasn't more than eighteen inches overhead, slick and dripping with moisture. It seemed dark and cramped and confining. "This doesn't bother you?" he asked.

Caroline shook her head. "Not as long as I'm in the water," she said. "As long as I have space to move my arms and legs, as long as I don't feel restricted, I'm fine."

Across the park, the alarms were shut off. The sudden silence was odd. It felt heavy and threatening.

"You did the right thing when Biffy approached you," Caroline said almost silently, her mouth against his ear again. "You didn't move quickly or panic."

Felipe had to smile. "I didn't move quickly because I couldn't move at all," he whispered back into her ear. "I believe what I did is called 'being frozen with fear.'"

"You're that afraid," Carrie asked, "yet you'd get into a tank with them?"

"I trust you," Felipe said, pulling back his head to look into her eyes.

Her hair was plastered against her head, and beads of water were caught in her long eyelashes. She looked so beautiful, so delicate, so small and fragile. She was all of those things, yet she was also the toughest, most determined fighter he'd ever met. He would have quit twice already tonight. True, he would have quit purely to save Caroline's life, to give her a chance to get away. But she wouldn't give up; she wouldn't give in.

So here he was, in a killer whale tank, praying harder than he'd prayed in a long time that somehow, some way they'd pull this off.

Caroline's arms were around him, helping him keep his head above the surface. Even though he was holding on to the side of the tank, the water dragged at his jeans and boots and the backpack, pulling him under.

Felipe could feel the muscles in her arms. Man, she *was* strong. She might've been little, but she could more than pull her weight.

She leaned forward to kiss him. Her lips, her nose, her face were cold against his, but her mouth was warm, and he closed his eyes, losing himself in her sweetness.

But then she pulled back, and he heard footsteps on the boardwalk above.

Carrie motioned for him to take a deep breath and sink beneath the water. All he had to do was let go of the side, and he sank nearly to the bottom of the tank. Carrie reached for his hands, and her added buoyancy pulled him back up a bit.

With her hair a cloud of gold around her face, she *did* look like a mermaid. A mermaid in overalls. She smiled at him, and right at that moment, he loved her so much, he could have wept.

Te amo, too, she said. She loved him, too.

Somehow she'd figured out the translation from Spanish to English. Somehow he'd given himself away.

Felipe's lungs started to hurt, to burn, yet still he and Caroline stayed underneath the water. He dragged his gaze away from her face and looked up to the surface of the water. As he watched, the shadowy shapes he could barely see through the slats of the boardwalk moved away.

Carrie was watching, too, and as he looked back at her, she nodded, gesturing with her head toward the surface. She helped pull him up toward the air, and silently, they surfaced.

Felipe could hear Captain Swick's voice as well as Chief Earley's. He recognized Captain Patterson as well as a number of detectives from the Fourth Precinct.

And then a new voice joined them—Jim Keegan's.

"The dogs have picked up a fresh scent outside the fence, south of the park," he said in his familiar New York accent. "Our theory is that they worked their way around the perimeter, climbing along the chain link of the fence, cling-ing to it, you know, so the dogs couldn't track them along the ground.''

Swick swore long and hard.

"That's why we lost their trail for so long," Jim said. "But the tracker thinks we've picked it up now. We've wasted a lot of time in here, sir. They're out there making good their escape. Shouldn't we get moving?''

"All right," Swick said. "Let's head south. Shut this place down.''

The voices moved away.

Felipe turned to find Caroline watching him, her eyes wide. "Someone intentionally led those dogs off the track," she whispered.

"Jim Keegan," Felipe said. "Diego. He came through for me.''

"He must really believe in you," Carrie said quietly.

Jim wasn't the only one who believed in him. Caroline believed in him, too.

Jim's loyalty wasn't a surprise—after all, he'd been Fe-lipe's friend for years. But only a few days ago, Caroline had been ready to run away from him, ready to think the worst. Now, not only was she willing to risk her life to help him, but she trusted him enough to let herself fall in love with him.

It was exhilarating, and terrifying.

She loved him.

It was enough to make him feel as if he owned the world—if he lived in the kind of world that could be owned. But he didn't. His world, his life, owned him.

Caroline loved him, but he could give her nothing in re-turn. Nothing but heartache and misery.

As Felipe listened, the police officers left the marine park. The gate was closed, the alarm system reactivated, and one by one, the lights were shut off, leaving only dim security lighting up and running.

Still, he clung to the edge of the killer whale tank, one arm around Caroline, listening and waiting, until they were sure they were alone.

Chapter 18

There were towels in the control room.

Carrie stripped down to her bathing suit and dried herself off. It was chilly tonight. She took an extra towel to dry her hair, shivering slightly at the cold concrete under her feet and the coolness of the air.

Felipe was quietly taking off his own clothes, wringing out his jeans and laying them out to dry with the other things that had been in his backpack.

He glanced at her in the dim light. His eyes were unreadable, but really, what did she expect? They'd just done a triathlon—running, swimming and confessing their innermost feelings. None of it could have been easy for him—certainly not knowing that she'd managed to translate his "untranslatable" Spanish phrase.

Te amo.

She'd suspected its meaning. She'd guessed and she'd hoped, but it wasn't until they were running for their lives that he'd said it again and she'd known.

Te amo. I *love* you.

As Carrie watched, Felipe stripped naked, quickly drying himself off and tying a towel around his waist. But still he didn't say a single word.

"How's your leg?" she finally asked.

He lifted the edge of the towel, turning to show her the wound. It looked angry and sore. "The salt water from the tank stung," he said. "But I'm okay. I thought maybe the stitches opened up from all that running, but they didn't." He looked over at her again. "Are you all right?"

She nodded. "You probably want to get out of here right away," she said. "We'll need something to wear. My wet suit's hanging by the dolphin tank, but there's probably one in here that'll fit you. George's or Simon's or—"

"No," he said. "No, we're in no hurry. I'd be willing to bet Tommy Walsh and his men are somewhere on the other side of that fence, on the off chance we're still in here. No, we'll stay here tonight and leave in the rush of the crowd tomorrow."

Walsh. Outside the fence, waiting for them. Carrie shivered again, wrapping the towel more tightly around her. "Won't Walsh still be watching for us in the morning?" she asked.

"Yes," Felipe said. "He probably will. And so will the police—particularly after they don't find us tonight."

Carrie was silent, letting his words digest. "So," she finally said, glancing up to find him still watching her, "really, what you're saying is we're not out of danger."

He shook his head. "I'm sorry, but no, we're not." He raked his wet hair back, out of his eyes. "I'm not going to lie to you, Caroline. There's a good chance we won't make it out of this park tomorrow," he said. "If Walsh is smart—and he is—he'll make arrangements for a sharpshooter to be near every entrance. And he'll have people watching for us—for me. It'll be a race to see who spots me first—Walsh's men or the police."

It didn't matter *who* found him first. Either way he'd be dead. He'd be killed immediately if it was Walsh who spotted him first, or he'd be killed later that day or the next if it was the police.

"Caroline." She looked up into the velvet blackness of his eyes. "I want to play that tape for you."

She shook her head. "There's no tape player," she said.

He stared around the room. "All this equipment, and there's no tape deck?"

"It's locked up in the main office," she said. She gestured around the room. "All this other stuff is underwater recording equipment and cameras. It doesn't have a lot of value in the local pawnshops. The tape decks, however, kept walking away."

He swore, then apologized. "I wanted you to hear this tape," he said. "It's a conversation between Lawrence Richter and Tommy Walsh. Richter orders Walsh to kill Mareidas and Dupree. It proves my innocence."

Carrie nodded, gazing steadily into his eyes. "I believe you," she said quietly. "I don't need to hear it."

His eyes filled with tears. He reached for her then, pulling her into his arms and holding her tightly against him.

This time tomorrow, Felipe could very well be dead. That wasn't a crazy, wild thought. It wasn't an extremely unlikely worst-case scenario. It was an honest-to-God possibility.

Carrie felt tears burning her own eyes, and she couldn't stop herself from speaking. She was well aware she might never have another chance.

"I do love you," she said.

She felt him draw in a deep breath as if her words had somehow stung.

"I'm sorry if you don't want to hear that," she whispered, fighting another rush of tears. "But I want you to know how I feel."

"I heard you when you said it the first time," he murmured. He kissed her gently on the lips, then pulled back to look down into her eyes and smile. It was shaky, but it *was* a smile. "Of course, you'd have every right to assume I'd have trouble with the translation."

Carrie stared up at him. He was making a joke. He had somehow found the strength to tease about something that he found so desperately serious and frightening as *love*.

"I'm not asking for anything in return," she told him softly.

He looked away at her words, unable to meet her eyes as she continued in a quiet voice.

"I know when you said you loved me—*te amo*—you probably only meant that you loved me at that moment," Carrie said.

He would've interrupted her, but she stopped him with a gentle finger against his lips.

"That's okay," she said. "It's more than I ever expected. Don't say things you think I want to hear, just because you think you won't be around to keep your promises."

Felipe shook his head. "I'm not going to die tomorrow," he said. "They're not going to catch me, and I'm not going to let them near you. We're going to get out of this park alive."

"Felipe, you just said—"

"That I wasn't going to lie to you. I know, but you've reminded me, *cara,* I've got a powerful reason to stay alive."

His hair had fallen forward over his face again, and Carrie pushed it back. He pressed his cheek into her hand, then reached up and moved her fingers to his mouth, planting a gentle kiss in her palm.

He loved her. Carrie had to believe that he loved her, but he didn't—or couldn't—say the words. Still, she could see it in his eyes as he gazed down at her.

She wanted to believe that they would survive tomorrow simply because Felipe wanted them to. But the real truth was, all they could be absolutely certain of ever having was right here and right now.

"Potato chips, popcorn or pretzels?" Caroline asked.

Felipe stared pensively at the row of vending and gumball machines. "How much change do we have?" he asked.

"Enough for two bags and one can of soda," she said, "with a quarter left over."

Felipe shook his head in disgust. He had nearly three thousand dollars in his wallet—in big bills. The smallest he had was a twenty. The bill changer took nothing larger than a five. "I'm hungry."

"I'm hungry, too. We *could* break into a machine," Carrie suggested.

"And have the police out here first thing to investigate?" Felipe said. "No thanks." He smiled at her. "We're going to have to distract ourselves until the concession stand opens in the morning, no?"

Caroline glanced at him over her shoulder, a small smile playing at the corners of her mouth.

She looked incredible. She was wearing her wet suit—a navy blue, form-fitting unitard that hugged her curves like a second skin. It zipped up the front and she wore it slightly open at the neck. Her hair was nearly dry, and it hung, shiny and blond, around her shoulders, down between her shoulder blades.

She looked capable and in control and utterly, totally feminine.

"Potato chips, popcorn, or pretzels?" Caroline asked patiently.

"I'll have the swordfish steak, grilled in lemon butter, with a baked potato and a house salad," Felipe said. "And I'd like to see the wine list, please."

Carrie laughed. "We have a very nice root beer, dating from December."

"If the lady recommends it, how can I refuse? My goal is to wine and dine her with this gourmet meal in the hopes of finding out exactly what she is wearing underneath that wet suit."

"Aha," Caroline said. "A meal meant to seduce. In that case, pretzels, my favourite."

She put the money into one of the machines and pushed the buttons that made two tiny bags of pretzels fall out.

"Shall we dine alfresco?" she asked, taking the root beer from the soda machine. She handed him the can of soda and the last of their change—a solitary quarter.

Felipe knew exactly what to do with it.

In addition to the snack and soda machines, there was a row of six or eight gumball and candy machines, many of which held inexpensive toys in clear plastic bubbles. One boasted action-hero pencil erasers while another had cartoon-show tattoos. A third contained a collection of cheap plastic rings.

"For such a fine meal, it's only fitting that the lady be properly adorned with fine jewelry," he said solemnly, dropping the quarter into the slot and turning the handle. One of the plastic bubbles dropped down. He flipped up the hatch and took out the bubble. Opening it with a flourish, he presented Caroline with a bright green plastic ring.

It was small, but it fit almost perfectly on her ring finger. She looked up at him, her sea green eyes wide.

And suddenly, this was no longer a game they were playing. Suddenly, this was real. She was in love with him, and God, he'd just given her a *ring*.

"I'll keep it forever," she whispered.

"It won't last forever," he warned her, so afraid he was going to break her heart. He felt his own heart already start to crack. "The plastic will break."

"Not if I take good care of it," she said. Her chin went up with that determined tilt that was becoming so familiar to him.

"It's not worth the trouble," he said. God, he wished the words he'd spoken weren't true. He wished he had a different life, a life that he could share with her. "It's worth nothing."

"I know what it's worth," she said quietly. "I know exactly what it's worth."

Carrie woke before dawn.

Felipe was still asleep, stretched out on the lumpy sofa bed in the dolphin trainer's room. He stirred and reached for her, wrapping his arms around her, holding her tightly.

Carrie felt safe in his arms, but she knew that that safety was only temporary. It wouldn't be long now before they'd have to wake up, get out of bed and get ready to face this day—and Tommy Walsh and his sharpshooters along with the entire St. Simone Police Department.

Last night, Felipe had called Jewel collect from the pay phones by the concession stand. She'd told Felipe that she had gone to see his brother.

According to what Rafe had heard, Lawrence Richter had raised the price on Felipe's head to a cool million, and Tommy Walsh had every available man out and looking for him and the angel—in other words, Carrie. The scuttlebutt was going around that things were going to get *really* intense. And word was spreading—if anyone sees Felipe Salazar, hit the dirt because bullets are gonna be right behind him. Rafe told Jewel to make sure Felipe knew what he was up against.

What *they* were up against, Carrie thought.

Jewel had talked Rafe into offering his halfway house to Felipe as a safe haven. That was good to know. That was *very* good to know.

Felipe hadn't done much more than report the contents of his conversation to Carrie, but she knew that Rafe's support—no matter how grudgingly given—was important to him.

Felipe had also told Jewel about the tape that incriminated Richter and Walsh in the Sandlot Murders, told her he'd hidden it underneath the sofa bed in the dolphin trainer's room here at Sea Circus. He'd told her to give this information to Jim Keegan, to deliver the message in person and written on a piece of paper so that no one could overhear.

And he'd told her to ask Jim to call him at Rafe's at one Thursday afternoon—*this* afternoon.

Richter's meeting with Captain Rat was to be at 3:30—two and a half hours later.

They were running out of time.

Felipe stirred again, and she could tell by the change in his breathing that he was awake.

"Good morning," she whispered.

"Is it morning?" he asked. It was still dark outside.

"Almost," she said. "It's nearly five."

"What time does the park open?" he murmured, running one hand lightly along the curve of her hip.

"Nine," she said, closing her eyes. "But the staff starts showing up around six-thirty or seven."

"Are you hungry?" he asked.

Carrie smiled. "Starved. And it's another four hours 'til the concession stands open."

"Hmm," he said. "I don't suppose it's any use, trying to distract you...."

Carrie turned to look at him. His eyes were half-closed, the lower part of his face was covered by a day's growth of dark stubble, and his hair was rumpled. He looked deliciously sleepy. He smiled, a slow smile that promised neither of them was even going to *think* about food—at least not for a while.

Chapter 19

There were four uniformed policemen, and God only knows how many plainclothes detectives, at each of Sea Circus's gates. They examined the faces of the people leaving the park, searching for Felipe Salazar—"Rogue Cop."

Felipe checked the clock over the main entrance. Eleven-thirty. Up to this point, there had only been dribs and drabs leaving the marine park. According to Caroline, the bigger groups wouldn't start to leave until after lunch—not much before noon at the earliest.

He scanned the parking lot outside the main entrance. This was definitely the way to leave Sea Circus. Both of the other gates had obvious places outside for a sniper to hide. This gate had only the flatness of the already-crowded parking lot, no trees or bushes or cover of any kind except for the rows of cars.

Of course, that also meant there'd be no place for Felipe and Carrie to hide, either, once they were outside the gate.

Caroline sat near him, cross-legged in the grass, off to the side of the crowded walkways. She was wearing Jewel's overalls over her bathing suit, with her pants rolled up to just under her knees. She'd put her hair up into a braid rather than the ponytail she usually wore. He'd bought her a pair of sunglasses and a baseball cap at the gift shop—there were quite a few of her co-workers around who could identify her—and she wore them with a certain attitude that made her look like a young teenager.

Watching her, Felipe had an idea.

"Those school buses in the parking lot," he said, sitting down next to her. "Did you happen to notice if any of them carried a group of high school students?"

Caroline bit her lower lip, thinking hard. "I saw some really little kids—first-graders maybe, and some older kids—ten-year-olds." She turned to gaze out through the fence toward the parking lot. "There's an awful lot of buses to-day—one of them *must* be for a group of high school kids." She looked back at Felipe. "Why?"

"We're going to leave with them," he said.

"If they're not seniors, if they're younger, we'll stand out," Carrie said. He couldn't see her eyes behind her sunglasses, but he knew they were serious.

"Cross your fingers," Felipe said. He leaned forward and kissed her lightly. "So far we've been lucky."

She lay back against him, her head in his lap.

"I'm scared to death," she admitted, peering through her dark glasses to look up at him. "We're sitting out here in the open like this, and I keep thinking someone's going to see me, someone's going to recognize me. Or *you*. Lord, your face has been all over the papers and the TV."

"People see what they expect to see," Felipe said. "They don't expect to see St. Simone's most wanted sitting on the lawn near the main entrance to Sea Circus next to the dol-phin trainer. They expect to see some Hispanic kid from the 'hood and his pretty girlfriend sitting around in the shade, wasting time. So that's what they see." He touched the side of her face, stroking her cheek lightly with his knuckles. Her skin was so soft, so delicate.

"Maybe we should separate," Carrie said. "Meet back at Rafe's by one o'clock."

"No." The word came out with more force than he'd in-tended, and he made himself smile to soften its impact. "We stay together."

She was quiet, and he intertwined her fingers with his.

"I'm still scared," she finally whispered.

Felipe nodded. He was scared, too.

Looking up into the vast blueness of the sky, he prayed. He prayed for Caroline's safety and for his own successful escape. And, failing that, he prayed for the ability to accept his death, to die at peace, knowing he had lived his life as best he possibly could.

But had he?

He couldn't help but wonder how differently his life might've turned out had he gone back to Sea Circus and introduced himself to Caroline Brooks that day after he'd locked her in the trunk of her car.

"Hello, my name is Felipe Salazar and I'm really a detective with the Fourth Precinct. Will you forgive me...and have dinner with me?"

She would have. Maybe not that night, but eventually she would have forgiven him.

And, as surely as she'd done over the past few days, she would have stolen her way into his heart.

And then...

What if...

What if Felipe had said no thank you to the assignment to bring down Richter? What if he had said it was time to take some greatly needed—and greatly earned—vacation time? What if he had spent that time, a month, maybe two, with Caroline, living a regular, *normal* life? What if he'd taken her out to see movies and go dancing? What if he'd moved his toothbrush and an extra change of clothes into her apartment? And what if...what if he had *liked* it?

What if his job had posed no threat, no danger? What if he had stayed away from undercover assignments for a while? What if he had transferred out of vice?

He could imagine this Felipe, this other Felipe, spending much more than twenty-five cents on a ring that was neither green nor plastic. He could imagine this other Felipe taking Caroline Brooks someplace unbearably romantic for dinner, and after sitting down at the small, secluded table, he would take her hand and gaze into her eyes and...

He could imagine their wedding day. Diego would stand up for him, slap him on the back and embrace him, happy that his best friend had also found what he and his wife, Emily, shared.

Felipe could imagine saving their money and buying a house close to Caroline's beloved ocean. He would plant flowers in the yard and bring her one every evening. And every night, he'd make sweet, perfect love to her and sleep with her in his arms.

He could imagine her round and heavy with his child. A familiar flame of fear flickered through him and he squelched it. Small women married tall men all the time. Perhaps the baby would need to be born by cesarean section, but perhaps not. Caroline was strong and tough. Either way, he'd see that she received the best possible medical attention and all the tender loving care she could possibly need.

Time moved faster in his mind, the years blending together, their children growing tall and strong. Sons he could be proud of, daughters with his dark hair and eyes and their mother's beautiful smile. His life became a blur of happiness and love, a blend of passion and tenderness, a mosaic of laughter and song.

Felipe stared up into the blue, blue sky, allowing himself to live that life, the life he had not chosen.

The life he never would have chosen—because he never would have turned down the assignment to put Richter away. He knew damn well that if he hadn't taken on Richter's organization, no one else would have. And he couldn't have lived with himself, knowing that such a man continued to run free, hurting innocent people.

But...

There had been something else, some part of his fantasy...

He closed his eyes, trying to rewind his daydream until at last he touched upon it.

What if he had transferred out of vice?

Felipe sat up suddenly, and Caroline, who'd been dozing, jumped.

"What?" she said. "Is something wrong?"

"No, shh," he said. "It's all right."

But his heart was pounding. What if he transferred out of vice? Not had—*did?* What if he did? Damn, if he lived through this mess, he'd *have* to transfer. There wouldn't be a crime lord or a drug dealer this side of Florida who wouldn't recognize his face. However he looked at it, he was washed up as an undercover detective for the vice squad—unless he moved to another town, another state. And he couldn't see doing that. St. Simone was his home.

He *would* transfer out of vice.

And *what if* he transferred to a less dangerous job, one that would pose less of a threat to Caroline, one where revenge and counterhits weren't part of the norm?

Jim Keegan had done it. He'd left vice and was happy with his new job. He was still making a difference by being a police detective.

Or hell, who said Felipe had to be a detective? He could transfer to youth services, follow in his mentor's, Jorge Gamos's, hard-to-fill footsteps.

The possibilities were endless.

He looked down at Caroline. She was watching him, concern on her face.

What if...? What *if?*

"What's wrong?" she asked.

He didn't know how to answer. He didn't know where to start. But when he opened his mouth, the words that came out were the words that he'd been unable to speak for so long. "I love you," he said simply.

She was quiet, just gazing up at him.

"Do you think..." he started to say. He cleared his throat and began again. "Do you think, after this is over..."

"Yes," she said, no hesitation in her voice.

Felipe had to smile. "You don't even know what I'm asking," he said. "How do you know I wasn't going to ask you to spend four solid weeks with me making mad, passionate love?"

She grinned back at him. "Well, *that's* an easy yes."

She took off her sunglasses and he marveled at the love he could see in her beautiful eyes.

"I want to spend time with you after this is over," he said quietly, seriously. "I want to find out if you'll still love me without all the intrigue, without all the danger."

There was another big if here—an if they both weren't bothering to mention: if, after this was over, Felipe and Caroline were both still alive.

But Caroline was thinking about it. He could see it in her eyes.

Death. His death. Her death.

The possibility was very real.

"Are you asking me to dinner or to move in with you?" Caroline asked. She was trying desperately to ignore the shadow of the Grim Reaper that was hanging over them.

Her words caught him off guard. Move in with him? His mother would have a heart attack. His father would turn over in his grave. But Felipe hadn't meant dinner, either. What *had* he meant?

Felipe knew what he meant—he just couldn't say the words. But the thought that after today he might not be alive to speak loosened his tongue.

"I'm asking," he said slowly, "for you to think about...considering the possibility of...marrying me. Taking my name, bearing my children."

God, he wanted that so much. He wanted that life he'd imagined, that sunlight and laughter. He wanted the warmth of Caroline's love forever.

Except...who was he kidding? The odds were that he was going to die. Tommy Walsh, or one of his men, was going to blow a hole in his head and that would be that. No marriage, no children, no laughter.

He'd have the forever—in the form of eternal rest.

And Caroline...God, Walsh would kill her, too.

Felipe closed his eyes, unable to stand the sight of the hope that was blooming on Caroline's face.

God give him the strength to die gracefully.

But Felipe knew with a powerful sense of certainty that if in the course of the next few hours he were to leave this world, he'd go out kicking and screaming and fighting every step of the way.

* * *

At seven minutes after twelve, Felipe could hear them coming. At least three busloads of teens, ranging in age from fifteen to eighteen, were heading directly toward the Sea Circus main entrance. He hastily rose to his feet.

Caroline sat up, and he held out a hand to help her up. Still holding on to her, he led her down the sidewalk toward the sound of the shouting, rap music and laughter.

There were nearly a hundred kids, wearing a hundred different, brightly colored shirts and jeans and caps. They were carrying backpacks and purses and listening to boom boxes and Walkman stereos. They were talking—all at once—to each other, at each other.

Felipe stood with Carrie in the middle of the sidewalk and let the teenagers surround them. Like a herd of wild horses, the kids parted and flowed around them.

Then Felipe turned and began walking toward the entrance, in the same direction and at the same pace. It was crowded and someone jostled Carrie. He looped his arm around her, pulling her closer to him.

His mouth was dry and his eyes were drawn to the big clock that hung above the main gate.

Nine minutes after twelve.

Were these the last minutes of his life?

Around them, none of the teens seemed to notice that there were strangers in their midst. And if they noticed, no one cared.

As they approached the gate and the watching policemen, Felipe let his hair fall forward into his eyes. *Please, God, let this work.* He didn't want to die. He didn't want Caroline to die. Without even looking at her, he could feel her fear. She gripped his arm even tighter.

"I love you," he breathed into her ear. "Whatever happens, I love you. Don't forget that."

"My answer is yes," she whispered back.

He glanced at her questioningly.

She explained. "I thought about it, and yes, I'll marry you."

Felipe laughed in disbelief. "Caroline—"

"Stay alive," she said, gazing into his eyes. "Whatever happens, stay alive."

He turned and kissed her on the lips.

Was that their last kiss? Maybe.

She was thinking the same thing; he could see it in her eyes. She clung to him, but he gently pulled away from her to pass through a revolving door made of metal bars. It was a one-way door—exit only. He turned, waiting for her to follow him.

There were police officers ten feet away, staring hard at the back of his neck.

Please, God . . .

Caroline came through the door and her smile was an explosion of sunshine. "Come on, give me a piggyback ride, Carlos!" she called out, loud enough for the watching police officers to hear. She pulled her cap off her head and shook her hair free from its braid.

Felipe barely had time to brace himself before she launched herself up and onto his back. Laughing, she clung to him, and he forced himself to smile and laugh, too. They were just a couple of kids having some fun.

Caroline leaned her head forward over Felipe's shoulder, and her long, shiny hair covered part of his face. With Caroline on his back, Felipe walked past the officers. They didn't give him a second glance.

And then they were in the parking lot. They were outside of Sea Circus. They were past the police. Now they only had to worry about Tommy Walsh.

Only worry about Walsh. The statement was a paradox.

Felipe felt the hair rise on the back of his neck as he imagined the sight of a long-range rifle aimed at his head. Every one of his senses was on edge.

He could only pray that if he was hit, Caroline would have the sense to get away from him, to get down, stay out of range and flee to safety.

As the river of teenagers approached the waiting school buses, Felipe pulled Caroline out of the crowd. They ducked down behind a row of cars.

Carrie's eyes were bright and she was breathing hard. "We made it," she said.

"So far," he said, searching the surrounding cars for a model that would be easy to hot-wire.

An ancient white Volkswagen Rabbit bearing the bumper sticker that read I Love Lee had been parked with its windows open. Felipe opened the door and, on a whim, searched under the floor mats. Caroline slipped into the passenger seat.

There was no key under the mats. He'd have to do this the hard way. Or the not-so-hard way, he realized, seeing a set of keys dangling from the ignition.

"Do you think they *want* the car to be stolen?" Carrie asked.

Felipe started the engine, then tried to roll up the windows. It soon became obvious that there were no windows to be rolled up. The driver's-side door didn't even shut properly. It had to be held closed with a piece of wire.

"Could be," he said.

Still, the old car ran smoothly. Felipe pulled it out of the Sea Circus lot and onto the main road.

The cars he could see in his rearview mirror looked innocuous enough. Just the same, he couldn't shake the feeling that Tommy Walsh was out there somewhere, following them.

This had been too easy. Too simple.

And when dealing with Tommy Walsh, nothing was *ever* simple.

Chapter 20

Highboy answered the door at Rafe's halfway house.

He didn't say a word, but he moved impossibly quickly for a man of his girth, throwing wide the door, pulling them both inside and slamming it shut again.

Carrie watched in silence as Highboy fastened every lock and bolt that was on that door. He would have let the alligators loose in the moat and raised the drawbridge if he could have.

When he turned to them, he finally spoke. "I will take you upstairs to Raphael's apartment," he said in an oddly high voice. "The fewer who see you here, the better."

Silently, they followed the heavy man up the stairs. He knocked lightly on the apartment door, and Rafe opened it. He was wearing only a pair of jeans. Carrie tried not to stare at the large dragon tattoo that nearly covered his upper right arm or the ragged scar that sliced across his chest.

"Well, well," Rafe said, "if it isn't the walking million-dollar lottery ticket and the blond angel." He stepped back, so they could come inside. "Come on in. They're talking about you on the news again."

The TV was on, and sure enough, there was a picture of Felipe on the screen behind the news anchor.

"... latest word from the precinct is that the ballistic reports show it was, indeed, Salazar's police-issue handgun that killed Tony Mareidas and Steve Dupree last week in the downtown sandlot. In addition to this late-breaking news, a copy of a videotape that was delivered anonymously to the police several days ago has been released to us. On this tape, which is clearly dated the same evening as the slayings, Detective Salazar can be seen holding Mareidas and Dupree at gunpoint. Let's look at that tape."

Carrie sat down on the sofa, her eyes on the screen. Behind her, Rafe and Felipe were silent as they, too, watched the news report.

The anchor's face disappeared, to be replaced by the grainy footage from a home video camera. The tape showed three men coming out of an unmarked door in an unidentifiable city alleyway.

The television studio had enhanced the videotape, brightening the area around two of the men's faces. Even without the enhancement, it was clear they were Tony Mareidas and Steve Dupree. The videotape was frozen in place, and the station superimposed clear, labeled photos of the two men in the corners of the screen. Yes, those men were definitely Mareidas and Dupree.

Then the tape continued to roll and the third man turned. He had a gun aimed at the two other men, and he was, indeed, Felipe Salazar. The cheekbones, the hair, the set of his shoulders were instantly recognizable. The hard set to his mouth, however, was not. Still, it *was* Felipe.

"What is this videotape?" Rafe demanded, voicing the doubt that was flooding through Carrie. "Man, you said you had nothing to do with these murders."

Felipe shook his head. "This video was taken months ago, back when Mareidas and Dupree first got into trouble. They came to see Richter, but Richter wouldn't even talk to them. I escorted them out of the building. I walked them to their cars, and that was that."

"The date on it says it was made last week," Rafe said, his doubt rapidly turning to disbelief. "Have you *lied* to me, little brother?"

"No." Felipe answered his brother's question, but his eyes were on Carrie, begging her to trust him, imploring her to keep her faith in him. "I didn't kill those men. Tommy Walsh killed them. The proof is on an audiotape I found at Captain Swick's house."

"Where is this tape?" Rafe pressed. "Play it for me."

"It's hidden at Sea Circus," Felipe said.

"Did you hear it?" Rafe asked Carrie.

Wordlessly, she shook her head.

"Perfect," Rafe said sardonically. "There's a tape that clears your name, only you're the only one who's heard it, no? Sounds a little too convenient if you ask me."

"Why do you doubt me?" Felipe asked quietly.

Rafe gestured toward the television. "I see with my own eyes that you were with these men, right before they died."

"That tape was made in October," Felipe said evenly. "I did *not* kill those men."

Carrie moistened her dry lips. "Would you tell us if you had?" she asked. "Us," she'd said, not "me." She was siding with his brother.

He couldn't hide the disappointment in his eyes. "Ah, *cara,* don't *you* believe me?"

"Would you tell us?" she persisted.

He shook his head with a laugh that held not a breath of humor. "Probably not."

"Definitely not," Rafe said, crossing his arms.

A commercial ended and the news anchor reappeared on the screen along with a picture of Carrie.

"To date, there has been no word of Caroline Brooks, the young woman taken hostage by Salazar four days ago at Schroedinger's restaurant," the woman said. The picture changed to that of a familiar-looking man holding a press conference. Carrie leaned closer to the TV. "Despite an impassioned plea from Robert Penfield, Caroline's fiancé, Salazar has not let his hostage go, or even communicated in anyway with the police."

"So the angel has a name," Rafe said. "*And* a fiancé?"

Robert Penfield? Her *fiancé?* Carrie nearly burst with indignation. "I met this man exactly *once,*" she said. "He's *not* my fiancé."

"Are you sure?" Felipe probed, his eyes burning holes into her with their intensity. "After all, don't you believe *every*thing you see on the TV news?"

Good Lord, he had a point. If Penfield could go on the air as her fiancé, then the rest of this so-called news story could also be pure fiction.

"Please," Bobby Penfield III said tearfully into the TV camera, "*please,* Detective Salazar, if you have any sense of decency at all, please let my dear Caroline go."

Oh, blech. And all of Florida actually believed she was going to marry this guy...?

"Despite that plea, there was no response from Felipe Salazar at all," the news anchor said solemnly. "And no word on whether Salazar's hostage is even still alive." She paused for only a split second before continuing. "We now go downtown, where Brett Finland is talking to the newly appointed chief of police, Jack Earley. Brett?"

"Thank you, Mary," the reporter said, and Carrie turned to look at Felipe.

He was standing behind the sofa, watching the screen, listening to the reporter. Surely he felt her eyes on his face, but he didn't so much as glance in her direction. His face was expressionless, but she could see the muscles jumping in his jaw.

She'd hurt and surprised him by not flatly discounting this news report. Hell, she'd surprised herself with how quickly she'd doubted him.

Salazar's hostage. That was as ridiculous a label as Penfield's fiancée.

Wasn't it?

On the television, Chief Earley's wide face looked tired and strained. He seemed distracted and the reporter had to keep repeating his questions.

"It's a hard job, tracking down Felipe Salazar, a man who once was one of St. Simone's finest," Brett Finland said, wrapping up the report. "Jack Earley has clearly lost some sleep over this, his first tough assignment as newly appointed police chief of this city. But Chief Earley, a man who started his law-enforcement career by tracking and trapping the enemy in their hideout tunnels in Vietnam, a man known as one of the marines' legendary 'tunnel rats,' should have no problem finding one rogue cop. This is Brett Finland, reporting live from downtown. Mary?''

"Madre de Dios!" Felipe exclaimed, his eyes still glued to the set. He fired off a rapid stream of Spanish to his brother.

Rafe frowned and shrugged, then answered, also in Spanish. He pointed next to the television. A pile of old newspapers lay there, and Felipe nearly leaped over the sofa to search through them. He scanned the tops, looking, it seemed, for one specific date.

"What?" Carrie said. "What's going on?"

"I need to find the paper that had that article on Chief Earley," Felipe said, still searching the pile.

"Why?" Carrie asked, but he didn't answer.

"Ah! Here it is." He sat down next to her on the sofa, and she moved closer, trying to read over his arm. He folded the paper so they both could see it better.

"Earley served in Vietnam as a *captain,*" Felipe said. For some reason, that news really excited him. "Yes!" He looked up into Carrie's eyes. "Don't you get it?"

Puzzled, she shook her head.

He pointed to the text. "Look! It says it right here. Jack Earley served for ten months in Vietnam as an explosives expert. He went down into the tunnels where the Vietcong had been hiding, clearing them of booby traps. 'It was one of the most dangerous jobs in the entire Marine Corps, and not for the faint of heart or claustrophobic,'" he read aloud, glancing over at Carrie for that last bit.

"'Chief Earley and his men were known as the tunnel rats.'" He smacked the paper with his hand. "Captain Rat! *Earley* is Richter's Captain Rat."

"The police chief?" Carrie was shocked. It couldn't be.

Felipe checked the time on Rafe's VCR. It was a little after one o'clock. "Okay," he said. "Listen, Diego's going to call any minute—"

"No, he's not," Rafe interrupted. "He called about an hour ago—said he was going to be tied up, that he wouldn't get a chance to call without a lot of people listening in."

Felipe swore under his breath. "Man, I really could have used his help. But…all right. I can still do this. We still have time."

"Time for what?" Carrie asked.

"We're going to go down to police headquarters," Felipe said, "and follow Earley to his meeting with Richter." He turned to his brother. "You still want to help me?"

"Even if you killed those guys, I don't want you to die," Rafe said.

"That's not the blazing endorsement I would've liked, but it'll do," Felipe said. "Can you get your hands on some film and a camera? Maybe one of those disposable ones?"

"I got an old Instamatic," Rafe said, crossing to the closet and pulling a box down from the shelf. "It works okay. It's got half a roll of color film already in it."

He fished a small black camera out of the box and handed it to his brother.

Felipe would've turned away, but Rafe caught his arm. "If you killed those men," he said, "you better head for Mexico."

"I didn't kill them."

Rafe ignored him. "If you head for Mexico, I probably won't see you again."

Felipe shook his head. "You'll see me again."

"If I don't," Rafe said, "I just wanted you to know… how sorry I am that I…I let you down all those years, all those times."

Felipe was silent. Carrie could see the tears that had suddenly filled his eyes. She turned away, not wanting to intrude.

"I hope someday you'll forgive me," Rafe said almost inaudibly. "And maybe then, someday, I'll forgive myself, no?"

"Forgive yourself, Raphael," Felipe said, his voice husky with emotion. "I forgave you a long time ago."

"*Gracias,*" Rafe whispered. "Go with God."

Felipe held out his hand, and Rafe took it. The two men, the two brothers, clasped hands, and each gazed into dark brown eyes so like his own.

And then Felipe turned and headed for the door.

"Good luck," Rafe added. "Keep your head down."

Carrie followed Felipe down the stairs. He checked his gun as he went, making sure it was properly loaded. Then he tucked it in the back waistband of his jeans, covering it with the hem of his T-shirt.

"Felipe," she said.

He glanced back at her, but didn't stop. "Yes."

"Please don't be mad at me."

He stopped by the front door then, his hand on the knob. "I'm not mad," he said. "Just . . . disappointed."

"I'm sorry," she said.

"How can you say that you'll marry me when you don't even trust me?" he asked, then shook his head before she had a chance to speak. "No, don't answer that," he added, rubbing his forehead as if he had a headache. "I honestly don't want to know."

"I keep wondering what if I'm wrong about you," Carrie admitted. "I see all this hard evidence against you and I can't stop thinking what if I've fallen in love with a man who's deceiving me."

Felipe was watching her steadily, his dark brown eyes echoing the disappointment she'd heard in his words.

"I can't help you with that one, Caroline," he said quietly. "It's something you've got to work out on your own. Let me know what you decide, though, okay?"

"Felipe—"

"Right now, we've got to move," he said, opening the door. "Stay close to me. We're getting in the car as quickly as we can."

Felipe took Caroline's arm, and together they went out into the bright afternoon sunlight and down the steps to the sidewalk.

Felipe felt the hair stand up on the back of his neck. Something was wrong. Something was seriously wrong.

Everything looked the same as it had when they'd arrived less than an hour ago. Children still played out in the street. Old men still sat, talking, on their stoops. People sauntered along the sidewalks, moving slowly in the sunshine.

The old white Volkswagen they'd "borrowed" from the Sea Circus parking lot was halfway down the block. Felipe moved quickly toward it, trying to shield Caroline with his body, praying his sixth sense that told him trouble was coming was wrong.

Caroline had thrown him for a loop back in Rafe's apartment. Her admission that she still didn't trust him had hurt even more than he'd let on. She needed time, he reminded himself. In time, she would learn he truly was everything he said he was.

Please, God, give him that time.

Out of the corner of his eye, Felipe saw a shadow move, and instantly, everything kicked into slow motion around him.

He turned his head and looked directly into the cold steel of Tommy Walsh's pale blue eyes.

Tommy had his gun out, hidden under a jacket he was carrying over his arm. It was pointed directly at Caroline.

If Tommy intended to kill them right here in the street, in front of all these people, they'd already be lying there dead. Still, Felipe knew if pushed too hard, Tommy would shoot. The time to move was now, while he was expecting Felipe to hesitate.

But Felipe wasn't going to hesitate. Not with Caroline's life hanging in the balance. No way was he going to let Tommy kill her. No way.

He pushed Caroline behind him and reached for the gun that rested against the small of his back. He drew smoothly, watching Tommy's finger tighten on the trigger at his sudden movement. But Tommy moved in slow motion and Felipe was faster. He aimed and fired.

The noise was incredible, as was the look of total shock on Tommy Walsh's face as the big man fell to the ground, a neat little bullet hole in the center of his forehead.

Stay detached, Felipe ordered himself. That wasn't a man he'd just killed, it was a monster. There'd be enough time later to suffer over the fact that Tommy Walsh might have a mother, maybe even a wife and children, who would mourn him. There'd be enough time—if Felipe could stay cool and concentrate on getting himself and Caroline out of there.

Somebody screamed—maybe it was Caroline—and suddenly the world moved again at its regular speed.

He stepped over Tommy's body and the blood that was pooling on the sidewalk. Stay cool. Don't look at the blood. Don't think. Just get Caroline away.

He wrenched open the door of the Volkswagen and pushed Caroline inside. Vaulting over the hood, he had the key in the ignition and the car in gear and halfway down the street before he even got the driver's-side door closed.

"My God," Carrie gasped. "My *God!* You *killed* him!"

"Fasten your seat belt," Felipe said calmly, as if he hadn't just fired a bullet into another man's head.

He'd killed a man.

An *unarmed* man.

With sickening clarity, Carrie remembered her surprise when Felipe had suddenly grabbed her arm. She could still see that awful, almost inhuman look in his eyes as he drew his gun. They had been filled with a cold, unearthly, unfamiliar savagery that was echoed on his face. His lips had been pulled back from his mouth in a wolfish snarl as he'd violently taken another human's life.

Who was this man, this Felipe Salazar?

Did she really know him at all? Lord knows she had never seen this side of him before—*never.*

Carrie felt sick to her stomach. How could Felipe kill someone and then just…keep going? He'd stepped over the body as if it had been nothing more than a spilled bag of garbage, an inconvenience.

Unless killing was something he'd done before, something he took lightly....

My God, was it possible he'd killed those two men in the sandlot after all?

The police had all that hard evidence against Felipe—a ballistics report that proved his gun was the murder weapon and a videotape of Felipe holding the two victims at gunpoint. Felipe claimed the tape had been made months ago and that the ballistics report was doctored. But ballistics reports were done scientifically. It wouldn't be easy to falsify information....

All her doubts, all her uncertainty came rushing back, hitting her full force in the stomach.

Maybe it was possible that Felipe *had* killed those men. Maybe he *had* been the one who'd shot them in the back of the head execution-style. That savage man she'd had a glimpse of, that man with the deadly flat eyes, had certainly looked capable of such an awful deed.

She took a deep breath, trying to steady her shaking hands, trying to stop the flood of tears that was streaming down her face. She'd been following her heart for the past several days, refusing to allow the cold hard facts to interfere with her feelings for Felipe.

But now those cold hard facts included one very dead man, and she couldn't ignore them any longer.

"Are you all right?" he asked, still in that same quiet, almost unnaturally calm voice.

"No," she said. "I want to get out of the car."

"We will in a minute," Felipe said. He looked into the rearview mirror. "I just want to be sure that none of Tommy's men are following us. But then we *should* ditch this car. The police will be looking for it."

In the distance, Carrie could hear the sound of police sirens moving toward them, getting louder. A patrol car passed them going sixty miles an hour.

Felipe turned down a side street.

"No," Carrie said again. "You don't understand. I want to get out of the car—*now*."

"Caroline, we can't—"

"Not 'we.' *Me*. I want you to pull over and let *me* get out."

Carrie felt him turn and look at her, *really* look at her. She stared down at her feet, unable to meet his gaze.

"I can't do that," he said quietly.

She did look up at him then. "Can't . . . or won't?"

The muscles in the side of his jaw were working hard again. This time it was Felipe who wouldn't meet her gaze.

"What difference does it make?" he returned.

"Am I your hostage?" she asked, trying to keep her voice from shaking. "Have I been all along?"

He made a sound that might've been a laugh. "What do *you* think?"

"I don't know." She *didn't* know. Had he been manipulating her right from the start? Were his words of love really empty promises, designed to make her trust him, keep her from running away? And what about her feelings for him? Was this really love she felt, or was it some kind of warped attachment of a hostage for a captor?

"Please," she said softly. "If you care anything for me at all, please let me go."

Felipe was silent as he took a left turn onto McCallister Street. "So," he said, just as quietly, "you've decided not to trust me, huh? That's too bad."

"Please," she said again. "Prove I'm not your hostage, Felipe. Let me go."

"As much as I'd like to prove that to you," he said, "I'd rather you remained alive. As long as there's a threat from Lawrence Richter, you're staying with me."

Carrie gazed out of the window, unable to speak.

"And now you're thinking, 'Ah, I *am* his hostage.'" Felipe's velvet voice surrounded her. "I have to tell you one more time, Caroline, that everything I've ever said to you is God's own truth."

Carrie closed her eyes. "I don't know *what* the truth is anymore." She only knew the facts. She'd seen him kill a man without a second thought. A ballistics report tied him to the murder weapon. A videotape showed that he was with the two men before they died.

As they stopped for a red light, Felipe reached over and picked up her hand, the hand with the green plastic ring he had given her.

"*This* is the truth," he said. "Open your eyes and look. *Look* at me!"

She opened her eyes and looked directly into the eyes of this man that she thought she knew so well, but perhaps didn't know at all. His face was so familiar—high cheekbones, lean, smooth cheeks, long, elegant nose, full lips, dark, mesmerizing eyes. She'd thought she'd seen him in every possible way. She'd seen him relaxed and laughing, tense and worried, cool and calm, thoughtful, angry, unhappy, joyful. But not murderous. At least, not until this afternoon.

Felipe took her hand, the same hand with the ring, and placed it on his chest, over his heart.

"*This* is the truth, Caroline," he whispered. "But if you don't want that truth any longer..."

As she watched, his eyes started to fill with tears, but he blinked them back, forced them away. He returned her hand to her lap.

"It's almost all over," Felipe said, putting the car into gear as the traffic light turned green. "A little bit longer, and then I won't stop you. You'll be free to go."

Chapter 21

Felipe was getting the job done.

He'd ditched the white Volkswagen near the parking lot of the Fourth Precinct. He'd found Jim Keegan's car in the lot. The key was hidden on top of the right front wheel, exactly where Jim had said it would be.

Now he sat outside police headquarters in Jim's gray Taurus, waiting for Chief Earley to leave for his meeting with crime lord, Lawrence Richter.

Yes, he was getting the job done.

He was trying very hard not to think about anything besides the pictures he was going to take of Earley and Richter's meeting. He was trying hard not to think about that small, permanent hole he'd put in Tommy Walsh's head or the nausea he felt as a result. And he was trying desperately not to think about Caroline Brooks.

That wasn't so easy to do, because she was sitting right next to him, and because, while he was busy getting the job done, he was having to take care that she didn't try to run away.

They had come full circle. Apparently, her doubts and suspicions had come out the victor in an emotional wrestling match. And, apparently, her love for him hadn't stood up to the test.

That hurt more than he would have believed possible.

So okay. He tried to harden his heart, tried to think about this practically, tried not to care. So he wouldn't leave the vice squad. He'd merely leave St. Simone. So what if it was his home? He hadn't lived here *all* his life. His parents had come here to make a new start. So now *he'd* go somewhere else to make his own new start. There were a lot of cities out there where his face wasn't known. Maybe he'd go up to Diego's New York, become a New York City cop. Now, *there* would be a job that was on the edge, that was filled with high risks and danger. He'd fit right in.

Man, he should be feeling lucky. Here was Caroline, ready to walk away from him, exactly the way he'd wanted their affair to end a few days ago. He wasn't going to have to worry about her safety. He wasn't going to have to deal with the restrictions that a permanent relationship would bring. Man, he was getting off easy. He'd had his fun. He'd had a series of intense sexual experiences with a beautiful, vibrant, passionate woman. He had the added satisfaction of knowing that he'd saved her life. He should be more than ready and willing to let Caroline Brooks simply fade into a fond memory as he continued on with his life as he knew it.

He should, but he couldn't.

Something had happened these past few days. Something had opened his eyes to the fact that his life wasn't winning any awards or prizes for Most Fulfilling. Yes, he was making a difference out on the streets. Yes, he was good at what he did. And yes, sometimes he even liked it. But he didn't like it all the time—and lately, he didn't like it at all.

The sorry truth was that the something that had opened his eyes had been Caroline Brooks. Caroline had shown him firsthand everything he'd been missing. She'd gone and made him fall in love with her and opened his eyes to a future that was impossibly joyful.

Impossibly indeed.

She stirred in her seat, and he couldn't keep himself from glancing at her.

She didn't trust him.

He was angry and hurt and even insulted by her mistrust, but the ultimate insult was that these emotions didn't make him stop loving her. He wanted to fall on his knees and beg her to believe him. But pride kept him in his seat.

He wanted to see her smile, hear her husky, sexy laughter. He wanted to know, just from looking in her eyes, that she'd be in his arms again tonight, surrounding him with her warmth and love. But there was not a chance in hell for that.

He wanted to weep for all he'd lost—for the love he'd probably never really had in the first place.

Because how could she have truly loved him without trust?

She was quiet and her face looked pale. She hadn't spoken a word to him since they'd taken Jim's car from the parking lot.

But now she looked up, actually meeting his gaze. The mistrust and trepidation he could see in her eyes burned like acid in his soul. But he didn't look away. He couldn't.

Maybe seeing her looking at him that way would make him love her less. But probably not.

"How many people have you killed?" she asked.

Her question caught him off guard. Of all the things he'd expected her to say to him or ask him, that wasn't one of them.

But he answered honestly. "Five," he said. "Tommy Walsh was the fifth."

"How do you sleep afterward?" she asked. "How do you do it? How do you live your life knowing that you took someone else's?"

Felipe was quiet for a moment, wondering how to answer. But there was really only one way to answer—with the truth.

"You don't sleep," he finally told her. He watched the entrance to the police station as he spoke. "Not at first. You lie in bed going over it and over it in your head. You try to figure out where you went wrong, where you made the mistake, what you could've done instead to make it turn out differently. And then, after about a week of not sleeping, when you feel like hell and you can't handle it anymore, you go visit the counselor—the precinct shrink. And then you start to work through it until you accept the choices that you made—the choices that led you to pull that trigger and take that life.

"You talk to people who were there, who witnessed the shooting," he continued. "You hang out with the person whose life you maybe saved by firing your gun and killing the perpetrator. Or you come face-to-face with the fact that it came down to the guy you killed or yourself. You look at yourself in a mirror and you remind yourself that *he* was the bad guy, not you. If he had been a little faster or a little smarter or a little luckier with his own gun, then it might very well have been *your* family holding that funeral service instead of his."

"And if he didn't have a gun?" Carrie whispered.

Felipe shook his head. "They all had guns. Starting with Benny Hammett. He was eighteen years old, just a kid, freaked out on crack. He had his father's handgun and was taking potshots at the children in the playground next to his house. One kid was dead—four years old—and two others were badly wounded. The medical teams couldn't get in to help them. The SWAT team was on its way when Hammett hit a fourth kid who'd been hiding behind some bushes. I was one of the cops who climbed down to his window from the roof and took him down. My bullet killed him.

"Then there was Thomas Freeman, age forty-seven. Took his hunting rifle and went back to where he'd been laid off, killed his boss's secretary and threatened to wipe out the entire office. I went in as a deliveryman, took him out before he killed the mail room clerk.

"Hans Thorne, thirty-eight, escaped convict, tried to hold up a convenience store that Diego and I happened to be in. I stopped him from blowing Diego's head off.

"T. J. Cerrone, twenty-three years old. I believe you had the honor of meeting him at Sea Circus. When we busted him on drug charges, he and his friends decided they'd skip jail and go right to hell. Unfortunately, they took a few of my friends on the force with them. T.J. had access to an Uzi submachine gun when I ended his life with my .45."

Felipe kept his eyes on the entrance to the police station, but he could feel Caroline watching him.

"And Tommy Walsh?" she probed. "Where was his gun?"

Felipe turned to look at her. "It was aimed at you," he said. He could see the doubt in her eyes. *Madre de Dios,* was it possible she didn't know Tommy had been armed? "You didn't see his gun?"

"No."

"You think I would kill an unarmed man?" His voice rose in disbelief. What kind of monster did Caroline think he was anyway?

"That's what I saw."

Felipe's heart broke into a thousand tiny pieces. "Maybe you saw what you expected to see," he said quietly. "You've already decided I'm guilty, that I'm a killer. But you're wrong, and I'm going to prove that, even if it's the last thing I do."

Numbly, Felipe stared at the door to the police station. He'd lost Caroline. He'd totally lost her trust—if he'd ever even had it in the first place.

Everything around him, his entire life, seemed to be circling the drain.

Everything, *every*thing—his freedom, his reputation, his life—was riding on his conviction that Chief Earley was Lawrence Richter's partner. Everything now depended on his being right about that.

God help him if he was wrong.

Ten minutes after three, and Earley still hadn't left for his alleged 3:30 meeting with Lawrence Richter.

Carrie risked a look at Felipe. He was getting more and more tense by the minute. He muttered something in Spanish, then glanced at Carrie, but didn't bother to translate.

"What if you're wrong?" she asked quietly. "What if Earley's not involved?"

"I drive you to Montana," he said, "then come back and start over again. If Earley's not this Captain Rat, then someone else is. Sooner or later, I'll find him."

He stared across the parking lot at the entrance to police headquarters. His mouth was set in grim determination and his face was lined with fatigue. His dark eyes were even more unreadable and mysterious than ever.

Where was his gun? she'd asked.

It was aimed at you, he'd said.

Was he lying?

He'd spoken with such conviction, such absolute certainty. There was a gun. She simply hadn't seen it. If he hadn't killed Tommy Walsh, Tommy would've killed her.

What if he was telling the truth? What if all along he'd been telling the truth?

Everything I've ever said to you is God's own truth.

If he *was* telling the truth, then, Lord, how she'd let him down by doubting him.

It was her head versus her heart. Her heart wanted to believe him. But her head couldn't reconcile the cold, hard facts.

And Carrie didn't know what to believe.

Felipe sat forward, gripping the steering wheel tightly in his hands. "My God," he said.

"Is it him?" Carrie tried to see where he was looking. She couldn't see anyone out on the sidewalk who looked like Chief Earley.

"It's Lawrence Richter," Felipe said. "He's going inside." He turned off the engine and unlocked the door. "Come on."

"We're going to *follow* him?" Carrie exclaimed. "Into the *police station?*"

"Yes." Felipe took the paper lunch bag that held Rafe's Instamatic camera, then grabbed her wrist. He pulled her across the bench seat and out the driver's-side door.

"Do you know how many police officers are in there?" Carrie asked in disbelief. "Do you *want* to get caught?"

"I'm not going to get caught," Felipe said shortly, pulling her with him across the parking lot toward the wide stairs that led up to the main doors. "But if anything happens," he added, "get down behind me out of the way. Do you understand?"

Carrie dug her heels into the gravel of the parking lot, and he turned back toward her impatiently.

"Felipe, don't go in there," she said. "Someone's going to recognize you and—"

"How nice that you should care," he said without expression.

"I *do* care—"

He grabbed her shoulders and all the emotion he'd been hiding erupted to the surface. "Then *trust* me, dammit!" he hissed. "Trust me, Caroline, and know that I *have* to go in there if I want this to end."

"I don't want you to die," she whispered, staring into the burning depths of his eyes. "I don't know what you've done or not done, who you've killed or not. I don't know whether or not you've been using me right from the start. I don't know whether you deserve to go to jail or get a medal for bravery, but I *do* know that I don't want you to die."

He touched the side of her face, his hands suddenly gentle, his eyes soft and sad. "I truly have no control when it comes to you," he murmured. "I should despise you for losing your faith in me, but all I want is to kiss you, to touch you. I must be one hell of a fool." He shook his head. "You can help me, Caroline," he added, talking low and fast. "We can get in and out and no one will ever know. I need to do this. I need your help. Please."

Helping him would be aiding and abetting. She could go to jail for that.

"Please," he whispered again, and she nodded. Her reward was a small smile, a mere shadow of Felipe's normal exuberance. "Put your hair under your hat," he said. "Hurry."

She obeyed, stuffing her long blond hair up underneath the baseball cap she was still wearing.

This was crazy. Felipe was crazy. *She* was crazy for going along with this.

He opened the door to the lobby and pulled her inside.

She should scream, run away, do *some*thing to call attention to herself. *Hello, I'm the hostage you've all been looking for all this time!*

Felipe was staring at the elevators.

"Richter got in one going down," he said, pulling her toward a door marked Stairs. "Come on." He pulled her into the stairwell with him, then started down. "Quickly. I don't want to lose him," he said, taking the stairs two at a time, all but swinging Carrie up into his arms to speed her along.

But he stopped running before he pushed open the door on the basement level. He opened it slowly—just in time to see Lawrence Richter walk sedately past.

They followed the silver-haired man into a cafeteria that was open to the general public. And the general public was there in all their various sizes and shapes. That was good. With these strange-looking people around, no one would give Felipe a second glance.

Near the door, there was an empty table against the wall, and Felipe sat down in one of the metal-framed chairs. He pulled Carrie onto his lap.

She didn't want to sit there. She didn't want to be so close to him, to be reminded of the way she had let him love her. She struggled to stand up, but he held her tightly.

"At least *pretend* you like me," he whispered.

Carrie stopped struggling. "Felipe—" she started to say.

"Shh. Richter's got a cup of coffee. He's going to sit down. Put your arm around me, for God's sake."

Carrie looped her arm around Felipe's neck. She wished she wasn't sitting here like this, so close to him, touching him. She wished she were back at Sea Circus or out on her boat, alone with the sea and sky, or hell, she even wished she were back in Montana. She wished she were anywhere but here.

Because she also wished that she could kiss him. Her attraction to this man was still there, powerful and strong. Her love was there, too, even stronger.

Head versus heart, it all boiled down to a matter of trust. Was he the Sandlot killer? Carrie didn't want to believe that he was. But wanting simply wasn't enough.

Felipe reached around her to put the lunch bag on the table. He poked a hole in the bag for the camera lens and aimed it at the table where Richter was sitting with his coffee.

And then, without any warning, Felipe kissed her.

It was a long, deep, achingly fierce kiss that caught her entirely by surprise. It left her weak and even more off center than she'd been before.

"Sorry." Felipe quietly apologized for the kiss almost before their lips had parted. "I'm sorry—Richter looked this way. I didn't know what else to do."

Oh. That hadn't really been a kiss. It had been a diversion, a form of cover.

"What is Richter doing?" Carrie asked when she finally found her voice. Sitting the way she was, her back was to the man.

"He's picked up a newspaper from the table," Felipe said. He reached out and laid one hand on the paper bag holding the camera and took a picture of Richter. "Put your head against my shoulder and you'll be able to see him. But don't stare. Look past him, not at him."

Carrie turned slightly and leaned back against Felipe. Richter was reading the newspaper. As she watched, he took a sip of his coffee.

Felipe's hand moved on the paper bag. "Did you see that?" he murmured into Carrie's ear. "He just put an envelope in between the pages of the paper."

He did? Carrie hadn't noticed that at all.

"I got it on film," Felipe said. "Now we wait for Earley to show up... ah, he's right on time."

Looking harried, Police Chief Jack Earley, in a white short-sleeved shirt and a loosened tie and carrying his sport jacket over one arm, came into the cafeteria.

Felipe nuzzled Carrie's neck, hiding his face from the man who was leading the statewide intensive search for him.

Earley walked past Felipe and Carrie, past Lawrence Richter—who didn't even glance up—and over to the coffee vending machine. Casually, the police chief put some money into the machine and pressed the buttons for decaf with sugar, no cream.

As the cup was filling with steaming dark coffee, Lawrence Richter stood up, straightened his tie and calmly walked out of the room.

"He left," Carrie whispered to Felipe. "Richter left before the meeting!"

"He didn't take the newspaper," Felipe murmured. "It has that envelope inside it. Just watch. Earley is going to pick it up off the table."

Almost before he stopped speaking, the police chief walked past the table where Richter had been sitting. For a moment, it looked as if the man was simply going to walk on by, but then he stopped, lingering to look down at the headlines of the sports pages.

He glanced at his watch as if in a rush, then took the paper with him, hurrying out of the room.

Felipe hustled Carrie off his lap and grabbed the bag that held the camera. Holding her hand, he pulled her along with him down the hall about fifty feet behind Jack Earley.

Earley stopped in front of the elevator and pushed the button. He took a sip of his coffee, made a face and tossed the cup and its contents into the garbage. The newspaper soon followed.

"Got it," Felipe murmured in her ear, and she realized he was holding the bag with the camera in front of him. "He put the envelope in his jacket pocket."

"I didn't see that," Carrie said.

"That's okay," Felipe said. "I got it on film."

"Now what?" Carrie whispered.

"Now we find a one-hour photo place," Felipe said.

"Holy hell, it *is* you," a voice said loudly. All across the basement lobby, heads turned in their direction. A bald-headed man in an ill-fitting suit fumbled for his sidearm. "Felipe Salazar, *you* are under arrest!"

"Or maybe we'll skip the photo place," Felipe said quietly, pulling Carrie close to him. "Play along."

From around the lobby came a murmur of voices and a wave of movement as civilians backed away and police officers began to draw their weapons.

But Felipe was ahead of them all. His gun was already drawn. He backed up until he hit the wall next to the closed elevator door. "Keep your hands up and guns down," he warned them. "I don't want to have to hurt the girl."

Play along. But was this fantasy or reality? It sure *seemed* like reality. The entire area was frozen like a tableau.

"Come on, Phil," the bald cop said, still trying to get his gun free. "Don't let's do this the hard way. Let me bring you in. I'll see that you get fair treatment."

"Put your hands up, Andy," Felipe said. "And back away."

"Someone get hold of Jim Keegan," the cop named Andy called out, lifting his hands with a sigh. "We got us a hostage situation here." He turned back to Felipe. "Phil, this is a royal pain in the ass."

This was all happening so fast. Carrie could barely breathe. Felipe had his gun pressed against her ribs. *Play along.* She didn't have to pretend to look frightened.

"Tommy Walsh killed Mareidas and Dupree," Felipe told Andy. "Not me. It was on Lawrence Richter's orders. I have proof of this."

"Richter?" Andy said, squinting as he tried to place the name. "Isn't he the guy who owns that chain of fish restaurants? My cousin got salmonella from eating there."

"He owns the restaurants—and runs a major crime syndicate," Felipe said. "Guess who else is involved?" He turned to look at Jack Earley. "You get the first guess, Chief."

Chief Earley's face was pale, his mouth a grim line. "Let the girl go, Salazar. You don't really want to see her killed, do you?" He turned to speak to his men. "He's clearly delusional. Get back and clear these civilians out of here."

"You're going down, Captain Rat," Felipe said to Earley. "I have the proof I need. When Jim gets here—"

Next to them, the door of the cargo elevator slid open, and a janitor blinked owlishly out at them from behind a dolly carrying large trash barrels.

Earley made his move. He lunged for Felipe, pulling both him and Caroline back into the big elevator.

"Get out!" he shouted at the janitor, who scrambled out the door. "The man's insane! *Get out!*"

Felipe hit the wall hard and fell to his knees, taking Carrie with him. He fired his gun, and the noise was deafening. She heard herself scream, felt Felipe try to cover her with his body.

Lord, this was it. They were going to die.

* * *

Felipe had missed.

He'd had one shot at Earley, but he'd missed. The bullet tore up into the soundproof tile of the elevator ceiling as the door slid closed.

Earley was back behind the cover of the trash barrels in the other corner of the elevator. Felipe tried to shield Caroline from the chief's gun, but it was no use. His body would act as a shield for only so long at this close a range.

"Put your gun down," the chief shouted. "Put it down!"

Slowly, Felipe lowered his gun. He had no choice. Not with Earley aiming his own gun directly at him . . . and at Caroline.

Earley reached up to the elevator controls and pushed the stop button, halting their journey up to the first floor.

"Heroically, Chief Earley pulled Salazar and his hostage into an empty elevator, risking his own life for the sake of the crowd's safety," Earley said, straightening up and coming out from behind the barrels, his gun aimed levelly at Felipe. "The papers are gonna have a field day with this one. I couldn't've planned it better myself. Put your gun on the floor and kick it over to me."

Felipe set the gun down, but instead of kicking it to Earley, he slid it underneath the dolly that held the trash barrels. Caroline's eyes were wide as she looked from Felipe to Earley and then back.

"It really is a shame when a good cop turns bad," Earley mused, shaking his head.

"You should know," Felipe said. He could see his future in Earley's eyes, and it wasn't going to be a long one. Earley was going to shoot him, and then shoot Caroline with Felipe's gun. And there was nothing Felipe could do about it.

Or was there?

Jim Keegan's Rule Number One: Nothing is impossible.

Felipe's Rule Number One: If you're going to die, die fighting.

The big cargo elevator was about eight feet long by seven feet wide. The dolly holding the barrels cut off one corner of that space.

"Let go of your hostage," Earley said as Felipe slowly rose to his feet, pulling Caroline up with him.

"Te amo," Felipe said to Caroline, brushing the side of her face with his lips. "Get down behind the barrels," he breathed into her ear.

"Very touching," Earley said impatiently. "Now, let her go."

Felipe pushed Caroline hard, away from Earley and toward the trash barrels, as he leaped at Earley. "Get down! Get back!" he shouted again at Caroline.

The gun went off with a roar as he hit Earley in the face. He felt a slap, heard Caroline scream, saw a spray of blood hit the elevator wall.

Felipe had been hit. Where, he couldn't begin to say. All he knew was that the bullet hadn't killed him—he was still alive. And until his heart stopped beating, he was going to fight like the devil himself to save Caroline's life.

He hit Earley again, and the chief's gun flew out of his hand and into the corner.

Earley fought back, trying to get to his gun. He used his hands like a club, striking Felipe hard on the shoulder.

God, he knew now where that bullet had struck him. Earley hit his wounded shoulder again and again and Felipe reeled back in mind-numbing pain. Somehow he managed to kick out at the older man, and his foot connected with Earley's knee. The chief went down with a grunt but scrambled quickly to his feet, assuming a street-fighter's stance.

"Freeze!" Caroline shouted from behind the barrels. "I said *freeze,* dammit!"

She was holding Felipe's gun, and she had Earley's gun behind her on the floor.

Earley straightened up, lifting both his hands as she pointed the gun from him to Felipe and back again.

"Good job, miss," Earley said, starting toward Felipe. "We've got him now."

"Don't you move!" Caroline warned him. He froze.

"You're kidding, right?" Earley said. He gestured toward Felipe. "This man's the known felon. He's the kidnapper, the *murderer.* He's the one who's been holding you hostage all this time."

Caroline's eyes flicked from Earley to Felipe.

Felipe didn't say a word. What could he say? He just looked at her. *Trust me.*

She looked into his eyes, searching for answers, searching for the truth. He hoped she could see it—the truth was clearly there, written permanently in his heart.

Te amo. I love you.

Earley started forward. "Give me the gun, miss."

She turned sharply, pointing the weapon at St. Simone's chief of police.

"Don't come closer, mister, or I'll put a hole in you," she said.

Relief flooded through Felipe. Caroline had followed her heart and trusted him.

He staggered slightly—his knees felt odd, weak. He realized that his shoulder was still bleeding quite heavily. Blood ran down his arm and dripped onto the floor from his fingers.

"You're hurt," Caroline said to Felipe, her eyes still locked on Earley. Her voice shook slightly, but her hands were steady. "Is it bad?"

Felipe shook his head. "I'll live," he said. He moved across the elevator and reached over to take back his gun.

She glanced up at him then. "So will I," she said. "Because of you, I think."

"Hands on your head," Felipe ordered Earley. "Sit down. There, in the corner."

"You're not going to get away with this," Earley said.

"You wanna bet?" Felipe said.

Overhead, an intercom speaker clicked on.

"This is Detective Jim Keegan from the Fourth Precinct," came a familiar voice. "Felipe, are you there? Pick up the telephone in the control panel."

The metal panel swung open with a squawk, and Felipe picked up the red receiver.

"Diego?"

"Phil! *Yes!* I heard a shot and I was afraid—is everyone all right?"

"I've been hit," Felipe said, "but I've cornered my Captain Rat."

"Jack Earley?" Jim said.

"That's right."

"The chief of police."

"Uh-huh."

Jim Keegan laughed. "You got proof?"

"Uh-huh. Photos of him accepting a payoff from Lawrence Richter."

"Well, isn't that dandy," Jim said. "That and the tape you left for me at Sea Circus should just about change your tag from Rogue Cop to Local Hero. I'll have the boys bring in Richter and his pals."

"That's cool, but meanwhile, I've got Andy and the entire police force ready to blow me away when these elevator doors open," Felipe said.

"Go on up to the first floor," Jim's voice said. "Captain Swick will be waiting for you there. Believe it or not, he's one of the good guys. That's why he had that tape of Walsh and Richter planning the Sandlot Murders. He was holding it to clear your name when the time came. He was working *with* you on this case, and he'd suspected Earley for some time now."

Felipe pulled out the stop button and the elevator started with a jerk.

"Keep your hands on your head," Caroline warned Earley.

"This isn't over," Earley hissed.

"Yes," Felipe told him, "it is."

And the elevator doors slid open.

Felipe was sitting on the lobby floor, leaning against the wall by the elevators, waiting for the paramedics to arrive.

A man Carrie recognized as Andy, and several other police officers, were around Felipe, trying to stem the flow of blood from his shoulder.

Earley had been taken away and reporters were gathering outside for an enormous press conference. In a matter of hours, word would hit the newsstands and TVs that Felipe

Salazar was *not* a menace to society. His name would be cleared.

As Carrie watched, Felipe glanced around the lobby, looking for something or someone. Looking for *her*. His eyes landed on her, and he visibly relaxed.

He held her gaze. She could see pain in his dark brown eyes and at the edges of his mouth. His shoulder hurt more than he was letting on. Hell, for all *she* knew, his wounded leg still hurt him, too.

The ambulance was on its way. The paramedics would arrive and take Felipe to the hospital.

What then? Was she simply free to go? Should she just walk out of the police station, hail a taxi and go home to her apartment?

Andy approached her. "Uh, excuse me. You're Caroline, right?"

She nodded.

"Uh, Phil was wondering if you'd mind coming over for a sec before you go," Andy said.

Before you go. Felipe expected her just to walk away, to leave. It was over. All of it. Including any future they might've had together. She'd destroyed that with her doubts and mistrust.

Still, as she walked toward Felipe, she tried to smile.

The other police officers moved tactfully away.

"You trusted me," Felipe said, looking up at her from his seat on the floor. He patted the tile and she sat cross-legged next to him.

"I didn't for a while there," she said. She looked at her hands clasped tightly in her lap, unable to meet his eyes.

"When it came down to the bottom line—" Felipe's soft accent seemed to caress her "—you were there for me."

"No," Carrie said, closing her eyes. "You were there for *me*. All along, you protected me. You risked your life for mine."

"I was glad to," he said simply.

"I let you down," she said. Her voice shook and she couldn't hide it.

"It was hard for you to trust me," he said gently. "The way we started..." He shook his head. "I don't blame you, Caroline."

Carrie nodded. She still couldn't meet his eyes. "I'm so sorry."

"I am, too."

"It could've been really good, couldn't it have?" She risked a glance up at him. His dark eyes were serious and as mysterious as the midnight sky.

He nodded slowly. "Yes," he said. "It could have been remarkably good."

He was just sitting there, watching her. She wanted desperately for him to reach out, to touch her, to pull her into his arms—or at least the one that wasn't hurting. But that wasn't going to happen. Their love affair was over. She'd killed it, smothered it with her mistrust.

"Now what?" she asked quietly.

He held out his hand—his good hand—to her. "Hello. My name is Felipe Salazar," he said, "and I'm a police detective with the Fourth Precinct. I'm with the vice squad right now, but I won't be for much longer. I'm thinking about putting in for an assignment as an urban youth officer." He brought her fingers to his lips and kissed them one at a time. "You've got to be the most intriguing woman I've ever met. Will you have dinner with me tonight?"

Tears flooded Carrie's eyes and hope flooded her heart. "You want to start over?" she whispered.

"I would love to start over," he said. "Will you have dinner with me?"

"Oh, Felipe, can you really forgive me?"

"If we're starting over," he said, with a small smile, "there's nothing to forgive." His eyes were liquid brown and so very warm as he gazed at her. "Even though we've just met, would it be forward of me to ask for a kiss?"

With a trembling smile, Carrie shook her head.

Felipe leaned toward her, careful not to jar his shoulder. Carrie met him halfway in a kiss so sweet, so pure and tender, it brought a fresh rush of tears to her eyes.

"This may be the shortest courtship in the history of the Western Hemisphere," Felipe breathed, desire sparking in his eyes.

"I hope so," Carrie said.

He touched the side of her face as he looked searchingly at her. "Caroline, there *is* a catch to this. I'm about to go into protective custody. As the chief witness against Rich-

ter and Earley, I'll have to be kept safe until after the trial.
For your own safety, you should come with me. Richter may
figure out he can get to me through you. But it's your
choice. You don't have to come. If you choose not to, I
won't be able to see you until it's over and done. It could be
nine or ten months. Longer."

Carrie was silent for a moment. Not see him for nearly a
year? "I'd have to quit my job," she finally said.

"A leave of absence," Felipe said. Hope lighted his eyes
and he leaned forward to kiss her again. "Your position
would surely be waiting for you when you returned."

"Returned from where?"

He smiled. "I don't know. Where do you want to go?"

Carrie smiled back at him, her heart exploding with love
for Felipe Salazar, who was man enough to give her a second chance. "Someplace where we can go out on a boat,"
she said. "Someplace near the ocean."

"I know of this great beach house on Sanibel Island,"
Felipe said. "The owners are friends of mine. Although we
may need to go farther away from St. Simone, this beach
house might be a good place to start."

Carrie kissed him, closing her eyes and drinking in the
softness of his lips, the sweetness of his mouth.

"It would be the perfect place to start."

* * * * *

COMING NEXT MONTH

MILLION DOLLAR SWEEPSTAKES (III)

Are your lips succulent, impetuous, delicious or racy?

Find out in a very special Valentine's Day promotion—THAT SPECIAL KISS!

Inside four special Harlequin and Silhouette February books are details for THAT SPECIAL KISS! explaining how you can have your lip prints read by a romance expert.

Look for details in the following series books, written by four of Harlequin and Silhouette readers' favorite authors:

Silhouette Intimate Moments #691
Mackenzie's Pleasure by *New York Times* bestselling author Linda Howard

Harlequin Romance #3395
Because of the Baby by Debbie Macomber

Silhouette Desire #979
Megan's Marriage by Annette Broadrick

Harlequin Presents #1793
The One and Only by Carole Mortimer

Fun, romance, four top-selling authors, plus a FREE gift! This is a very special Valentine's Day you won't want to miss! Only from Harlequin and Silhouette.

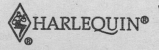

INTRODUCING...

A collection of award-winning books by award-winning authors! From Harlequin and Silhouette.

Falling Angel
by Anne Stuart

WINNER OF THE RITA AWARD
FOR BEST ROMANCE!

Falling Angel by Anne Stuart is a RITA Award winner, voted Best Romance. A truly wonderful story, *Falling Angel* will transport you into a world of hidden identities, second chances and the magic of falling in love.

"Ms. Stuart's talent shines like the brightest of stars, making it very obvious that her ultimate destiny is to be the next romance author at the top of the best-seller charts."
—*Affaire de Coeur*

A heartwarming story for the holidays. You won't want to miss award-winning *Falling Angel*, available this January wherever Harlequin and Silhouette books are sold.

For an *EXTRA*-special treat, pick up

TIME AND AGAIN
by
Kathryn Jensen

In January 1996, Intimate Moments proudly features Kathryn Jensen's *Time and Again*, #685, as part of its ongoing Extra program.

Modern-day mom: Kate Fenwick wasn't looking for a soul mate. Her two children more than filled her heart—until she met Jack Ramsey.

Mr. Destiny: He defied time and logic to find her, and only by changing fate could they find true love.

In future months, look for titles with the EXTRA flash for more excitement, more romance—simply *more....*

IMEXTRA3

HEARTBREAKERS

We've got more of the men you love to love in the Heartbreakers lineup this winter. Among them are Linda Howard's Zane Mackenzie, a member of her immensely popular Mackenzie family, and Jack Ramsey, an *Extra*-special hero.

In December—HIDE IN PLAIN SIGHT, by Sara Orwig: Detective Jake Delancy was used to dissecting the criminal mind, not analyzing his own troubled heart. But Rebecca Bolen and her two cuddly kids had become so much more than a routine assignment....

In January—TIME AND AGAIN, by Kathryn Jensen, *Intimate Moments Extra:* Jack Ramsey had broken the boundaries of time to seek Kate Fenwick's help. Only this woman could change the course of their destinies—and enable them both to love.

In February—MACKENZIE'S PLEASURE, by Linda Howard: Barrie Lovejoy needed a savior, and out of the darkness Zane Mackenzie emerged. He'd brought her to safety, loved her desperately, yet danger was never more than a heartbeat away— even as Barrie felt the stirrings of new life growing within her....

INTIMATE MOMENTS®
Silhouette

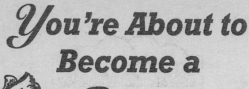